Fallen

RHR HANDLEY

"Hell is empty and all the devils are here"

William Shakespeare

Dedicated to MSB

ISBN: 979-8-6666-8472 6

CONTENTS

ACKNOWLEDGMENTS

Many thanks are in order for this book. Practically, a big thank you to the talented Fiona Leitch for the wonderful, evocative cover – a witty and funny writer herself

https://smile.amazon.co.uk/Fiona-Leitch/e/B07HYZLQ57?ref=sr_ntt_srch_lnk_1&qid=1594888357&sr=8-1

Thank you to Script Angel editing services for honing my writing skills over the years.

Thank you to ‘ugglemamma’ for the cover image, taken from pixabay

https://pixabay.com/photos/angel-lucifer-horrified-2332116/?fbclid=IwAR07dVAQX5mThE5CdbxjBKdE5vbsn8j3BrS0rsEQqD-vwxSgDA1YNPJPPIk

And my heartfelt thanks to my family for their love and support, especially Maddie a patient, keen-eyed critic in a teenager’s body, and to Peta for kindly reading and improving my story.

This will not be the last journey for Danni, and more of her books will appear on my Amazon page, or via my website www.rhandley.com

Run

Danni knew the instant her father died.

She'd had the creeping sensation that *they* were closing in, and ordinarily she would have run away, immediately, but she had met someone. And in the end, it wasn't her they were closing in on.

She'd been in Glasgow for 3 weeks. She was a gardener in a municipal green space at the edge of a large social housing estate. For the last week she'd noticed a little girl of 9 or 10 who came every day after school and sat on her own until the park closed. Fear radiated from the child and a dark miasma surrounded her. Something had sunk its claws into her.

Danni had, as she always did, cultivated a small haven in the park, planting runes under flowers that radiated peace and some measure of safety. The child had been drawn to them for the last week, and Danni had worked closer to her each day.

"They're coming." Danni's inner voice had whispered. She would have to leave, and soon, so it was now or never with the child.

"The worst lie they tell children is that monsters aren't real." Said Danni in a lilting accent from the Scottish

Highlands. “But we both know they are, don’t we?”

The child’s heart skipped a beat and she jumped to her feet – but she didn’t run, not yet. She wasn’t ready to leave the peace of her little spot.

“Piss off!” She replied in a broad Glasgow accent.

“Ach, I normally take my time building up to this.” Danni had a small bonsai tree in her bag and she carefully brought it out, “but I have to leave. So, would you like me to hide you from the monsters that are after you?”

“What are you on about? Are you a pervert?” The child sneered full of bravado - as her little heart pounded in her chest.

Danni shrugged, creeping closer, plant in hand. “I can help you, but it has to be right now.”

“I’ll get you sacked! Get you locked up.”

“Lassy, I can see that a devil has sunk its claws into you.” Said Danni, desperate to help and worried about the passing time.

“Monsters ain’t real.” Shouted Amy, a mantra she’d repeated many times.

“How come you’re so terrified then?” Danni realised that the child was about to bolt, and Danni would be gone when she came back, so she moved in, praying nobody would see them. She grabbed the child’s shoulders and held her, to stare deep into her eyes.

"And you're right to be scared, because one of them has placed its mark on you." Amy's heartbeat accelerated as Danni continued, relentless. "And when it comes back, which it will, there's not a thing you can do to stop it."

Amy was mesmerised and terrified, and fat tears welled in her eyes as her bravado collapsed. Danni could see her retreating inwards, back in time, to the day the monster had visited. Danni saw shadowy claws reach out for Amy's little soul, which squirmed and ran away from them, retreating deep inside her body. Danni pushed aside her rage to focus on the task in hand. She squatted before Amy and thrust the bonsai tree in its little pot into the child's hands and wrapped her hands around the pot.

"What's your name? Quick."

"Amy." Whispered the child.

Danni breathed over the tree, whispering her name and quiet words that activated 2 tiny runes on its trunk – symbols that she'd carved into it the day before, that were now bound to Amy. The runes glowed and shivered in Amy's hands, the leaves rustling.

A great weight was lifted from Amy's soul and she cast an astonished look at Danni, who smiled with relief. The runes' glow was fading but Danni pointed to one of them in the shape of a harp with 2 horizontal lines through it.

“That is for protection.”

Danni was in her early 20’s. Wild, strawberry blond red hair and blue eyes – for today. A blond wig and blue contact lenses hid her real appearance. She wore, as usual, overalls over a long-sleeved top, but now she rolled up her sleeves, to show her forearms, covered in tattoos from the wrist up. She pointed out several tattoos of the ‘harp’ shape.

“See, I wear it too.”

Danni then pointed to other tattoos on her arm, multiple eyes with the lid closed, then pointed at the same rune on her bonsai. “And this one hides us.”

“Us..?” Whispered Amy, still not quite believing what was happening.

Danni smiled sadly, “Aye, there’s something ‘special’ about us, Lass, that calls out to them.”

Danni reflected that this was a curse nowadays, with so many broken families without elders to instruct their children. She pushed a strand of hair from Amy’s face.

“I’d bet you’ve no got a Granny or Gandpa to guide you?”

Amy’s expression turned pensive as she thought about her home – her parents always out at work, one set of grandparents dead, the other alienated from her argumentative mother. Danni read her expression and nodded.

"Amy. Sleep with this wee tree in your bedroom, and..."

"RUN!" Shouted her father into her head with his last breath as the Fallen caught him in Norway, thousands of miles away.

A spike of adrenalin flooded Danni. A cloud passed over the sun and the temperature dropped so their breath clouded the air, as Danni's connection to her father was severed forever. Danni and Amy stood in a circle in the park in Glasgow, now surrounded by cloud. Through the mist, dark figures roamed, their shadows passing pressed against the barrier.

"It's here!" Whimpered Amy, eyes wide with fear, clutching the plant tight.

"RUN!" her father's urgent warning echoed in her head.

"No, Amy, they're hunting but they're no here yet."

Danni whispered chants, old words taught to her by her father, plus some she's created herself. She pulled a bracelet from her pocket, made of small, wooden beads that she'd painstakingly carved with protective wards, weaving magic into them. She slid the bracelet onto Amy's wrist – and the temperature rose as suddenly as it had dropped, and the sun came out again and their circle expanded, out of Otherworld, back to the real world.

"RUN!"

"Wear this *all* the time, touching your skin." She patted the bonsai tree. "And you tend this wee tree, keep it alive. You'll be invisible to the bastards that're after you. I promise."

Danni got to her feet.

"Wait! Don't leave me!" Begged Amy, who felt safe and more – peaceful. For the first time in months the shadow was gone. She flung her arms around Danni's neck and burst into tears. Danni was painfully aware of the passing seconds, but she returned her hug, holding her close.

"Hush, Lass, you're safe now, but I have to go. I have monsters after me too."

"Fight them! You can fight them? You've got magic, just fight them."

"RUN!" The urgent warning was getting louder.

"Ach, I cannae. Mine are much more powerful than your wee bastard. If I stay I'll bring them on you too."

"Please?" Begged Amy.

"You'll be safe now." Danni disentangled herself and

stood up. Later Danni knew she would feel terrible remorse at having to leave Amy so ill equipped, but staying would be far worse.

"RUN!"

"If I were you, I'd no tell anyone about this."

Danni ran to her van and drove off, her skidding wheels flinging gravel behind her, her survival instincts now screaming for her to run. In her rear-view mirror she saw Amy, gripping her tree, staring after her, tears streaming down her cheeks.

Danni lived in her van and now she drove it to a storage facility on the outskirts of Glasgow. Her lockup only held 2 suitcases, registered to one of her many identities. She grabbed the cases and headed south, parking under a flyover, away from cameras. Danni did not panic, but she did hurry, first changing the registration of the van, then adding stickers for 'JD Plumbing' onto the sides. She got into the back of the van and changed into a no-name tracksuit. Last to come off was her wig. She was a natural redhead, but her own hair was shaved, and she put on a long, black wig and baseball cap and sunglasses, then she clambered into the front and drove off.

She drove all night, stopping in Yorkshire to change the registration again and swap the stickers from JD

Plumbing to 'Aquarium Supplies'. She skirted London on the M25, ensuring the traffic cameras recorded her, and stopped once for fuel, paying with a credit card. From the services, she used the card to book a plane ticket from Heathrow to Los Angeles. Near to Heathrow airport, she changed registration plates once more, and drove to Dover where she managed to get a last minute ferry crossing to Calais, travelling under the name 'Ellen Grove'.

"RUN." The desperate warning still echoed, but it faded as she got further south.

In Calais, she drove to a corporate chain hotel, where she registered for a room with halting French, still using Ellen's ID, before driving to a car breakers, where she sold the van and caught a cab back to the hotel. Inside her room, she decanted the contents of the cases into a bag with wheels, then ... disappeared.

The Fallen

Around five thousand years ago, Uruk was built in Mesopotamia - the world's first ever recorded city.

But before Uruk, another settlement had existed. Mud brick houses sprang up as a few families joined together, expanded to dozens of people, which soon became hundreds, inching towards city status. It would have been the first city in the world, were it not for the dead inside one of the houses.

The remains of 20 people - great-grandparents, grandparents, parents and their children – were splattered on the walls and ceiling in a homogenised mess of blood, gristle, bone and organs. 20 people, ripped to shreds.

The town's residents stood outside the house in horrified silence, beside the lone survivor who had snuck out to screw his girlfriend. He would not be a survivor for much longer, nor would his lover. Soon the residents of the town would bludgeon him to death – not because he believed him guilty of killing his family. They turned on him because he had caught the eye of devils and brought them to their homes.

Their actions wakened the sleeping devils, who inflamed their blood lust so they turned on each other in a bloody, violent massacre that raged through the city like a forest fire. Those who escaped the madness abandoned the city, the dead left behind to rot where they'd fallen. News spread, and all records of the town were erased from history.

It was not the first time that the ungodly had reached out for people, it would not be the last.

Over the next thousands of years, the ungodly cultivated many relationships, with whispered promises of power and riches, always in exchange for life blood. Hundreds and thousands of people were sacrificed to – or by – the summoned who would rip and shred hated human flesh into gristle, bone and organs. When a village was attacked and 600 souls were savagely murdered in the Indus Valley, humanity became more careful about their relationship with the ungodly. They began defining rules of engagement and while the ancient Egyptian civilisation still sacrificed humans, they targeted their gods carefully and never fed them too much at once. Human sacrifices were given a fighting chance under the Greeks and Romans, but then the we forgot and ungodly whispered their poison again. The mighty Aztec and Incans ascended on a wave of blood, until the organised religions discovered them, and quashed them. The secretive Order, encompassing all religions in an uneasy alliance, became a formidable force against them.

Some called them demons or devils. Some call them Fallen. They still search for their way into our world, still whispering into receptive ears.. and some still listen.

Louisiana, USA, twenty years ago.

The wail of children carried over a still night. 12 of them, tied together on a flat-bottomed boat moored up in a fetid swamp. Lilith released them, one by one – and one by one their screams were cut off as their blood poured into the stagnant waters.

She was in was in her 40's, sexy and voluptuous, with long, red-varnished nails that matched the crimson of the children's' blood. She read from a grimoire, guttural words that slithered off her tongue and seemed to sink into the water around her.

When the last child was dead, she closed the book.

"Abaddon!" She shouted. "Abaddon you fat lump, it's time to wake up!"

The silence was deafening as not even insects dared venture into this patch of swamp. Then the stagnant water swelled as somebody, or something, very large waded through it. Snakes swam along the surface, rushing to hide between weeds, and a huge man appeared from the gloom.

He sniffed the air, smelling the fresh blood, and accelerated, moving far too quickly for a man of his size. He approached Lilith with a deadly, hungry intent – but stopped as a shaft of moonlight fell on her face.

"Lilith?" He voice was curiously unaccented and high pitched.

"Abaddon. It's time to wake up."

Huangshan, China, fifteen years ago

A bucolic scene. High snow-tipped mountains, fields of rice, a wide, slow river and a house on stilts beside it. Silence apart from the excited buzz of flies, drawn by the steady, red drip-drip of blood through the floorboards of the house, and the bodies inside. Lilith sat on the stoop and stared out at the rising sun. She didn't appear to have aged, still voluptuous in a deep red cheongsam, which did little to disguise the blood that covered it and splattered her arms and face.

As the sun broke, Armers arrived and she got to her feet.

"I've been waiting all night." She complained. "I was beginning to wonder if you'd heard me."

Indeterminate age, tall and rake-thin, Armers's gaze drifted to the blood dripping under the house.

"Where's Abaddon?" He asked.

"He's still sating his appetite." Replied Lilith. "Abaddon, Armers's here!" She shouted.

Abaddon waddled from the house, covered in gore, his age anywhere from 40 to 60.

"Armers, what a delight to see you again!" He called in a curiously high pitched voice.

Armers merely turned away. "I've brought
said as he walked off.

Lilith and Abaddon followed. It would be da,
young woman would travel to visit her family in the mountains, when she would find the remains her entire family, 4 generations. All had been murdered, had their entrails removed (while they still lived). Animals and insects had feasted on the remains, but there was evidence that human teeth had bitten the youngest, tenderest members of the family – while they still lived.

The walls of her family home were covered in their blood which had been used to write Satanic summoning runes that permeated her nightmares for the rest of her life.

The Chinese government tried to hide the news, but the Order had contacts everywhere, and Brother Ailwyn and Brother Anders were dispatched to record the scene. Ailwyn and Anders made an unlikely couple, and a casual observer would never have identified them as monks. Both in their 50's, Anders had greying, sandy hair, Ailwyn had the bent nose of a brawler, both men well-muscled and fit. Both men used to violence.

They had difficulty gaining access to the scene, with Chinese authorities wary of foreigners at the best of times, and now furious that occultists had dared to interrupt their ordered, communist ideals. The monks managed to bribe local officials for a copy of the file, and snuck in the night before the house was demolished to record the images left behind.

Mexico City, ten years ago

An old part of town, with huge buildings of stone and brick. A distant bell clanged urgently, a constant ding-ding-ding, competing with rapid-fire, automatic weapons. In the shadows of a narrow, dark street, Lilith waited as a blood-splattered young woman ran towards her.

"Tarel, it's good to see you again."

Tarel was in her early teens, blond, already curvaceous and beautiful. She giggled as Lilith wiped a smudge of blood off her cheek, then hooked her arm through Tarel's and guided her to a well-maintained residential side street, where Armers waited by an expensive car with tinted windows. He leant against the car, looking as if a strong wind would blow him over, and Tarel offered him a seductive grin before Lilith hustled her into the car.

It would a few hours yet before the news broke about the murder of 12 children in an abandoned factory. Their sacrifice, surrounded by the accoutrements of a Black Magic ritual. When the Coroner deemed that their hearts had been pulled from their little bodies while they still lived, even the gangs in the city were appalled. The news was so shocking that it drowned out the other news, of a gang that had imploded the same day, as members turned on each other in a senseless massacre.

Tarel's former gang, for her nature had drawn her to criminal life. Dormant but still corrupted, Tarel had lived with the gang until Lilith woke her up and she unleashed hell.

Brother Ailwyn and Brother Anders were again there afterwards, moving from the factory to the former gang headquarters, where they found numerous photographs of Tarel, posing for the camera. Later, via the police, they found pictures of Lilith on a CCTV camera as she sat in a square. Headscarf, sunglasses, elegant suit, she seemed to not have a care in the world. As she crossed the square to leave, she took off her sunglasses and looked directly into the camera, knowing full well the Order would track the footage.

Severomorsk, Russia, five years ago

On a bitterly cold night, Brother Ailwyn and Brother Anders parked a battered old car beside a black body of water. From their vantage point over Murmansk Fjord, they surveyed a frantic crime scene. Military police and medical vehicles came and went at great speed. They knew Russia was the next target and had been nearby when the Order's Russian Orthodox office intercepted the urgent request for emergency response in Severmorsk.

Through binoculars, they focused on the warehouse. It

was a hive of activity, multiple emergency services vehicles, whose lights reflected harshly on the black waters of Fjord; red, flashing blue, the white of headlights and hastily erected spotlights. Ailwyn watched a young, uniformed Police Officer ran out of a building and vomit into the snow.

And as Brother Anders and Brother Ailwyn waited for access to the crime scene in Russia, Lilith found Belial in a brothel in Moscow.

She strode into the brothel and when a bouncer asked her what her pleasure was, she shot him in the balls, before stepping over his screaming body. Alerted by the shots, more men ran out and shot at her, but she dodged their bullets with inhuman speed, blazing a deadly path up the stairs.

Unerringly she headed along a corridor to the fourth door on the left and pushed it open on a bedroom with 2 occupants. Belial, a totally naked, beautiful young Mongolian man, and a middle-aged man, tied up on a bed. Having castrated him, Belial was in the process of stripping the flesh off his fingers – with a pair of nail scissors. He grinned with delight when he saw Lilith.

"Lily, you woke me!"

"Belial, it's been far too long." She replied with a sexy smile.

She gestured for him to follow, but he pouted, not

finished with the screaming business man. Lilith sighed and shot the man in the head.

"Get dressed." She said, and left. "There are more important things to do."

Belial eyed the man regretfully, then shrugged it off and followed Lilith. Lithe and graceful, he pulled on a robe and stepped delicately over moaning, dying men. A door opened and a woman, Nadezhda, peeked out at his retreating back. He froze and she squealed and hastily retreated from the door, her heart hammering. He turned, having decided to kill all the fellow prostitutes he'd lived with these past few months, but Lilith hurried him on.

"There'll be plenty of death," She encouraged, "but the police will be here soon."

The next afternoon, Brother Ailwyn and Brother Anders met with Brother Alexi. The priest in an Orthodox church had contacted the Order after Nadezhda had run there for sanctuary. She explained how she'd felt a shadow enter the building around midnight the night before, like all the light had been snuffed out in the whole world. She'd worked across from Belial's bedroom and she'd felt his terrible, hungry rage radiate from the room, along with the screams of his client.

Oklahoma City

Marbas was a tall, handsome man in his 40's. He wasn't considered anything special in the FBI – he excelled in all his exams but only got above average results when it came to arrests. He could have closed many more cases but he let some crimes slide, even to the point of evidence tampering, following a desire he didn't fully understand. He wasn't driven by justice and hadn't joined up to track bad people, so he found he didn't care much either way. He'd been pulled towards law enforcement because, if he was honest – which he rarely was – he was titillated by violence. It gave him a thrill that he first noticed when he was 10 and his parents and older siblings had been murdered in their beds. A crime people whispered about behind his back, nobody sure how he'd survived, everyone aware that he was 'wrong'. He'd already been an unpopular child, unnecessarily cruel and spiteful, and his life became unbearable after that – or so the authorities thought.

He'd been moved out of state and given a new name, but he'd had never found new, adoptive parents or foster parents prepared to keep him. Not that he minded, he'd been happy enough in care homes and had learned to hide his unpleasantness under a veneer of charm. He became a serious, studious child who'd had no friends, but no outright enemies.

His entire life he'd had feverish dreams that lingered as he woke, and he still wasn't entirely sure if he had been the one to kill his annoying family, which his dreams seemed to indicate. The problem was that the dreams had receded as soon as he came fully awake, leaving a feeling that he was supposed to be somewhere –

supposed to be doing something. 15 years before, after finding an article on the massacre in China that got his skin tingling, he'd switched from Oklahoma Police Department to the FBI. 10 years ago, when the ritual killings had occurred in Mexico, he'd got a thrill and experienced even more vivid dreams – though they still faded as soon as he woke. Then five years ago, when Lilith found Belial, he'd found the photos of the three crime scenes – including the ritualist writing that called out to the Fallen. He'd fallen asleep on his couch with the folders in his lap and when he'd woken his dream hadn't receded. Marbas had woken to his true nature.

He contacted Lilith and it was agreed he would stay in place and work for his Fallen brethren from within the FBI, recruiting and canvassing the corruptible with care, paving the way as Lilith continued with her plan to wake their brethren.

Europe

Danni had hacked the hotel network, located an empty room that she'd reassigned to a fake guest, then turned off the CCTV and activated the hotel fire alarm. Then while everyone evacuated, she'd switched rooms. Her conscience niggled about leaving Amy, but her presence around the child was too big a risk. She just hoped she'd done enough to divert her trace away from Scotland to France via London. She had left a breadcrumb trail to Calais and estimated that she had a maximum of 4 days before they tracked her, and a minimum of 24 hours. She would be gone within 12.

Mentally and physically exhausted, Danni used chalk to draw basic protective wards on the walls and floor, then fell asleep, fully clothed.

She woke, 8 hours later, and braced herself to shower. As she undressed she shed a fine mist of dust from her tattoos, which had lost their vibrancy. She stepped into the shower and watched her tattoos wriggle, then lift from under her skin. The running water first washed away the tattoos on her head, then her torso and arms, forming black streaks on her skin that slid down to the drain. Her stomach, thighs and finally her calves, the ink a black cloud around the drain before it washed away, leaving Danni totally unmarked. She had known that helping Amy would negate some of her wards, but watching her protection wash away so thoroughly, she realised *they* must have performed a ritual with her father's blood to trace her.

Her father– who of course was not her real father. Father Richard had never told her who her real parents were, nor where he 'found' her. When she'd questioned him about her parents, about him and his life before her, about why he'd rescued – or kidnapped – her, his replies had been terse. He had never been cruel to her, but he had never lavished love on her either. From the moment she could talk and walk, he had 'crafted' her. Every day they had lessons – in the morning it was trades, skills or physical fitness, then each afternoon she would study cultures and languages, then meditation in the evenings. As she got older, he'd allowed her to take different jobs, nurturing her ability to fit in, support herself and become invisible in a crowd. And always they moved.

He had taught her how to create new identities and how to inhabit each new persona with different mannerisms and appearance. She recalled a small town in the US where they had lived for 5 months when she was 15, the longest they'd ever stayed anywhere. Long enough for her to develop a crush on a boy and go on a date with him, promising to see him the following weekend for a drive-in movie ... then they'd absconded overnight.

One thing she had never questioned was the need to move. Her memory was extraordinary, and she even had recollections from when she was a baby, when she'd felt the urgent need to move whenever the 'monsters' scented her. And her memory wasn't the only extraordinary thing about her. Danni picked up skills and languages instantly, as if the knowledge slept within her, waiting to be activated. Father Richard had told her that pretty much everyone in the world wanted that ability – wanted her. His old employers, who he called the Order, and the legion of devils and demons, headed by the Fallen. Other than warning that neither party must ever find her, that was all he was prepared to tell her.

Now he was dead.

Danni dried herself off and got out her tattoo gun, a small, battery powered unit. She had reapplied her tattoos 5 or 6 times before in her life, her father having applied them when she was just a baby – and he had been the one to re-tattoo her back. She began re-applying the tattoos to the parts of her body that she could reach, starting with her freshly shaved head. She kept thinking of the little girl in Glasgow, and her desperate appeal to stay.

"Fight them! You can fight them."

Danni had often thought about it, and in truth was tired of running. She often daydreamed about standing her ground and fighting back, but her father, who seemed bonded to her thoughts, had always lashed out at her. She risked more than her own life if she was caught, she would be exploited and countless people would be hurt. He never seemed concerned that she, herself, would be hurt – just the damage to others. And now he was dead and his nagging voice was silent.

Danni made her way to Paris and studied local websites for student tattooists. She met a heavily pierced and tattooed young man called Charlie in his small but spotlessly clean bedsit, and produced hand-drawn tattoos to go on her back, buttocks and upper legs.

"Charlie, you must promise me something before we start." Said Danni in fluent French with a flawless Parisian accent. "These tattoos are secret. They're gang tattoos."

Charlie looked up from his preparation.

"And worse." Danni held out papers and he examined them – a series of runes and symbols. "You cannot take any photos of these, you cannot use these in any other tattoo design."

"Some of these are... strange. Some are beautiful." Charlie examined the images and whistled in appreciation. "They are very original."

"Charlie, if you or somebody posts a photo of these on the internet, some very nasty people will come after you asking questions."

Danni could see the calculation in his eyes. Charlie was

obviously an artist, and the designs intrigued him.

“Charlie?” He nodded agreement - reluctantly – and resumed setting up his inks, and Danni stripped off for him to start on the backs of her legs.

“Charlie, I escaped from a gang, a very nasty gang.” Charlie’s expression turned compassionate.

“My God!”

“These symbols are secret to them.” Danni shivered, in genuine fear, “Sacred even.”

“Why do you want them on your body?” He asked.

As usual, Danni edited the truth. She didn’t tell him that they were an ancient language that kept her hidden her from devils, instead she grinned savagely.

“As a fuck you! I’ve altered them, in my own way.” She replied, which was partly true at least, and he grinned in return.

“Charlie, I am serious about these, they are really pissed off that I escaped, they want to find me again, they hunt for me. If they see these images in your tattoos they will recognise them instantly and punish you for using them, then torture you to see if you can lead them to me.”

She grabbed his hand and looked into his eyes, and he nodded with more conviction. He cancelled his classes to complete her legs and back. That evening they drank wine and ended up in bed together. Danni relished the intimacy and allowed herself a full night in Paris. In the morning she tried to pay him from her meagre remaining funds, but he wouldn't accept. He walked her to the metro and kissed her goodbye, and she was alone again.

She got a metro to a coach station then she got a ticket to a random destination where she stole a car and drove to Switzerland. She dumped the car and caught another coach, then a train, without a ticket, barely avoiding the inspectors. She caught coaches and trains in a random zig-zag pattern and ended up in Amsterdam, where she headed to a PO box and picked up a new ID, this one a German student called Mila.

She was always drawn to plants and she found a job picking tulips that included accommodation in giant dormitories mostly filled with backpackers, though there was a section where Romani lived in their caravans. One evening as Danni left the shower block she encountered a woman from the Romani camp. The woman had hissed at her and made a sign against the evil eye, and Danni did her best to avoid the Romanis after that – but she didn't have to for long. The foreman announced, to his obvious consternation, that the Romani had all gone. He asked the backpackers if they could 'put the word out' to their friends for more pickers.

Danni had listened at the window outside the foreman's

office and overheard his confusion. The Travellers had picked tulips every year for as long as anyone could remember, but they had packed up and gone, saying the tulip farm was cursed. Word had spread in the Traveller community and everyone now refused to come there.

The Romani

Everyone except one family. They'd moved off the farm with everyone else, then came back in their cars and waited until Danni was alone, catching her late at night. Two men stepped into her path, another two stepped behind her blocking her retreat.

Danni waited for them to speak – or attack, for there was a menacing quality to them. Then a tiny, elderly lady joined them, her face wreathed in wrinkles, her eyes bright and piercing.

"She has one foot in Otherworld." She stated in Romani, making a sign against the evil eye.

"Won't she make it worse?" Asked one of the men, radiating anxiety and barely concealed aggression. "Maybe it's her fault."

"Ioana's troubles started before she got here." Said the old woman, eyeing Danni venomously. "What choice do we have, Florin?"

"I can understand you." Replied Danni in Vlax Romani. "What do you want?" She continued, switching to

Balkan Romani, correctly identifying their accent.

The group's animosity grew and the old woman stepped forward. "My granddaughter has been infected by one of your kind."

Danni sighed. Of all the people she met, the Romani could somehow see through her wards, no matter what symbols she used, and they always assumed the worst of her. She avoided them and so far they'd never attacked her, but she'd felt their animosity when she did encounter them. She cursed herself, she should have moved on the second she'd seen their camp. She waited as the old woman, whose name was Kezia, signed to Florin, encouraging him to go ahead and ask her.

"I can sign too." Stated Danni. "And I didn't hurt anyone."

"A devil has laid claim to my daughter," Said Florin, belligerent, "You will help her."

The men came closer, one of them brandishing a rope to bind her, to Danni's annoyance.

"Why did you not protect her, Old Woman?" She snapped at the old woman. "I can See your Black Blood, you should have protected your grandchild."

In the darkness her eyes flared orange. She hid her strangely coloured, amber eyes behind contact lenses of different colours, but a blink ejected the lenses. It was petty of her she knew, and she could see it pained the old woman and frightened the men.

"It is... beyond me." admitted the proud old woman.

She eyed Danni with dislike, reluctant to ask her for help, "Ioana's only seven…." Danni waited, and the request finally came, "Will you help? Please?"

Danni eyed them as she considered – or pretended to consider. Her father had ordered that she never expose herself, and every encounter with 'tainted' children posed a threat, but she had never refused, despite the punishments her father had meted out. She would help the child, not these people who hated her on sight.

"Take me to her." The men released relieved sighs, not even aware they were holding their breaths. One of them stepped forward to grab her, but a glare made him step back.

She followed them to their cars and got in the front beside Florin. He drove her a few miles down the road to a small group of caravans in a layby. More stony faced men and women waited with their children who watched her in wide-eyed silence. The old woman and Florin accompanied her into his caravan and she instantly felt the taint. Ioana was crouched behind a chair, her hair pulled over her face in a desperate attempt to hide.

"Do not interrupt us." Said Danni, her heart going out to Ioana as she mentally sifted through wards that might help. She eyed the caravan and settled on a wooden spoon on a counter top – it wasn't ideal, but it would do. She grabbed it and rummaged through her pockets for a penknife to carve her runes.

Danni shut out the world - the child, Florin and Kezia - as she sat cross-legged on the floor and began to carve runes into the spoon. Danni opted for a mixture of Romani and Sumerian, starting with a rune that hid from Sight, then she extended the rune to incorporate protection, and a mist drifted up around her as she stepped into Otherworld.

Ioana crept forward, drawn to Danni's magic as Amy had been – as they all were. The mist expanded, tendrils reaching for the child, and Florin's mother had to hold him back. The mist solidified into a thick smoke, forming a circle around the patch of floor where Ioana and Danni sat.

"Ioana, I know you're scared," Said Danni in Hungarian, instinctively knowing Ioana would be most comfortable with this, "but I'm gonna help you."

Danni was aware of the presences on the other side of the mist as she wove magic into her carvings. Shapes came nearer to their barrier, puzzled by the scent of magic, unable to trace it.

BANG – a thud from outside the mist, and the mist

bulged inwards, and Ioana hunched into a ball.

"We're gonna kick this monster where it hurts, right?" Smiled Danni, "In the balls!"

Ioana peered at Danni through her hair, not quite trusting her. Danni focused on two words and wove them into her wards.

"Can you say *hide* and *free* with me, in Vlax Romani? Can you do that, Ioana?"

Ioana nodded but as Danni started to count to three, something butted against their barrier, and the child whimpered and backed away.

"Danyal?" Said a voice.

"On three, Ioana. One..."

"You're close, Danyal." Said the voice of Abaddon from outside the barrier. "I can smell you."

"Two."

"Where are you?" Abaddon's voice turned angry. "Why are you always so fucking annoying!"

"Three."

In unison Ioana and Danni said the words, and Danni bound the wards to the child, wrapping her in the protection. The mist faded and they returned to the room as Danni held Ioana's hands around the wooden spoon.

Silence for a few moments, then Ioana burst into tears and climbed onto Danni's lap.

"Ioana, are you alright? Papa's here." Said Florin. "Where did you go?"

Ioana sobbed and clung tight to Danni, as Florin squatted, ready to take his daughter.

Danni stroked Ioana's back, "You're alright now, you're safe."

"I was in a dark place, Papa. Danni came and got me." Ioana's arms wrapped tighter around Danni's neck.

Danni eyed the old woman, expression stern.

"How did this child attract the attention of a demon from the fourth circle?"

Kezia crumpled into a seat. "I will deal with it."

"Whatever you've been dabbling with nearly lost you your grandchild!" Snapped Danni, and Florin cast his mother an angry look.

"It wasn't me, we were cursed," She made eyed contact with Florin, communicating something, and he nodded to her. "We know who it was. They will pay."

Danni could feel the tingle in the air as Kezia cast a curse against someone, starting a feud that would last generations no doubt.

"I'll need to teach you how to renew these wards, Ioana. You and..." Danni turned to the old woman. "Is there anyone else?"

The old woman shook her head, "Our magic passes to women mostly, and her mother is dead."

"You and Grandma then." Ioana nodded, "You'll need to cover the entire caravan, though they needn't be visible, in fact paint them on all the caravans, then cover them in white paint or wallpaper so nobody can see them."

Danni tapped the wooden spoon, clutched tight in Ioana's hand.

"And make sure you're always wearing something with these symbols on, sweetheart. Sown onto clothing, knitted or woven into fabric. I usually give children beads on a necklace or bracelet but they take too long to make." She eyed Kezia, "And you have the ability to recreate them yourselves anyway."

Kezia nodded as she squinted at Danni, revising her opinion of her - somewhat. Danni gave a weary sigh. She would be getting no sleep tonight and she doubted that these people felt any more kindly towards her. She never took money to help children, it made the act feel... tainted somehow, but she would take payment this time. They would check her tattoos and replenish those that had faded because of her help, and because... she shivered as an image of a bloated Abaddon came into her head.

She shoved the thought aside and made them practise the wards she'd created, drawing and re-drawing them until the symmetry was perfect, before she taught them the words to activate them. Then they burnt any imperfect wards and painted runes on the caravan walls.

The sun was coming up when she finally stripped off and asked Ioana to check her spells, finding that all the tattoos on her back had fallen away. As Kezia re-created them, under Ioana's watchful eye, Danni was struck by a thought.

"How can the Romani See me? Through my protections?" She asked.

The old woman debated telling her. Romani secrets were sacred, but her family was in her debt.

"It is said that in ancient times, our King made a deal with an angel." She said reluctantly. "We can See your kind, whatever your disguise."

"My kind?" Her words unsettled Danni. "You think I'm one of them? A demon?"

The woman squinted at Danni, then looked away with pursed lips, earning a reproachful look from Ioana.

“I don’t know what you are.”

“Fuck you.” Said Danni as she got dressed.

The old woman looked at Ioana. “Wait.”

Her vision became unfocused as she called on old magic. A debt was, after all, owed, and the Romani always paid their debts.

“There will be a woman who talks to the dead. She might help you find your path.”

New York

Emergency services filled a wide lane beside a row of warehouses on the waterfront, a harsh disco of lights in a cordoned off area. Detective Henry Boswell was in early 60's, and thought he'd seen it all. He resembled an owl with his tufty hair that stuck up whatever he did with it, and his large eyes behind thick glasses, that blinked slowly whenever he thought deeply. People assumed he was slow witted if they didn't know him, helped by the look of puzzlement that resided on his features, and he'd learned to use the look to his advantage when interviewing suspects. His suit was cheap and crumpled, while his partner Detective Sam Carter, in his 30's, was smartly dressed. Blond, athletic and tall, his expression was habitually cheerful – more varsity footballer than detective, which he also leveraged in his job.

Today both of them were ashen with horror.

"What sick fuck would do this?" Asked Sam.

They stood outside the door to a warehouse as a shocked medic left. Sam's hands shook as he examined a cigarette, while Harry intercepted the medic. "There aint no-one alive, you need to clear the scene."

The medic blinked, dazed, then nodded, as Harry noticed Sam and swatted his cigarette away.

"Don't start up on them again, Sam!"

Sam struggled to get himself under control. “Jesus, Harry - children!”

Harry’s face set and he turned to face the crowd of emergency workers. “People, we need to lock this down, FBI’s on its way!”

Sam eyed his cigarette, but dropped it unlit as Harry approached a young policeman by the police tape. “Get these vehicles out and make damn sure nobody comes in.”

“Make sure no press get in, and don’t say a word to anyone!” Added Sam.

“Thank Christ I’m retiring, I can’t cope with this shit.” Said Harry, re-joining Sam.

Sam stepped closer to speak in an undertone. “I wanna put these fuckers away.”

Harry looked up as a black, unmarked car parked and two suits get out – Marbas and Stella, who was late 40’s, both in suits.

”That’s FBI, Sam.” Sam’s expression turned truculent.

“This is our patch, Harry.” Replied Sam, eyeing the FBI, reluctant to let it go.

The Order in Brooklyn

Ailwyn and Anders were in the crowd gathered beyond the crime scene cordon. Under black overcoats they wore the white of a dog collars of the clergy.

"Every five years, Anders, how many Fallen is that now?" Asked Ailwyn, his Welsh accent unsoftened by his years in the US.

"Have faith, Brother." Replied Anders, his accent Scandinavian.

"I'm going into the crime scene, we need-."

Anders restrained Ailwyn, "Brother Ailwyn, we have to wait for them to ask us."

"We're wasting time, Brother!"

People in the crowd eyed the 2 men, and Anders dragged Ailwyn away before he could make a scene and draw any more attention to them.

Inside the Brooklyn warehouse, the bodies of 12 homeless children lay entwined by their entrails. Each little face was frozen in a rictus of terror and agony. On the walls, painted in their blood, were the black magic symbols for naming spells. Lilith, Abaddon, Marbas, Tarel, Belial, Beleth and Danyal.

The Fallen in New York

In an expensive apartment in Manhattan, Abaddon ate dinner at a mahogany table. Belial paced the room, fidgeting and bored, while Tarel played solitaire with a pack of cards.

"How come I have to babysit Beleth, Abaddon?"

Abaddon ignored him to keep eating.

"I thought the ceremony was supposed to make him whole?"

Abaddon wheezed, the mere act of sitting an exertion. Dark bags under his eyes, his skin deathly pale - a man very ill. Belial sat down beside him with an exaggerated sigh.

"What's wrong with him anyway?"

Abaddon's stare turned glacial. "Don't worry about Beleth, worry about tomorrow. Is everything ready?"

Belial refused to be diverted though. "Is Beleth ever going to recover?"

"He will, when we've offered enough blood."

"He was supposed to recover after Brooklyn, but Abaddon got distracted by Danyal as usual." Interjected Tarel.

"Danyal is crucial." Blood rushed into Abaddon's cheeked. "I nearly had her!"

"And Beleth isn't? He'd better not be 'cos he's totally mad! He's no good to us, we should kill him and start again. And fuck off this hunt for-."

Abaddon leant forward over Belial - who didn't shrink

away. "This plan is a millennium in the making, you little shit."

"Except that we never sacrifice in the same country, never mind the same city, twice in a row. We're supposed to wait for the occult pattern or some shit." Said Tarel, turning over cards, "You know, just in case they catch us."

Belial nodded agreement. "You fucked up, Abaddon. I vote we move on."

Abaddon's placed his huge, filthy hand on Belial's arm - long, dirty nails digging in. "You don't get a vote! You don't get to question the plan." Abaddon leant in, close enough to kiss, his spittle on Belial's cheek. "If you deviate from our design... if you threaten it in any way..."

He let the sentence trail and Belial looked away. Lily and Armers entered the room with Marbas, and gave Belial frosty stares. He yanked his hand free and sat back, surly but subdued.

"Everything's exactly as you ordered." Mumbled Belial.

"Good. Danyal will come and Beleth will remember who he is, each sacrifice makes us stronger." Abaddon resumed eating.

"Go and play with corpses, Belial." Said Lilith, "You too, Tarel."

Belial and Tarel shared a look, but got to their feet obediently enough. Tarel reached out and took Belial's hand, and they left together, leaving the older Fallen.

"He's right that you got distracted." Stated Marbas.

"It would have been worth it to catch Danni." Replied Abaddon.

"No. We have Beleth, and at the moment we can't use him. We must focus, Abaddon." Replied Lilith.

"Don't lecture me about focus, Lilith!" snapped Abaddon, "You're more obsessed than I-."

"Shut up, both of you." Interjected Armers. "There are specific targets for each sacrifice and we must stick to them. Because of both of you, we have to sacrifice again and risk exposure."

Lilith and Abaddon didn't reply, "Our agents will find Danni eventually, or we will summon her when we're stronger. Either way, we're closer than we've ever been and we can't afford fuck ups. Just stick to the plan."

They reluctantly dropped it and looked to Marbas, who filled them in on the FBI investigation, and assured them that the Order were clueless. Nobody had any idea what they were planning, nobody was on their trail. Nobody would realise they hadn't left New York, nor that they had planned another ritual so soon.

Tarel and Belial listened at the door, then made their

way to the master bedroom, which held the bodies of the apartment's former occupants. A wealthy couple whose money and success had come from membership of a cult. They had been on several charitable foundations, including one for homeless children, and had helped round-up kids for the sacrifice in Brooklyn.

They just hadn't read the small print on the contract when they sold their souls and hadn't realised that they too would have to pay the ultimate price.

Harry

Sam and Harry sat at a corner table in a 'police' bar, empty at that time of day, but with sympathetic staff who left them be. Gruesome crime scene photographs and reports filled the table – an array of corpses, always piled up in a circle - most of them children, with their throats and torsos butchered. Photos from Huangshan, China, 15 years ago, Mexico City, 10 years ago, then again in Russia, five years ago, then fresh photos from Brooklyn.

"Christ, this has been happening all over the world?" He picked up a photograph from Russia, then eyed his partner. "Where the hell did you get these anyway?"

Sam examined photographs. Close-ups of runes on the walls of crime scenes.

"An ex-girlfriend, now FBI." He spread out just the photos of runes and hieroglyphics. "They all have these, like a ritual."

"Black magic." Harry shivered and shoved aside the photos. "This is way over our heads, Sam."

Harry grabbed his beer and took a deep drink as Sam pointed to the older crime scene photos.

"These kids were all kidnapped from one place in one go." He tapped the folders from China, Mexico and Russia, then held up the report of the New York crime scene. "Our scene, the kids were rounded up slowly.

They took their time."

He found a list of people and pulled out sheets clipped together - names, criminal records and mug shots.

"See?" He asked as he handed the paperwork to Harry to inspect, a photo of a waif-like teenager topmost bearing the name JO JO. "Jojo, Harry. They killed Jojo."

Harry paled further as he recognised the street child him and his partner had tried to help. He took the folder and flicked through it, flinching as he saw another name he recognised.

"And Jessie! Shit, she was supposed to be off the streets. God, I didn't even recognise them at the scene." Harry felt nauseous when he remembered that atrocities committed on these children that society had rejected and utterly failed to protect.

"These kids weren't ever in one place, Harry. I've been asking around and the word is a religious outfit offered a clean bed and hot food, no questions asked. I think the sick bastards groomed them. And they took their time 'cos they're based here. Took homeless kids nobody would notice."

"Where? Where did they hold them?"

Sam slumped, "I found a flier but there was no address. A coach came and picked them up, but Harry, these kids were street wise. It must've been someone who won their trust."

Harry flicked through, sorrowful as he recognised more homeless kids. "Jesus, as if their lives weren't hard enough." He sat back - sickened. "But why kill them, Sam? And why like this?"

Sam opened his mouth but Harry changed his mind and waved him off. "No, second thoughts I don't wanna know and nor do you!"

He grabbed their empty glasses and got to his feet. "This is sick shit but the FBI have it and we're off the case."

Sam produced a business card - slapped it on the table.

"What's this... a professor? No!"

"A professor of ancient languages."

Harry leant over his partner, "I'm just shy of retirement and I ain't gonna screw it up."

Sam eyed his partner, not backing down, and Harry jabbed a finger at him. "You've got your whole career ahead of you!"

Sam crossed his arms, stubborn, and Harry sagged, realising he'd get nowhere.... Realising that he also wanted to get the sick fuckers who'd tortured then murdered 12 homeless children.

"I need more beer."

Sam checked his watch, "Make it quick, we're meeting a homeless woman named Tilly who might have a lead on the minibus they used to round up the kids."

Sam and Harry left the bar as night fell, with no clear path to follow, but determined to track down the sick fuckers if they were still on their patch. They traced Tilly who told them a frumpy couple had been feeding homeless kids for weeks. They'd never asked for anything in return, hadn't preached any hellfire and damnation, and had built up trust with the most vulnerable kids, before inviting them to a new hostel their church was opening. The couple hadn't been seen since, and Tilly confirmed that the dead children were the ones the couple had groomed.

Harvey drove a school coach and loved his job. In his 30's and engaged to be married, he hoped to have kids of his own soon, and the little kids he took out on their day trips were a delight to him.

He slowed for a red light and Lilith tapped on the door as he stopped. Sha hadn't aged in 15 years - still voluptuous and beautiful. She simpered and looked apologetic.

"Can you help me?" She asked in a plummy English accent.

He glanced at his watch but levered open the doors "I'm sorry, Ma'am, but I have a tight schedule."

She grabbed the handrail, "I'm just a bit lost." She said, batting her eyelashes. "Could you just show me where to go? I'll be jolly quick!"

She smiled and hurried onto the bus.

"I..." Whatever he started to say were his last words as Lilith shot him in the chest, sending a little puff of blood onto the windscreen. She pulled him from his seat as the lights changed and cars started to honk, then climbed into the driver's seat and drove off. Cars on either side, engrossed in their own lives, and pedestrians jogging over the road, all failed to notice the murder committed right under their nose.

Lily detoured to move Harvey's body and change into a uniform, before driving the bus to Thomas Moore Elementary School, only a few minutes late. She smiled with delight as she saw 25 excited children lined up, ready to board.

The Call

Danni had stayed on at the tulip farm after the Travellers left. Her instincts were quiet and she felt safe – relatively safe. She'd been out all night, drinking, smoking and having sex under the stars with a young man called Stefan. She was just drifting off to sleep when an insect crawled over her arm. She swiped it off, but the itch persisted. Coming fully awake, she stared at her left forearm, at the rune she'd created herself. It was her early warning, tied to her 6th sense. She thought of the rune as a little hook on edge of a giant web that felt the vibrations when an insect landed, and a fat spider began stalking its prey.

Danni got her phone out and scrolled for breaking news. There might be nothing there yet… but no, front page of every news website around the world. A school bus with 25 children and 4 adults had gone missing in New York. Cold dread settled in her stomach and she *knew* with certainty that the Fallen had them and were preparing another sacrifice. She was surprised by the date and made a mental note to check the records, but didn't think she was wrong. The Fallen sacrificed to fuel powerful summoning spells, which included coded details for their next sacrifice. She'd deciphered the last crime scene, 5 years before in Russia, and her faultless memory put their sacrifice at… the time she'd helped Ioana. Her stomach clenched when she realised she'd forgotten. Her flight, her father's death, Ioana's distress.

She shoved the thought aside. Her father always contacted the authorities after she deciphered the message, so they must have reacted and knocked their schedule out... but then another news story caught her eye from New York and she clicked into it. The brutal slaying of children in Brooklyn in what was reported as a Black Magic ritual.

It had happened, as predicted, at the exact moment she'd helped Ioana.

Her instant reaction was rage. More innocent lives taken by monsters that she was powerless to stop. Her rage dampened and sweat broke out as she thought about how vulnerable she'd been, with one foot in Otherworld, *while* they performed a summoning. It was the closest she'd ever come to capture, totally unprepared and distracted, they should have caught her. Danni had to conclude that something about proximity to the Romani must have helped her, and she put the thought aside to study later.

Her presence must have made them lose focus on their spell if they were preparing another ritual already. Patterns were everything in the occult, and their schedule was every 5 years. Now they were angry with her, even angrier, she amended, and about to perform another ceremony. She had to protect herself... but she couldn't leave those children, could she?

Stefan woke up beside her and reached for her, but she

pulled away and got dressed.

“Hey, Babe, we’ve got time before work.” He grinned.

Danni examined his face. He was handsome, he had a lovely cheeky grin, and although arrogant, was fully self-aware of his failings. “If you had the choice to rescue children, or even just one little child, but it meant probably losing your own life, what would you do?”

Stefan lit a spliff and applied serious thought to the question. “I’d like to say I’d sacrifice myself, but I’m not sure I’m that generous.” He took a deep drag, then grinned, “Besides, I’d be depriving everyone of my gifts.”

Danni smiled, realising he was only partly joking.

“See you around.” She replied, knowing she wouldn’t, then jogged off to the huts.

Danni collected her pay then headed into Amsterdam, to an internet café and idly studied a map of Europe, ostensibly debating where to go, but she had a browser window open on the unfolding case of the children, and soon a photo of 25 kids popped up. She studied each of their little faces, her heart going out to them.

She pulled up charts she’d saved in the cloud and did some calculations. The sacrifice would be less powerful than their previous ritual, but, if they were quick, it would still be potent. She then traced the detectives from the 'Brooklyn Massacre', as the press had dubbed it, and using a disposable phone, she rang the NYPD precinct assigned to the case and placed an anonymous tip that the children had been kidnapped by the same cult, and that they had 48 hours to find them.

Danni blanked out the world around her. Her senses quietened and she thought... The Fallen were in New York, so she had to run as far away as possible. But her stomach cramped when she thought of all the children she'd met, scarred by demons, and the Fallen were the very worst of them. She felt physically sick when she visualised what would happen to the 25 children they had kidnapped.

If she had access to the crime scene photos, she might be able to help. Without giving herself time to reconsider she booked herself on the next flight to New York.

Over in New York, Harry and Sam were in their car, Harry driving while Sam examined photos of runes.

"Hey, we got real cases too, Sam."

Sam waved off his comments as his cell rang.

"Yvonne, how you doing...?" He tensed, his skin turning ashen. "Thanks."

He disconnected and turned to his partner. "The missing school coach. A member of a Satanic cult just had a pang of conscience or something. She rang in to say that the cult took them. The same people who killed our homeless kids is going to kill them in two days."

Harry turned on his siren, "Let's go visit that professor of yours."

Harry and Sam sat in the dining room of Professor Brewer, a woman in her 60's. On her table were the photographs from 3 crimes scenes, starting in Mexico, then China, then Brooklyn. In one photo, children had been piled into a heap in a circle around a large, scorched section of floor.

Brewer winced as she peered through reading glasses. "Oh God!"

"Do you recognise this writing?"

She pushed aside her distaste and picked up a photograph of hieroglyphics. "Some, though it's a strange hybrid of languages. Egyptian beside Mayan, Arabic…." Her gaze caught on the glassy stare of a child and she swallowed bile to examine runes on the wall behind it.

"But these aren't Sumerian or Egyptian hieroglyphics. They nearly are and they're all jumbled up." She dropped the photo.

“Can you guess at their meaning?”

She shrugged as she wiped her fingers on her top, distaste etched on her face.

“These runes are familiar but I can’t read them.” She used a pen to tap photos of runes, unwilling to contaminate her hands again. “If I had to guess, I would say these are Satanic runes, and that this is a name.... Lucifer.”

Harry crossed himself.

“A Satanic rite?” He asked.

“I can’t tell you their provenance.”

She took out her cell phone and pushed away the photos.

“I’m a historian of dead languages, you would be better talking to a scholar of the occult.” She searched on her phone address book. “There’s monastery on Long Island.”

She wrote down a number and turned to face them, wincing when she saw the pictures again. “Ask for Brother Ailwyn.”

In a deserted arches full of litter, a squad car pulled in beside the missing school coach. Two police officers called it in then approached it warily, guns ready.

"Police! Come on down off the bus."

There was no response and they stepped closer, but nobody was visible through any of the windows. The door was open and first officer stepped onto the bus and did a quick scan, but it appeared empty. He stepped along the coach, scanning each seat, but nobody was there. What he did detected was a faint, unpleasant smell.

The second officer got a wave from her partner and walked around the outside, drawn to the back, attracted by a smell. When her partner joined her, she opened the baggage door – and jumped back as flies exploded from Harvey's corpse.

A high brick wall, mounted with cameras, stretched into the distance, topped with iron spikes. Harry drove his car through sturdy, wrought iron gates, Sam beside him, and they both peered into the distance. Behind them the gates swung closed.

"You sure this is a monastery and not a prison, Sam?"

Harry drove slowly, up a gravel drive to a huge Gothic building of grey stone. Immaculate and flat, the lawn stretched for miles, the high stone boundary wall receding into the distance. A monk waited at the door for them and he escorted them, in silence, to an office, then let himself out – all without talking. The room was large and simple, whitewashed walls, tapestries - a picture of monastic study, with the soothing background sound of rushing water audible through thickened glass windows.

Sam moved to the casement window, drawn by the sound. “Would you look at that!”

The window looked down onto a large quadrangle with covered walkways and a giant fountain in the centre - a granite outcrop, water hurled high into the air, to cascade down into vast grates. Monks surrounded the waterfall, prostrate in prayer. Harry joined him, impressed despite himself.

“Hey, that looks like a Buddhist?” Sam pointed to one of the kneeling monks in saffron robes. “Wait, I think it’s a woman too.”

“And that one looks Sikh.” Harry pointed to a man in a turban.

Ailwyn entered, now in a brown cassock.

“All denominations and creeds are welcome at this monastery, though I myself am Church of England.” He said, smiling warmly and crossed the room to meet him, hand extended.

“Thanks for seeing us, Brother, er...”

“Al-win. It’s Welsh.”

Ailwyn shook hands with them and gestured for them to sit.

“What’s with the giant water feature and all the monks?” Sam grinned, gesturing to the window.

“A fountain of Holy Water.” Ailwyn was matter of fact and Sam gave an ‘of course’ smirk.

Moving onto business, he opened the folder to spread photos of hieroglyphics on the table.

”So, like I explained on the phone, I’d like you to read these.”

Ailwyn leant forward to see the pictures, “Crime scene photos from China, Mexico, Russia and most recently...” He moved the pictures as he spoke, “America, Brooklyn to be precise.”

The men eyed him in surprise, having not mentioned the other crime scene photos.

“The FBI already showed me. Which I believe places this outside the NYPD provenance.”

“The latest massacre of children happened on our

patch!" Angry, Sam leant in towards Ailwyn. "The CIA, FBI, Interpol, fuck, even the KGB..." Harry winced as his partner swore before the monk, noticed by Ailwyn. "... Combined, they haven't caught these bastards in fifteen years."

"And you intend to?" Asked Ailwyn.

"Damn right!"

Ailwyn raised an eyebrow, sceptical.

"They're in New York and we know the streets, we have informers-."

"They *were* in New York..."

"No, New York's a different MO, they didn't just scoop up the kids, they took their time - they're based here, at least for now."

"We've been told that they're behind the kidnapping of the school children." Interjected Harry, and Ailwyn eyed them keenly.

"Told by whom?"

"Anonymous tip. We traced it to Europe, a disposable cell phone."

Ailwyn considered then nodded. "These are names. I'm still deciphering what they mean, but..."

"Lucifer?" Asked Sam, earning a look from Ailwyn.

"It's best not to name them, young man." He said, then got to his feet.

"Combined with the runes and child sacrifices, they form..." He searched for the word. "Summoning spells, if you will."

Ailwyn crossed to a sideboard and picked up two simple, metal crosses on chains.

"So they're what, witches?" Asked Sam.

"The people performing these rituals look normal, they'll act normally when they're in public - they'll be almost impossible to trace."

"No black, pointy hats then?" Asked Sam.

Ailwyn turned to face them, deadly serious. "They are pure evil."

He re-joined them at the table, a cross in each hand, but Sam automatically patted his holster.

"They'll react to a bullet."

Ailwyn dropped the crosses into the men's laps. "Maybe."

The men stared at their laps - nonplussed and unsettled. Ailwyn relaxed and smiled. "Aye, they will. And I think you're right, they'll stay in New York to perform a second ritual. I think your informant is right, they kidnapped those children."

"Jesus." Said Sam and Ailwyn frowned at his blasphemy.

"One ritual fifteen years ago, one ten years ago, then again five years, now two in the same month. There's a pattern somewhere, that's what I'm working on. The Occult is all about patterns, if you know where to look."

"But can you help us find those children, Father Ailwyn?" Asked Harry.

"I'm not a priest, Detective. Brother Ailwyn technically, but I prefer just Ailwyn." He flashed a tired smile at Harry, "I will certainly try. We need to stop their ceremony."

Ailwyn held out his hand to shake, the meeting over. "I'm still deciphering these, but I will let you know what I find, without informing the FBI that you're in the loop."

"Our informer said we had 2 days."

Ailwyn nodded. "I think she's right. Would you do me the favour of letting me know your progress? I'd be particular interested if your anonymous contact gets back in touch?"

"OK, Fa.. Ailwyn." Said Harry. "Anything to save those children."

"My concern is what they might be summoning."

Replied Ailwyn.

Back in the car the huge gates to the ground swung open for them, and they both breathed a sigh of relief.

“I feel like I’ve just been to see the head teacher at school.” Said Sam.

“And I’d like to know how Brother Ailwyn knew our informant was female.”

Danni in New York

A mental clock ticked in Danni's head as she flew to New York, the count-down to the sacrifice of innocent lives. At the airport, as she'd gone outside for a taxi, she'd been hit by their rank presence immediately. A fat cockroach dropped from an awning, narrowly missing her hair. A trash can exploded with flies when she passed. When the taxi dropped her at Harry's precinct, she'd opened the door to find a cat's corpse in the gutter, alive with maggots. The Fallen were here, in New York, and if she could feel their presence, she suspected they'd feel hers.

At Harry's precinct she learnt the case had been handed over to the FBI. However much she'd risked coming so close to the Fallen, but she couldn't risk the FBI. She waited outside the station until Harry and Sam finished their shift, then followed Harry home, the streets around her full of the stench of decay and corruption.

He lived in a rundown tenement with a broken security door. She headed up to a narrow, dirty corridor, poorly lit from a small window onto the street. Danni now wore a blond wig, jeans and jumper - a preppy look. She knocked at a battered front door and waited.

There was no answer, but she'd seen him enter the building. She knocked again, louder, and waited. When there was still no response she raised her hand to knock again and the door was yanked open, the barrel of a gun in her face. Harry, in shadows, kept his gun level, and Danni raised her hands.

"I can find the missing children." She said.

Harry didn't bother to hide his annoyance - and disbelief. "So go down the station."

Danni warmed instantly to him, despite his scowl. "Nobody can know... Just give me five minutes? Please."

A moment of silence greeted this. "I'm not on the case."

"Yes you are."

Another moment of silence while he tried to compose his features into a scowl. "What's your name?"

"Emma." Said Danni instantly, but Harry raised an eyebrow.

"Emma, huh? Take off your bag, face forward, hands on the wall."

He gestured with his gun and she stepped into his apartment and swung her pack off, then placed her hands on the wall, above her head. Harry kicked her bag away then placed his gun against her head while he performed a practised pat down of her body, pockets, upper legs. When he was happy he stepped back, gun still in hand.

"Turn around."

Danni turned and he gestured with his gun for her to go

ahead, along the corridor, scooping up her bag as he passed. They entered a neglected room with battered second hand furniture, papers scattered everywhere. Harry sat on a chair opposite Danni, a coffee table between them. He plonked Danni's bag on it.

"Five minutes then I'm calling uniforms. I don't like people coming to my home uninvited."

"Open the bag."

Harry hesitated, then unzipped her pack and pulled out a thick folder. Father Richard had collected records on the Fallen for years and she'd printed them off at an internet café before coming to see Harry.

"The man who raised me was a scholar."

He sifted through documents, grouped with paperclips: crime scene photos and newspaper clipping from around the world, some duplicates of the files he'd already seen, some much older, going back 100+ years.

"Specifically, a scholar of dead languages and the occult. He spent his life studying the cult that has these children."

Harry glanced at images from China, Russia, Afghanistan, Africa, England... Richard's contacts had given him photos of all Fallen massacres, but his contacts had vanished with Richard's death so she had nothing from Brooklyn.

"They have existed for a very, very long time, spread over the world."

He sat back, unimpressed. "I know."

Danni went absolutely still. "You've met The Order?"

"I've met a monk who specialises in this shit. So, if there's nothing else you can leave, and not come back."

"Did they tell you that they leave instructions at their rituals? The location of their next sacrifice?"

Harry's eyes narrowed and Danni reached for the documents, selecting a file on Mexico from which she pulled out 2 photos, each with circles over portions of walls where runes and hieroglyphics had been drawn, then grabbed a pen and paper. Her father had made her translate them 10 years ago, when she was only 12. He hadn't baulked at explaining what they meant, or where they were found. He said that he'd passed the information on to the authorities in Mexico, but if so, how come the sacrifices had even happened? It was only after his death that she was discovering how much he'd kept from her.

"These were taken in Mexico City, ten years ago. These are numbers, the latitude and longitude for the next sacrifice, date and time. " She copied the symbols and translated them into numbers - latitude and longitude directions.

"Look them up, Detective." She tore off a sheet of paper. "Should give you Severomorsk, in Russia."

She grabbed the topmost stack of documents, from Russia, scanned photos until she found 2 with areas circled and went through the same process, giving him another series of numbers, "The date and time with directions for the attack in Brooklyn."

"How do I know you're not just making it up? They look like squiggles to me."

"Do you really think I can memorise dozens of coordinates?" Snapped Danni – though of course she could. "I'll do it for all of these if you like. Just try it, please."

Harry grabbed an old laptop from his coffee table. "*If* this is true, why the hell didn't your dad tell the police?"

"Richard wasn't my real father, and he did, well, the FBI." She hoped that part was true. She wasn't yet ready to think that he hadn't contacted them. "Within two hours of making the call, he was dead." That of course was not true, but she did wonder now why he hadn't tried harder. Or why the Order hadn't…. unless they hadn't been able to decipher the runes?

"If I see the Brooklyn photos, I can find where their next ceremony is." She said desperately as Harry entered the numbers on his computer, then sat back with a sigh.

"The Order want to bring down this cult, but they don't care about these kids, not in the bigger picture." She waited for him to look at her. "Let me see the crime scene photos. I can read Sumarian, Egyptian, the ancient hieroglyphics, Latin, Arabic..."

Unsettled, Harry waved her into silence.

"Give me more coordinates first."

The factory had been abandoned for nearly a decade and the Fallen had their captives locked in a small room in the basement, the children asleep in a tight bundle around the four adults. Abaddon and Belial entered the room. Abaddon shuffled, wheezing and gasping, while Belial sauntered, taking his time, studying them, an evil blade in his hand. He stopped before Miss Cooper, who woke with a start. She eyed him with wide, scared eyes. "I need Katie."

He smiled at Miss Cooper's alarmed glance at the sleeping Katie.

"Please don't hurt them, please-."

"And Marianne, Rodrigues and David." He shouted, waking them. Belial played with the knife, as the children cried and whimpered, and adults tried to hug them all close. Abaddon meanwhile sat heavily on a chair, his breathing laboured.

"Come on, it's time for some fun!" Belial pointed to Katie. "Brave Katie, come on up."

He grinned, handsome and reassuring, and Katie got to her feet.

"Marianne, Rodrigues and David too, come on you little misfits!"

Three children got to their feet and the teachers tried to give reassuring smiles. They picked their way through the other kids to line up before him, and he dropped to his knees before him.

"Can you guess why I picked out you, darling little children?" They eyed him in defiant silence.

"Well, let's see. Katie, molested by your stepfather... Rodrigues, physically and mentally abused by your mother" He tapped his finger on their chests as he spoke, in turn, "Marianne," He laughed, "Just about every one in your family beats on you!" He moved onto the last child, "Ooh, David, watch out for your brother Peter. Your dad had him carnally before he was locked up and now Peter's full of lust for you."

The children all looked at their feet, frightened and ashamed.

"You see, your anger and self-loathing makes you particularly ripe for us." Belial eyed the other children gleefully, "But don't y'all worry. Innocence is equally alluring."

Katie grabbed hold of Rodrigues's hand, defiant.

"Good! Don't get pissed on all your lives, kids, learn to fight back! Not that they'll be very long lives." He winked at her, "Shall we visit your would-be guardian angel? She's right here in New York!"

Belial looked to Abaddon who had finally recovered his breath. Abaddon nodded and Belial sliced, cutting Katie across the palm. He then grabbed her hand and squeezed her blood into a bowl, then moved on and did the same to the other children. Several of their classmates screamed but none of his victims cried out and he eyed them with approval, before dancing back to Abaddon with the bowl.

"You're sure this isn't another flight of fancy, Abaddon?" Sneered Belial.

"She's here." Replied Abaddon.

Back in Harry's apartment, Harry slept in an armchair but Danni continued working. She sat on the floor by the coffee table, a table lamp over documents and she used a magnifying glass to read the scripts, pen and paper beside her full of notes.

"You're reading our secrets, Danyal." Said Abaddon from close to Danni. She sat up with a start and scanned the room. She'd known it was a risk to get involved, but she'd never imagined they could trace her.

"I can almost taste you, you're very close... you're in New York." Laughed Abaddon with a curiously effeminate laugh.

She felt hot breath on her neck twisted to face backwards to see Belial's face, inches from her own.

"Belial." She breathed, his name resonating within her. Abaddon, Armers awoken in China, Tarel in Mexico, Belial in Russia... and Lilith.

"Why won't you join us?" Said Belial, "We have lots of fun, don't we, Katie?"

For a second Danni got a view of the children, the four lined up, Katie's head held high in defiance, the others huddled behind them with the adults.

The children vanished and Belial's hand appeared and he stroked her lower lip, his eyes lidded. Danni grabbed his wrist and pulled it away from her cheek, her nails digging into his flesh. "I am not one of you."

Belial grimaced in pain and tried to pull his arm away. "Come to us and we'll let the children go."

Danni uttered a curse as she dug her nails in deeper, drawing blood - and Belial vanished with an angry cry.

Back in the deserted factory the children were all awake, all silent, staring at Belial who knelt before Amy, Rodrigues, Marianne and David. Armers had joined them and kicked Belial, who snapped his eyes open and jumped to his feet, holding his right arm, in pain.

"That fucking bitch!" Five crescents from Danni's nails bled on his hand, but Armers scanned the prisoners.

"Where's the man?"

The teachers looked around in alarm – but the male teaching assistant was gone.

"Stop him escaping." Armers stood close to Belial, who fumed but nodded. The children scooted back to the others as Belial made circles with his hands. He started whispering under his breath and brought his hands closer together. A grey form appeared, and he expanded his hands again, moving them, shaping something. Smoke solidified and darkened, then a black dog formed with fire in its eyes and mouth.

"Kill." Said Belial, pointing to the door and the hound bounded off on silent paws. The children wailed and the adults tried to pull them closer, in a pathetic huddle as Belial fell to the ground, exhausted, his bloody hand close to his chest. Then a scream carried, long, agonised, and the children screamed.

The sun was just rising when Harry woke to see Danni, still on the floor, with tears streaming down her face.

"You ok?" He asked, not sure what to say.

"Ok?" She asked herself. *"I've tainted myself by touching their foulness, and they found me, they touched me back."* She shivered and wiped her lip where that *thing* had touched her, contaminated her, *"I have looked on pure, dark, corrupted, vile evil... And I have seen those children, the captives of devils, and I can't help them. I can't help myself and I can't help them."*

"They'll die tonight, at midnight... but I can't find where."

Danni examined her hand, dried blood under the nails, in despair.

"What happened to your hand?" He asked.

"It doesn't matter. I failed." She packed her bag, defeated. "I'm sorry."

"But..." Harry eyed her with suspicion, sure now he'd

spent an uncomfortable night in a chair for some perverse, thrill seeking teenager.

"I wasn't lying!"

She snatched up a pile of papers.

"Look, it's right here!" She drew the symbols that appeared in all crimes scenes. "Life, live, force, energy...." More symbols, "circle, ring, bind, prison, captive," more runes, "enter, freedom, liberate, doorway" she drew more runes and started to draw arrows between them. "Life, with this becomes death, the taking of life... this linked to this rune means to offer a captive to free another captive, they're the summoning element of the spell. These are names, the names of those they are calling to, demons from the deepest pits of hell, and it's an open offer. They aren't closing the doors afterwards, they're opening the floodgates and inviting them in." She scrabbled through the photos and lined up more of them.

"These are the coordinates. Using Hindu-Arabic numerals, these are Egyptian, this is Khmer numerals, this is a primitive tally system. The numbers are easy, the secret is work out their order." Danni was aware she was speaking too fast and that she was trembling, but she couldn't slow down. Harry watched her in bemused awe.

"The order depends on the date and time of the ceremony, and confluence – of the stars and the worlds.

Again, it's easy when you know the formula. Everything in the occult has a pattern," She said, unknowingly repeating Ailwyn's statement, "They're calling to their own kind," She stumbled over the word, "waking them up, telling them where to meet them, but the *numbers* are missing!" Danni searched frantically through the scattered photos. "Did they get everything? Maybe they didn't photograph it all?"

She looked up, half-hopeful, but Harry shook his head.

"No, they got everything... still, doesn't mean I have it. I'm not supposed to even have this." Creaky and groaning, he hoisted himself to his feet. "I need coffee."

Harry stretched, then reached for a photo - a list in Arabic. "Is Lucifer's name on here?"

"Never say their names aloud!"

She got to her feet, stiff and cramped. She wiped away her tears, her whole body language defeated. There was nothing more she could do and needed to leave New York, urgently. They were closer than they'd ever been.

"I'm sorry I wasted your time, Detective. I'm sorry I couldn't save those children."

Harry stood there, awkward, as Danni re-packed her bag.

Lilith, Armers and Abaddon sat at the large table upstairs in the factory, with fancy take-out coffee and fresh pastries.

"She's still fighting us."

Abaddon huffed and shifted to get comfortable.

"If we push her too hard, we risk forcing her to suicide." Stated Armers, the most reasonable and patient of them.

Lilith nodded reluctantly, and her expression twisted with anger. "Always the brat."

"Always the key, Lilith. She's important." Abaddon put his huge, sweaty hand over Lilith's delicate, long-nailed hand, his own nails filthy.

"She's answered our call, whether she knows it or not. She's so close this time, and if she doesn't heed the call she'll come for the children."

Lilith pulled her hand free, lips curled with disgust, but she gave a reluctant nod.

Danni sat, hunched, at the back of a retro coffee shop in a booth. Untouched black coffee before her, she scrolled through images of the documents, photos taken on her phone. A couple sat close together on low sofas, the shop otherwise empty aside from a waitress. Danni debated if she could really leave those children. When they performed the next ceremony she would no doubt lose her protections, and they would find her. Perhaps she could save them if she gave herself up?

A THUD against the large glass frontage made everyone look up. An old man staggered against the window, clutching his chest. The couple on the low sofas gasped as he sank to the ground, and a bystander rushed to help, shouting for someone to call an ambulance.

Time seemed to slow. Danni watched colour drain from the world, turning it sepia as sounds became muffled.

The old man's hand fell away from his chest as a woman dropped to her to knees and checked his pulse. She shouted, her words lost, then began CPR as all colour drained from the world and it turned fully black and white. Danni watched, the only person still vibrantly colourful. She turned her attention to the couple in the coffee shop, noticing that they stood up in slow motion, freezing halfway. The waitress was by the door, frozen in time. Out on the monochrome street, all traffic had stopped and utter silence had descended.

Time stood still.

A tall, slender black man traversed the frozen crowd with the fluid grace of a dancer. His skin glowed but darkness surrounded him, like a cloud. Azrael, the angel of death.

He neared the old man and waited as his soul left his body, ready to be escorted to judgement. Soul in tow, Azrael turned away, then went completely still. He turned back to face directly into the café, to Danni's table, but she had gone.

Danni cowered in the restroom, sure Azrael would come for her. The world remained silent and monochrome – until colour suddenly flooded back and sounds returned. Out in the café, the waitress called out to say she'd phoned for an ambulance, then looked back inside, surprised to see that Danni's table was empty when she was sure it was occupied when she'd gone to the door. She shrugged it off as back in the bathroom, Danni leant back against the wall and caught her breath –struck by inspiration. She hurriedly dug her phone out of her bag and enlarged a photo of the Brooklyn scene. Had Azrael guided her? She somehow she doubted it. Bad things happened when Angels got involved with the happenings of earth. She shivered and dialed Harry's number.

In the monastery, a thoroughly modern room was a

stark contrast to the stone walls that enclosed it. A surveillance room with feeds from cameras around the world to a bank of TV screens, watched by half a dozen monks.

A young woman, Olive, in jeans and sweatshirt, sat before a bank of computers where a pop-up link appeared on screen. She clicked open the link to Harry's phone and listened in on Danny.

"Detective, I've found them! I'm in the cafe, by your apartment."

Olive snatched up a phone, "I might have something."

Danni tentatively returned to her seat and ordered fresh coffee. She didn't have long to wait for Harry, who entered with a carrier bag under one arm, the folders from the night before - then she nearly bolted when Sam followed.

"Sam's my partner, he goes where I go." Said Harry, cutting off her protest.

Sam flashed a lopsided grin at Danni, and slid in beside her, Harry on the other side, cornering her.

“I don’t have long as they’ll trace my phone call, but they’ve switched methods.”

“Who will have traced you?”

“Everyone.” Replied Danni, waving off the comment and got out her phone and enlarged a photograph - an animal hide with primitive inscriptions.

“They used Algonquian hieroglyphics, which is desecration of course.”

Harry and Sam exchanged a bemused look, as Danni snatched a folder from the carrier bag and rifled through to the photos from Brooklyn’s crime scene.

“It’s Native American.” She flicked through to the photo she needed - the hide. “These symbols mean First Place or Principle Place, otherwise known as Cutchogue, on Long Island.”

She turned the photo to show them. They eyed the squiggles, dubious, as Danni tapped the photo.

“These here translate to Old House.” She sat back with a relieved grin. “Built in sixteen forty-nine, the Old House is a museum in summer, but it’s available for private hire.”

Danni’s smile faded at their lack of reaction. “The children will be killed there, tonight, at midnight.”

“Really?” Asked Sam, highly sceptical. “You got that

from squiggles?"

"Not squiggles, a language. But you can't go too early, you'll scare them off and they'll kill those children anyway."

"This is utterly insane!" Said Sam.

"And anyway it's completely outside our jurisdiction." Said Harry.

"So tell the police there!"

"Tell them what? A young lady who reads ancient Egyptian told us to tell them that a Satanic ritual was gonna happen in... Old House?"

"I know it's career suicide, but I'm right! Can you live with yourselves if you ignore it? If you don't try?" She beseeched. "What if I'm right?"

"I'm having a hard time with this, Harry. I mean, why would they even do that anyway? Give away their location?"

Danni was crestfallen. She'd wasted all this time on Harry and risked everything, and they still didn't believe her. "Those children will be there tonight, and you can't call in the FBI, they have people working there. You have the chance to save their lives."

Danni pushed against Harry to get out as he debated.

"Sam, I ran her notes by the Prof and everything she wrote is right."

She pushed against Sam this time, getting more frantic. "Did you ask her just how many people in the world can read sacred, Native American writings? And Sumarian, and... basically anything ever written?"

Harry nodded thoughtfully, "The doctor wants to meet you in fact, Emma, you discerned whole new word associations she hadn't thought of, whatever that means."

She shot Harry a beseeching look. "This is one of the reasons why this cult want me, the FBI want me, the Order want me. I *have* to go! Please help those children."

Her top caught on the table, revealing her tattoo sleeve. Harry stared at a tattoo of a closed eye... which slowly opened.

"What the..?"

Danni pulled down her sleeve, panicked. "Let me out!"

Harry nodded to Sam, who moved to let her pass.

She bolted passed them, but paused. "If you go there, you will recognise them. You will know I'm right."

Then she was gone. Shortly afterwards, a young man entered the coffee shop at speed and looked around, noting 3 mugs on the table with Harry and Sam. He eyed them briefly, catching Harry's eye, before speaking into phone and hurrying from the shop.

Danni zigzagged her way across the city, changing her clothing and hair and gait frequently in a desperate bid to reach a coach or train station. At Penn Station, she noticed a pile of fat maggots on the steps, and altered course. Everywhere she went, the Fallen had posted people so she opted for a bus to take her out of town, but each time she boarded one she ended up headed towards Long Island.

She was wildly off kilter. Her father's death had set off a domino of events, with the Fallen ever closer – with Ioana, then last night at Harry's. They were close to catching her and her father had made clear that must never happen. She asked herself for the millionth time who she was and why they wanted her? They had called her Danyal, and that had struck a chord somewhere deep inside her. Then there was the 'pull' that Abaddon had mentioned, and she could feel something pulling her east again.

With determination she headed west, on foot, on coaches and buses. And everywhere she felt their presence. A police car screeched to a halt in front of her, but as she backed up, the officers jumped out to accost a young, black man and racially abuse him. People argued around her, cars hooted and people swore at each other, and the stink of corruption permeated the city. Insects, maggots and roaches erupted from sewers and trash cans. Filth and pollution lay heavy in the air, and she passed a house whose walls seeped a black, tar-like substance.

Feeling as if she was battling a gale that pushed her east, she fought the pull, but her head was filled with the photographs of the school children, heading towards death in Long Island. At around 10:30 that night, she gave up fighting the pull and hurried to catch a train to carry her east. Fuck the police. Fuck the Order and the Fallen. She could not run away from this crime without being complicit. Relief overcame her as she gave into the pull, now battling a concern that she might have left it too late to help.

Cutchogue, Long Island

At the point Danni began her journey to Cutchogue, Harry and Sam were already there, parked on the grass along from an old wooden house which blazed with lights. Sam nudged a dozing Harry when a black van pulled up outside and reversed up to the front door, to a tunnel made from a tent that hid the back of the van and the door to the Old House.

Sam grabbed the door handle, but Harry gripped his arm to wait, as Belial and Armers got out of the van. Something knocked against the handbrake in Harry's pocket and he felt inside, and found 2 little charms that Danni had slipped in at the café.

"I do not like the look of them." Whispered Sam, and Harry nodded, handing Sam a charm.

"From Emma?" He asked, and Harry shrugged.

"I feel like we fell down a wormhole somehow though, Sam." Said Harry and Sam nodded agreement, "It somehow makes me feel better."

Sam pocketed the charm, and felt a comforting warmth spread into his hand where he touched it.

The men vanished into the tent for about half an hour and they heard the rear van doors open, then a short while later close again, and Belial drove the van off, to reappear ten minutes later. Lilith came out to meet him and they had a brief conversation before Belial disappeared inside the house.

“It’s gone eleven, Harry. We need to call for backup now if we’re gonna do it.”

Harry puffed out a breath, then squinted. “What’s she doing?”

Harry focused night-vision binoculars as Lilith bent down and put ‘something’ outside the front of the house.

“I can’t see.”

He passed the binoculars to Sam. “I really don’t like it, Sam, any of it.”

“And I think she just planted a suspect package under the house.” Replied Sam.

Harry nodded thoughtfully, “That might be something we need to call in.”

Lilith went inside the Old House, but four people came out and went to stand at the 4 compass points around it. Time was ticking past.

“Decision time.” Said Sam.

Harry opened his car door. “Let’s take a look.”

Harry got out of the car and sauntered towards the old house, clicking on his police-issue torch, while Sam melted into the shadows. A man crossed the green to block his path.

"It's a beautiful old house, do you think I can get a peek inside?"

"There's a private function in there tonight."

Lionel Thompson was in his 60's. Slicked back silver hair and a haughty air that instantly annoyed Harry.

"I'm only here today, I'm sure the people inside won't mind."

"It's a private function and they would mind." Replied Lionel, blocking his path.

His wife, Alison, an equally haughty woman in her middle age wandered over to see what was happening, the other remaining two guards invisible behind the house, and Harry hoped that Sam would take care of them.

"How about I come back with a warrant?" He asked the haughty man.

Thompson threw back his head and laughed, an overly dramatic action honed by years of performing in court, "I don't think you'll be getting a warrant any time soon."

"You don't look like a security guard? Don't sound like one neither."

The couple bristled. "We're not guards, we're volunteers. We run the historical society-"

"And let me guess, you're a lawyer, right?" Asked Harry, and Thompson nodded, smug again now his authority was recognised.

"Tomorrow you'll have all the access you'd ever want." He sniggered to his wife.

Harry's hand fell on the amulet from Danni just as his torchlight was pointed at their torsos, and at that moment he noticed that neither the woman nor the man cast a shadow.

"You need to leave now." Added the woman.

Harry shined his torch upwards towards their faces, and for a brief moment the couple appeared to be something else – their eyes pitch black, their teeth bared – before they raised their hands to block the light.

"Hey!" Said the man, annoyed.

Harry thumped his torch over his head. Before he'd collapsed, he did the same to the woman, and they both fell unconscious to the ground.

Sam came around the back of the house, his 2 lookouts walking before him with their hands raised. Like the 2 on the ground, they cast no shadows. As they eyed the fallen couple in alarm, Sam shrugged, then hit both his captives to knock them out.

"We're in trouble now." He whispered.

They rifled through the clothing of the four unconscious people and withdrew hand guns. Sam got his cell phone out and rang 911 to request an urgent police response at Old House, Cutchogue, claiming they had just been attacked by 4 armed people.

They disabled the guns and threw them away, and withdrew their own firearms to approach the house. They checked underneath and swore when they saw a flashing light, and Sam redialed 911 to advise there was a suspected bomb under the house.

"How did you know it was a bomb?" Whispered Sam.

"I didn't!"

Sweat broke out on their foreheads. "Backup'll be here real soon, Harry, we just put a rocket under their arses."

"Or a rocket in my pension." Replied Harry.

The checked the time, aware that they were risking their careers and, given their assault of the guards, their liberty, all on the word of a lunatic young woman. But the whole situation felt off the them and they were both convinced that if the children weren't inside, something else nefarious was going on. The time was now 11:45 – 15 minutes until the sacrifice.

They slipped into the tent over the door, but a weighty oak door was closed. They ducked out and headed to the side of the house, to another door, then took position on either side of it. They did a silent count, then Harry threw open the door, careful it didn't bang on the wall, while Sam burst in, gun raised.

A huge fireplace, furniture moved back against the wall, but the room was otherwise empty, although voices carried from the room next door. Harry closed the door and they tiptoed through the kitchen, passed the front door and staircase, into the old 'parlour'.

A old table had been pushed against the wall and it's top was littered with paraphernalia of a black magic ritual – candles, a goblet and an array of blades from surgical knives to hunting knives. There was no sign of the children but Lilith, Abaddon, Tarel and Belial stood in a row, and pivoted as they entered.

Harry and Sam aimed their guns, hands steady. "Where are the children?"

"You stupid little men. You have no idea what you're messing with." Snarled Lilith.

A drop of blood fell through the cracks of the ceiling, then the sound of rapidly approaching sirens, and everyone exploded into action. Lilith, Abaddon, Tarel and Belial dived in different directions at lightning speed, including Abaddon who moved with grace and speed when required, despite his bulk. Sam shot wildly, retreating to the stairs, but Harry was calmer. He saw a detonation device as Belial grabbed it, and he shot it, shattering Belial's hand along with the device.

"The children, Harry, upstairs!" Shouted Sam.

Lilith was dodging towards him and he fired another shot before backing up, then running up the stairs, firing blindly behind him as he ran. Two rooms, and they checked each, but found the children on the right. Alive, gagged, with their hands tied in front of them, but 1 of the 3 remaining adults dead, her throat cut.

The children whimpered as Harry took up position at the door and Sam did a quick count, before heading upstairs to the attic rooms, which were empty. The sirens were close now, and downstairs seemed quiet. Mindful of the potential bomb, Sam hurriedly got the kids to their feet.

"You're safe now, but we gotta get out." He urged, yanking smaller kids upright feet as Harry stepped down the stairs.

The first 2 police cars screeched to a halt outside, headlights shining through the tent and through the open door, and called for the people inside to come out with their hands up. Harry did another check left and right, but the house was empty. He threw his gun outside then turned to help the first child down the steps.

"You hurry on outside now, the police are waiting. They're gonna take you home! You're safe now, you're all safe."

The children were tentative at first, worried by the strange men, worried about a trick, but Harry yanked them none too gently off the steps and thrust them through the door as they come down.

"You run now! Run."

More police cars pulled up, and police stood behind their cars, guns pointed at the house, but they lowered them in amazement as the first child stepped out, still bound at the wrists and gagged. Another child followed, then another, as Sam and Harry hurried the kids out of the house. Some of the children ran to the police, but others hovered on the grass, too scared to move. When all 25 were free, Sam and Harry emerged from the house, both with their hands up.

"Bomb!" They both shouted, and started running, herding kids before them.

The police responded instantly, running forward to pickup children as ambulances started arriving behind them. Harry and Sam hastily showed their badges and advised that they were the ones who'd called it in. They had discussed what to tell them, especially so far outside of their jurisdiction, and had opted for the truth. A young woman, expert in dead languages, had advised that the previous sacrifices held clues and she'd worked out where this location. They would be in trouble of course, not least for sharing confidential material with a civilian, but they wouldn't be crucified as the saviours of 25 children and 2 teachers. They both agreed that a visit back to Father Ailwyn was in order, after he'd failed to mention the markers left that pointed to the next locations.

Of the Fallen there was no sign, and their lookouts had also vanished. The 'bomb' under the house wasn't an explosive, but some kind of transmitter. It was picked up by the FBI, so Harry and Sam were unable to discover just who it was transmitting to.

A feeling like an electric shock jolted Danni the moment they began their summoning spell. The pull east became almost tangible, as if she was roped to a freight train and dragged along. Unbidden, the images of terrified children popped into her head, bound together on a wooden floor in an old house. She heard their cries and a wave of guilt washed over her – she could not possibly make it in time to save them and she hated herself for running away.

"You can fight them." Amy had said, and this time she would.

"I'm coming." She called out the children.

Pulled by guilt and the spell, her frustration and anger built to a ferocious rage as the spell got stronger. She could not save them, but she would make the Fallen pay. Her eyes flashed amber, shredding her contacts and lighting up the - luckily empty - carriage. A glow emanated from Danni as her hands gripped the seat, shredding the padding, and her face twisted in uncontrollable rage....

And suddenly the pull vanished.

The image of the children in the room faded away and her anger evaporated, and she *knew* that Harry and Sam had done it! They had saved them. She sagged back in her seat, drenched in sweat, dazed and disorientated. She'd never had such a strong compulsion and she wondered if she was more vulnerable since her father's death, or perhaps it was her proximity to them. She had never felt pulled to them before, just exposed and traceable for *them* to come to her. This anger was new too, stronger with Father Richard's dying, but she couldn't help but think that the Fallen were growing stronger and exerting more influence.

"What am I?" She thought.

The familiar fear kicked in as her rage vanished, with the instinct to run away overwhelming. Battered by emotions, she jumped off the train at the next station, ran over a bridge and got on a train heading back west as the doors were closing. After hours of adrenalin and fear, she was exhausted and too flustered to plan a route. She jumped on and off trains at random in a wild zigzag over the US, catching a few hours of sleep before waking with a start and jumping on yet another train. And all the time her emotions ran wild – guilt for always running, anger at herself and fear of the pull. Had she suddenly developed a conscience? Which implied she'd never had one before? Maybe her desire to save those children only been a product of the pull to go to the Fallen.

She dozed and daydreamed, and thought she was slightly delirious after her roller coaster of emotions. Driven by the urge to run and keep moving, her thoughts strayed to her own childhood.

She remembered being seven years old when her father had up and left their temporary home, which was a common enough occurrence, but they'd kept moving, never stopping for more than one night. He'd dragged her across Europe, sleeping in empty buildings or camping in fields and woodlands, as far as possible avoiding all people.

The same thing happened again when she 12, and Danni worked out that every 5 years, when the Fallen performed their rituals, he kept them mobile. She'd had tattoos since she was a baby, and after each ritual they would brush off and need replacing. During their sacrifices, while they were running, he would cover every inch of her skin, even her face and hands. Afterwards, at the ages of 2, 7, 12 and 17, they would need replenishing, and he taught her to tattoo herself, keeping the visible parts of her flesh clear for most of the time.

Between the rituals they would sometimes stay in one place for several months, and then they would always revert to the same routine of physical and mental exercises. Her father would take her hiking most days, rain or shine, to build her stamina. He made her practise the dance moves he would later incorporate into martial arts, and made her study runes and dead languages, and the local customs and politics of the country they were living in.

He had a secret underground network that he refused

to divulge to her, that vanished with him, but as she got older, he had included her more in his security arrangements. He would order identities, pay for them in advance, then collect them from lockers and safety deposit boxes – or leave them there for another day, and instruct her on locating and accessing them. As things went virtual, and 'the cloud' grew in prominence, he got rid of his coded notebooks and setup online accounts with linked clues to locations. He didn't like safety deposit boxes in banks and generally used anonymous lockers in medium to large towns and cities, and he had documents and money stashed all over the world. The whole time she lived with him, he'd never worked or earned any money, but he'd refused to tell her where the money came from.

She lingered on a memory from when she was 12, 10 years ago, not long before the Fallen performed another ritual. They had been living in Peru for a few months, in a shack high in the mountains. In a tatty, primitive kitchen, Danni, on the cusp of puberty, remembered herself sat at the table in patched clothes and a too-large jumper, her red hair wild, long and tangled. She remembered a tattered, stuffed bunny on the table beside her, that her father had thrown away not long after.

She had worked on a pencil drawing, precise, almost architectural in its detail: a huge Gothic monastery, The Order's HQ. The image had persistently presented itself in her mind, and in a daydream she'd started to draw it.

Her father come home and Danni had snapped out of her reverie, trying to hide the picture from him.

She remembered his thunderous expression as he'd snatched the picture off the table and ripped it to shreds. Without saying a word, he'd opened a plastic first-aid box full of medication and shaken out pills that he'd handed to Danni. He then poured her a glass of water and watched her take anti-psychotic meds. That was the stage where he'd experimented with shutting down her 'abilities' with medication, a period that had lasted nearly a year, that he'd abandoned when he realised the meds made her worse not better. After that he'd reverted to meditation to control her daydreaming – and he'd also removed her drawing materials and kept them under lock and key, only to be used under his watchful eye when she was practising protective runes.

He had also moved them on that very night, shaved her hair and started giving her wigs to cover the distinctive red of her natural hair.

At the age of 15, he'd pushed her to spend time without him, though he'd stayed close for the first year to keep an eye and correct her mistakes. When she reached 16 he'd distanced himself more, their meetings every few weeks then months, showing her how to find the stashes of ID's and money, and how to support herself without them – it was the only time he'd discussed money with her, when he warned that there was not enough to live on in perpetuity, and that one day they would run out unless she learned self-sufficiency.

By the time she turned 18, their meetings were down to once a year – or when she needed to top up her tattoos. Since then, 4 years ago, Father Richard had worked tirelessly to move around and create false trails or new identities for her. They had the ability to pick up on each other's strong emotions, even over great distances, which is something she'd only recently begun to question.

Then a year ago he'd told her that he was too old to keep moving. They'd met up in Venice and she'd been surprised to learn that he was 96 years old. As they had coffee in a small square, he'd seemed frail for the first time. The sunshine made his skin look papery and dry, mottled with liver spots, his wiry, grey hair thin enough to see his scalp, making him appear vulnerable. Danni chided herself for not noticing before, but knew secretly that she had, but hadn't wanted to acknowledge it.

He told her he was moving to Norway, to a remote fishing village, so she should never travel there. He'd said he could no longer make new identities for her, and that she should never try to contact him again. Then he'd simply got up and left, leaning heavily on a cane. No words of love or support, no physical contact, he'd just walked out of her life. Of course she'd still had her mental connection to him, mostly consisting of terse instructions or warnings...

His final ever words echoed in her head – run. She knew that he'd killed himself when he realised they had finally found him, which according to his religion was an unforgivable sin. He'd known they'd catch up when he stopped moving, and in a way it was surprising it had taken them so long.

Danni wasn't ready to examine her relationship with him, or his final sacrifice for her, and moved onto the thoughts of the child in Glasgow. Amy, who'd told her to fight... Fight for children. She'd been prepared to, but she also knew what Father Richard would have said about the children in Cutchogue. They were none of her business, and she was too important to risk... but she kept coming back to tortured Amy, and those children who'd died in Brooklyn – and nearly died in Long Island.

She was so self-absorbed that it came as a total shock when she eventually ended up in New Orleans. The city had magic in its bones, more in touch with Otherworld than any other 'new' city. In the old world, uncountable places had magic woven into their fabric, good and bad, but in New Orleans, many inhabitants still practised the Old Ways. So much so that her Father had ordered her to stay well away – so naturally it was the first place she visited as soon as she'd officially left 'home' aged 16. She'd hated and loved it, both enchanted and repelled, and had avoided it for the 6 years since that first visit.

And now she was back. The people here didn't have the ability to See her like the Romani, but if she spent long enough here, she was bound to bump into a practitioner with real magic who might spot her, which meant danger.

Danni was exhausted and desperately needed to eat and sleep, so she told herself she was too tired to move on straight away. Right now, she found the strange magic of New Orleans alluring. Perhaps she could hide within it, just for a night, amongst the other denizens of this fascinating city. Her first priority was food, and she ate at a small jazz bar and rested, until the music began to jar on her senses. She wondered aimlessly, eyeing the occult shops with wariness - from tarot to voodoo, but with very few of any real power. She was about to check into a budget hostel when her skin prickled and her tattoos itched. Black Magic.

She stepped into a recessed doorway and searched her surroundings, but detected no direct threat. Tourists bustled passed her, on their way out, or workers on their way home. Then a scream rent the air as a young child screamed in pain and terror – but nobody else noticed.

Another scream followed by a desperate sob, but the crowd kept moving – laughing, talking or just focused on their evening plans. She clamped her hands over her ears and squeezed her eyes shut, but more sights and sounds filled her head; the terrified sobs of children in Cutchogue, Amy in Glasgow, dozens of other children all over the world that Danni had met over the years…

they flashed before her eyes, haunted, chased and terrified, tainted by darkness.

“Are you alright, young lady?” Danni realised this was a real voice, speaking to her.

She took her hands off her ears and eyed an elderly black man. Immaculate in a linen suit with a halo of white hair and a gold-tipped cane, who was eyeing her with concern. He took in her wildness and fear and nodded.

“Plenty of people have demons to fight.” He tapped his head, “Up here, and some say out there.”

He gestured to the streets around them, and with his words the chaos on her head faded, leaving the very quiet sobs of a single child.

“That don’t mean you have to let them win. You can always fight back.”

Danni blinked and the strange old man was gone. She looked up and down the busy street but caught no sign of him in the crowd, and she shivered.

But she still heard the plaintive wail of a very young child in danger.

There was no compulsion, but Danni followed the sounds and anger lit up her eyes. She blinked her contact lenses away and yanked off her wig as she turned left. A right then another left took her off the main tourist strip until the quiet, heartbroken sobs led Danni to a house.

New Orleans

Isabella Pluchard's family were old Southern money who had prospered before the Union, had fought against it, but had accepted the results with good grace. They even advocated equal rights in public – as long as black and white rights didn't mingle. They chaired many charitable foundations that encouraged 'good family values', and were staunchly, NRA-supporting, Presbyterian hellfire sorts. Pillars of the community.

Unlike many of their piers after the abolition of slavery, their estates had flourished. There were rumours, in those early days, about vanished former slaves, but then many Southern white folk had skeletons in their closets that were best left undisturbed. They were a powerful family with friends in very high places, and people with grievances against them invariably came off worst. Or vanished.

The family were just lucky. Their enterprises always succeeded and their investments always seemed to pay off. And if they still had ties with the Klan, they were careful to be discreet about it. But their lip-service at church hid a deeper secret. A contract signed in blood, each generation, to ensure their continued good fortune. A contract with a devil who asked for blood in return – a contract they were only too happy to oblige.

Their house was set back from the road behind wrought

iron fencing. In this neighbourhood it must be worth a small fortune, thought Danni as she stood in front and examined the house. Downstairs, Isabella, an elegant woman in her 50's, stood at the window. She spotted Danni and frowned, but Danni's eyes roved up each window until she focused on the attic. Her tattoos prickled and anger grew as she instinctively knew a young child was trapped in there. Almost before she realised, her feet carried her to the front door and she knocked.

Some moments later a tall, muscular blond man opened the door. He eyed Danni, in her cheap jeans and scruffy hoody.

"Who is the child in your attic?" She asked, in crisp, British accent – though she had no idea why she'd chosen that accent.

Surprise flitted briefly over his handsome, arrogant features. "Get off my land."

"Fine, I'll just call the police then and tell them you have kidnapped a little girl and locked her up."

With mild curiosity but no alarm, he opened the door wider. "Boys, there's someone here who wants to meet y'all."

Two young white men appeared, in police uniform, with brutish, cruel features. Anger burned so fiercely that Danni had to clench one hand and dig her nails into her palm. Could she take on all these men, plus the man upstairs with the child... and do what with them, she wondered?

“Give me the child.” Danni stated, unaware that her eyes shimmered.

“We don’t know what you’re talking about. Go away. While you still can.” Stated the man.

“Not without the child.”

“Have it your own way.” The man eyed empty street beyond her, then grabbed her and pulled her inside, slamming the front door behind her.

“Were you seen, you idiots?” He asked them, and they shook their heads vehemently.

Danni reeled as she stepped into the house. Many centuries of evil had resided here and unspeakable acts had been performed. She instantly felt their connection with the Fallen, the pact with them that had benefited the family for generations. Danni had the sensation of a door opening, giving her a view of their depravity – their corruption of willing officials, their blackmail, their political agitation, their hate mongering. She saw meetings and rallies, full of extortions against foreigners, migrants, women – anyone who was weak and vulnerable – and the echoed shouts of hatred nearly drowned out the cries of the child upstairs. She watched Isabella’s ancestors encourage and participate in lynching, the abduction of young children, led below for dark rituals in the cellar downstairs. Successive generations, children, grandchildren, great-grandchildren – all of them had been happy to renew the contract.

All this flashed through her head as Isabella joined them in the hall.

"What is all this noise and fuss?" She asked, breaking the spell.

From her features, she was the mother of the 'doorman', and she sneered when she saw Danni.

"A contract with Asmodeous." The name popped into Danni's head, as Isabella looked in her eyes and her jaw dropped. She gasped and gave a little moan, almost sexual.

Without taking her eyes off Danni she gave a casual flick off her fingers at the policemen. "Leave us."

They cast a surprised look at the man, "Are you sure?"

Blood dripped from Danni's palm where her nails dug into her own flesh, and she realised that she wanted them to attack. She had years of training she'd never used and these people were as bad as humans came. Her eyes flashed brighter and the policeman's hands dropped to their guns. The woman laughed, delighted.

"I'll sponsor your membership tomorrow night." Stated

the woman, "Now go."

"Membership of the Klan?" Asked Danni.

"Indeed." The woman laughed, "Now get out."

The policemen backed out, clearly unhappy to leave what they saw as a clear threat to their benefactors. A scowl from Isabella sent them packing and when she was sure they were gone, she addressed her son.

"Charles, you are in the presence of a Master."

The woman performed a deep curtsy. Charles eyed Danni in surprise, then made a deep bow.

"My apologies, Master."

Danni felt a flare of concern at the title, but the wail of the child upstairs sounded again, loud and terrified, pushing the thought aside.

"Bring me the man and the child from upstairs." Ordered Danni, and Charles instantly ran upstairs, shouting.

"Henry?"

As he obeyed, a heady feeling of power added to Danni's rage.

"Why did you take this child?" She asked.

"She's just a coloured whose parents got above

themselves, putting together a case against us for corruption!" A momentary flash of outrage at their audacity, quickly replaced by pride in their achievements, "But she has power, Master." Giggled the woman, beside herself with excitement. "She's a sacrifice for the Morning Star!"

"Morning Star?" A cold feeling in the pit of her stomach. Danni's eyes flashed pure black and the woman moaned with pleasure again.

"Of course! As requested."

Danni's eyes returned to amber, but with small fires raging inside them that lit up the foyer. She should follow this up, she suspected, but her surroundings were making her nauseous.

"We hadn't heard from our master for years, but we kept up the rituals anyway."

"You've been murdering folk here for generations." Stated Danni.

"We've been sacrificing coloureds mostly, particularly their children." Continued the woman in delight, unaware that she was digging herself deeper and deeper. "We have served you all loyally all this time, feeding you, and we are happy to increase our offering when you asked."

Danni's gaze was drawn to her feet, to the cellar below,

where the reek of blood, spilled long ago and fresh, wafted up to permeate the house in corruption.

"Of course it's harder now than it used to be, with CCTV and camera phones," Isabella preened, showing off her dedication, "So we've used the Klan and extended our influence with the police."

Isabella gestured to the sitting room.

"Won't you make yourself comfortable? Or would you like to go straight down to the cellar?"

Charles and Henry came down the stairs with a terrified, tiny little girl of around four. They shoved the child, who tripped and fell on her knees, while Isabella almost hopped up and down with excitement.

"We are ready for our reward, Master. Our years of-."

Danni's rage exploded. She grabbed a vase and smashed it over the mother's head before throwing it at Henry. It caught him a glancing blow as Charles sprang to life. Young, fit and muscular, he jumped at Danni but she ducked and punched his jaw with an upper cut, before twisting around him and pulling an antique mirror from the wall and smashing it over his head. Henry ran for her and she rolled, grabbing a shard of glass, which she punched into his eye, before jumping up, then landing on Charles's back, to snap his snipe with a satisfying crunch.

She crossed to the woman, her eyes now blazing, and yanked her up to pin her to the wall.

"I don't understand, Master?"

Danni transferred her hands to the woman's neck. "The reward for evil is evil, and now you will choke on it."

The woman, still dazed, tried to fight back as Danni throttled her. Even as she twitched and died, Danni kept squeezing.

A door from the back of the house opened and she turned with a snarl as a tall, handsome black man entered. He knelt, arms out wide for the little girl, who was frozen by the stairs.

"You're safe now, Honey." The child ran into his arms and buried her face in his jacket, "Your muma and daddy are safe, Tandy, they're waiting for you along with Muma Alice." He said, holding her close.

He turned to face Danni, "Muma Alice sent me to fetch you." He said, scooping up the child as he stood, "And she said to burn the cursed house to the ground."

Danni's rage extinguished and she looked around in shock at what she'd done. Shaking as the adrenalin left her, she dropped the woman's corpse.

"I..."

"I've got gasoline, it's in the kitchen." Said the man, "If

you could help?"

Danni's eyes returned to normal and she blinked rapidly, trying to process. She caught sight of drops of her own blood on the floor, and looked to her hand. Crescent gouges had mostly healed already but she'd added a large cut from the broken glass at some point.

"My blood." She managed. Blood had great power and she could not risk anyone finding her blood and using it in a ritual.

One handed, the man brought in a gasoline can which he held out to her.

"We should hurry up." He said.

Danni poured the fuel over the bodies and into the carpet, in the hall and adjoining rooms, then closed the curtains and lit a match. The man led her out the back of the house and through the garden, still holding the child, then into a side street where he'd parked a car.

"This car's stolen so don't worry about anyone tracking it." He said as he put the little girl on the back seat and knelt to unlock her fingers from around his neck. "Tandy, I have to drive now but I'm taking you to your parents. You're safe, sweet child."

The child opened her mouth for a big wail, and the man ran one hand down her face, and she fell asleep. He gently lay her down on the back seat, watched by

Danni.

Danni backed up, worried if her legs were able to support her if she ran.

“Who are you?” She asked.

“Muma Alice will explain, but we need to go.”

A whoosh from behind and flame lapped the back of the house. Danni hesitated, bewildered by events, but realised she was too tired to run. She was covered in blood and stank of gasoline, and her head was a mess.

“I’m Alex.” He said, opening the car door for her. She got in and passed out.

Muma Alice

Alex drove out of New Orleans into the swamp. When Danni awoke he started up a stream of conversation - banter that ranged from the animals and insects of the swamp, the charlatans in New Orleans who ripped off tourists, and the magic of Mardi Gras.

Eventually he crossed a wooden bridge over a wide channel of water and Danni felt the pressure drop, then he drove up to a large house built on stilts over the water.

A young couple ran out and Alex handed them the still sleeping Tandy, and they quietly vanished back in the house, sobbing with relief and all the while trying to avoid looking at Danni. Then Alex took Danni inside to meet Muma Alice. A slender young black woman who, she explained, had recently inherited the mantle of 'muma' as her mother (and grandmother before her) had both died young. She took Danni around a wide veranda to the decking at the back of the house, with a spectacular view over the bayou as the sun came up, and explained how she'd come to send Alex to fetch Danni.

"We all know the Fallen are making some kind of move. Even before they took Tandy, I knew their followers would be stirring things up so I sent my brother to her, but we were too late. They took her from her school."

"The police took her." Said Danni and Alice nodded

sadly.

"Alex went into the city but we didn't know where to go 'til the very last minute."

"But you knew you'd know?" Asked Danni. Her tattoos were silent, but she was so overwhelmed she wasn't sure she could trust them.

"I hoped." Replied Alice.

"What do you want?" Asked Danni. She'd seen children's toys scattered about the yard, and caught fearful but curious children's faces peering through windows before parents pulled them away.

"I don't want anything from you, child." Alice was barely older than Danni, but it didn't seem incongruous calling her a child. With her Cajun drawl, somehow Alice had the wisdom of generations, and these previous generations were peering out through Alice's eyes.

"This is a little bit of respite. When you... intervened tonight, my visitors told me to ask you here."

Danni felt a gentle shiver, almost a caress, on her warning tattoo and decided to let the subject of finding her drop. She glanced at the house, thinking of the girl's parents, "I'm sorry Tandy had to see... what I did."

"Tandy will be just fine now, 'cos of you, and you did the right thing!" Stated Alice, leaning over to pat her hand. "Don't let their deaths linger on your conscience, those people were evil to the core. They signed their death warrants a long time ago and many times since."

Danni heaved herself to her feet. "Well, I might trouble you for a bed for a couple of hours, then a lift to the airport. I need to keep moving."

A plate of food was brought out while a bed was made up, then Danni staggered into a small, neat bedroom and collapsed. After the last few days she was surprised her sleep was deep and dreamless and she woke up refreshed, her wounds healed.

A shy little girl showed her to the bathroom, and she re-joined the others when the sun was low over the bayou. A large, extended family had set long tables out on the grass and had a BBQ fired up when she joined them, including Tandy and her parents, who approached her cautiously.

"I can never thank you enough." Said Tandy's mum, which made Danni uncomfortable. She didn't recall ever meeting a gifted child's parents before, so she focused on Tandy.

"I am so sorry you had to see what you did."

Tandy hid behind her parents as Danni rummaged in her back pack for the small beads she carved whenever she had time. She held out a four beads, but the girl was too shy – or too terrified of Danni – to take them, so her mother did.

"You don't have to have them, Tandy, but would you just try and pick one up?" Requested Danni, pointing to a bead with an ankh on it – life, love, a lock and also a key. The girl's mother placed the bead on her daughter's palm and Tandy's expression turned from fearful to surprised to overjoyed. Danni was totally unprepared when she ran up to her and threw her arms around her neck.

She threw a surprised smile at her parents, then pulled Tandy onto her knee and sorted through the other beads.

"These are for protection, Tandy, from the monsters." Danni pointed to each bead in turn. "I'm guessing you have Sight?" She looked to Tandy's parents, who nodded, "These will keep you hidden from those who seek you."

She looked to Alice, "Though you still need to be careful."

Alice nodded her understanding.

"Thank you." Said Tandy's father, but Danni waved him off. Those people were evil, she had felt their cores, but what she had done crossed all the lines her father had set her and she wasn't ready to talk about it.

"Just keep them beside your skin, put them on a wire and wear them as a bracelet."

"Thank you again, Danni. Those are powerful magic." Said Alice, "I should have thought to protect Tandy and the others with wards long before now. I'll make sure we all have them."

Alice tickled Tandy, who giggled, breaking the mood. Her parents took her, with more heartfelt thanks, then they moved off and Alice sat beside Danni, surrounded by happy bustle.

"I should go." Said Danni.

"Take a good look at my property with your Sight." Replied Alice.

Danni eyed the house then extended her vision to the marshes and water around them. A shimmer caught her attention, half a mile or so from the house and her breath caught at the scale of protective wards that ringed the house and grounds around it.

"A barrier?"

"Yes, ma'am. We been building that wall for two hundred years and it works on folks without Sight too. It's helped my ancestors more times than I can count, especially in the days of slavery. Not a person alive can find this place without an invitation." Replied Alice, before taking hold of Danni's hand.

The shimmering wall got thicker and darker, until they were an island of sunshine surrounded by mist. Shapes stalked the fog, dark and distorted shapes that roamed outside the ‘wall’.

“At the moment it keeps out Otherworld too, but it’s getting busier out there. However strong our barriers, a concerted effort would find us, Danni, so we’re real careful to keep a low profile.”

Danni snorted a bitter laugh. “I don’t believe I’ve ever been ‘low profile’.”

“No.” Alice released her hand and the world went back to normal. “But there’s words we need to have. You’re safe here for now, safer than you’ve been for a long while. Will you be my guest for tonight, then we’ll talk again in the morning before you go?”

“I don’t want to bring trouble on you.” She replied, hurrying on before Alice could object, “I don’t just mean the supernatural. The police will be following up the people who burnt down the house and … and killed those people. They had two officers there, at the house, who saw me…”

“But didn’t see Alex. He checked the property before he entered it last night, they had no cameras, and he got rid of the car today, somewhere they’ll never find it. He’s had a lot of practise running rings around corrupt officials. Besides, once the fire’s cooled, the police won’t be able to hide what they’ll find in that basement of theirs. It means the FBI will likely get involved, take it out of their hands.” She patted her hand again, “Don’t you worry. I wouldn't put my family into harm's way any more than necessary."

Danni exhaled slowly. She wasn't in a hurry to leave this sanctuary and all her senses confirmed she was safe here. She nodded her thanks and felt the tension drain away. Danni spent an evening surrounded by joking, laughter and family, for the first time in her life.

They ate and Danni stayed up, dragged into the singing and dancing, until it was just her and Alex left. Then she accepted his offer of a bed and fell into a deep, untroubled sleep much later, with his arms wrapped around her.

In the morning Danni woke up after everyone had gone off to work, except some seemingly ancient old people and some young children, including Tandy with her parents. Danni ate a late breakfast with Alex, who kissed her goodbye and said he'd be back to take her to the airport, or for another night's company, whatever she felt like.

Alice appeared as she was finishing and made a pot of tea which she carried onto the decking, and bade Danni make herself comfortable.

"Thank you." Said Danni.

"Thank *you*, Danni. You saved my Tandy, who's likely gonna be my successor when I die. She's powerful that one, the next Muma of Louisiana.

"My family's gift – or my curse – is that unhappy dead folk are drawn to us. Ghosts, who speak to us. My whole family has a touch of magic, but only who's truly powerful each generation."

Alice studied the swamp, deep in thought, "Many people think our magic is evil, but we fight the devils just as hard as the Order. Harder if you ask me.

"You see ghosts, in *this* world?" Asked Danni, and Alice nodded.

"You see lingering souls in Otherworld, Danni, and I meet them here. I am pulled to violence and depravity, the witness to crimes committed in the shadows. Some of it I tell the police."

Danni eyed her in surprise and she gave a sad smile, "They ain't all bad. Sometimes they even listen." Alice's face went serious again. "But one crime I cannot tell them."

"And this is what you want to talk to me about?" She asked.

Alice nodded, "There's a little girl who visits me, name of Sarah, she's very keen that I pass on her story to you. She seems tied to you somehow, 'fact I'm surprised you ain't felt her on your shoulder, she done gave me flashes of you all over the world!" Alice whistled in appreciation, "London, Paris, Amsterdam *and* New York, and I ain't never even left Louisiana."

"You were spying on me?" Asked Danni, and she struggled to calm herself as adrenalin flooded her system.

"The *dead* been spying on you." Replied Alice. "Demons use the blood of murdered humans to summon those they want, only when they finished with the dead, sometimes there's a residue that takes exception to the manner of their passing."

Alice's tone was light, but underneath Danni could still feel her anger.

"Sarah's been showing you to me for the last week or two and she told me yesterday that you were at the house of those demon-lovers." Alice peered intently at Danni, who had the unsettling feeling of generations of women staring at her. "We, my ancestors and I, seen a whole lot of you since you nearly-daddy died. Little Sarah is obsessed with you, especially how you saved those children up north."

Danni eyed her narrowly. "Did *you* bring me to New Orleans?"

Alice laughed, "I don't have that kind of power! And nor would I want it. Maybe what guided me to you also reached out to you."

A finger of dread at the mention of something bigger than her. "'*What*' guided me?" Asked Danni.

Alice chuckled, "People call 'It' all manner of names, and some deny it exists, but you and I don't have the luxury of not believing in Her, Him or It above. Just like we have to accept the It down below, and all the angels on both sides."

Danni didn't respond. It was a subject she deliberately avoided and it was worrying if 'it' was taking an interest in her. Maybe the Angel of Death hadn't ignored her after all in New York. Had Azrael given her that flash of inspiration... had he guided her here? She shivered at the thought as she recalled the strange old man who'd helped calm the chaos in her head, who'd then vanished. Who had he been?

She eyed Alice, this young-old woman who communicated with dead people, who was she really? Father Richard had been very clear in his warnings about the occult. Danni tested out her wards and Sight, none of which detected a threat from Alice, despite her unsettling words.

"Will you let me tell you little Sarah's story?"

Danni gestured for her to continue.

"The story starts hundreds of years ago, long, long before Sarah was born. Before my ancestors were dragged here in a slaving ship.

"There was a monster that lived in the bayou, miles from here, preying upon anyone, human or animal, who wandered into his domain. Over the years people sometimes hunted him down, and sometimes they'd catch him and kill him, but he'd always come back and then he'd track down his pursuers and they, along with their families, would meet a terrible end. So eventually they sealed off his swamp and left him be.

"Then, 20 years ago, 12 little children were taken to his bayou and sacrificed, and the monster up and left."

"Sarah?" Queried Danni, and Alice nodded.

"Sarah was one of them. She takes me to a bayou that even the 'gators won't go near. In the water are the bodies of those 12 children, and she warns me that he's free now. He's awake and unleashed on the world."

Danni shivered although the day was warm. The air filled with sounds of the bayou, but behind it, the sound of screams. Screams going back hundreds of years, people killed by... Abaddon. The name came to her and she felt as much as heard a sigh beside her, and Alice's glance moved off Danni to her left. Sarah was there.

And Danni knew. Abaddon had lived there for many years, torturing and killing. Then she heard the terrified, agonised screams of those 12 innocent little children, whose sacrifice had woken him to his true nature. Alice looked away from Sarah then, unable to face her pain.

"I know him." Stated Danni in a whisper, as tears prickled her eyes, along with fear and incipient anger.

“That’s not the most important part of what Sarah wants me to tell you. She says that in England, in 1875, a man called Aleister Crowley was born. As nasty a man as you’d want to meet. He travelled the world studying the occult until he finally found a supernatural entity. Or the entity found him. Sarah believes that this entity taught him the mysteries of summoning the Fallen. They roam around our world, waiting to inhabit a body after the rightful soul has passed, but they often don’t realise who they are. Cowley learned how to wake them, how to bring back their memories while they live in our world.”

Danni had an uncomfortable prickling feeling under her skin, which Alice either didn’t notice or didn’t mention as she continued.

“This was in the last year of his life, and the Order quickly killed him and took his notes before he could do too much damage.”

She waited for Danni to nod for her to continue.

“The Order was supposed to have destroyed this book, but it cropped up twenty years ago right here in Louisiana. Sarah said that you’d know who performed the spell that killed her with those other little children. The one the who looks like a fine, beautiful woman.” Lilith, thought Danni, the name popping into her head as Alice continued, “And they been doing it every five years since, sacrifices to summon their brethren, ready for a big confrontation."

"Lilith, Abaddon, Armers, Tarel and Belial." Thought Danni.

"Hush." Whispered a voice in her ear. "They'll hear you."

The two women sat in silence for a while, thinking.

"Do you know what this has to do with me?" Asked Danni eventually in a quiet voice, not sure if she was ready to know.

Alice nodded and poured the tea, without a strainer so the cup was full of leaves. "I'll tell you what I can... if you want me to?"

Danni hesitated for a second, but then nodded.

"Sip your tea so I can read your leaves."

Danni took a sip of tea then carefully drained the liquid and turned the cup upside down on the saucer, but Alice didn't immediately remove the cup.

"You sure you wanna know? People don't always like the answer."

"I want to know why everyone wants me. My father either didn't know or wouldn't tell me, but I'm getting tired of running, Alice. Since he died, it's getting harder too."

Alice nodded and lifted the cup off the saucer. To Danni

it felt as if the earth rotated a full day – the moon came up and flew across the sky, then dawn, then the sun in a rapid orbit into dusk, then night time again. In reality, it was a few seconds before she put the cup down.

"You're in the middle of maelstrom, the eye of a storm."

Danni laughed out loud. That was an entirely apt description. "Why?"

Alice let out a long breath.

"These spells every five years, they're opening doors from Hell to Otherworld and they ain't been closing them." This wasn't news to Danni so far, but Alice spoke slowly, picking her words. "You understand that Otherworld is a gateway between the worlds? A midway point."

Danni nodded – this much at least she also knew. She occasionally glimpsed more worlds beyond Otherworld when she stayed there too long.

"I know more... devils are crowding into Otherworld." She replied, and Alice nodded.

"But mostly they struggle to get into this world." Added Alice.

Danni tenses, aware that Alice was getting to the crux.

"You and me both got one foot in Otherworld, but

unlike me, unlike anyone or anything in this world, you *also* got that foothold in the worlds beyond. You could, if you chose, visit more places than just Otherworld."

Now Alice hesitated, choosing her words carefully. "Danni, I'm sorry to say that you are the key for all of those doorways, including Otherworld and here."

"A key? What does that mean?"

"*The* key. It means you can unlock the doors, to and from Otherworld. You can let the denizens of these worlds into our world. You can let *all* the demons in here."

Danni's heart sank "I would never do that! I don't even know how!"

"You may not do it voluntarily, Danni, but you cannot let the Fallen catch you. If it comes to it, you'll... you'll have to take your own life."

Danni's stomach rolled, her heartbeat accelerated – but it was exactly what her Father had told her. Father Richard had ordered that the Fallen must never find her.

"Wait, you said *may* not? I may not do it voluntarily..."

"You got a rage inside you. Sarah and others shown me how you help children, I seen the good in you, but..."

"But you've also seen the bad." Finished Danni. "Like

when I murdered the people in New Orleans."

Alice spat, "They were barely people they'd gone so far down the path of darkness, don't you worry about them."

"But I enjoyed killing them."

Alice grinned savagely, "I enjoyed you killing them too! You rid Louisiana, hell the whole world, of a very great evil."

"Alice, I think it's worse than you realise. The woman I killed... she called me Master?"

Alice look worried, but patted Danni's hand.

"The dead are scared of you, Danni, I won't deny that, but little Sarah has confidence. She says she's seen you in Otherworld and you shine like a bright light over there. And you seen how little Tandy loves you, and she's got even more talent than me!" Alice smiled at Danni.

"You do have a lot of anger inside you, and you have to keep that anger in check or it will develop a life all of its own. And you mind you don't let bitterness take a hold. People will let you down, all the time, they'll betray you. You just need to look at the history of black folk in this great nation to see that, and how we's still treated today." Danni again felt Alice's undercurrent of anger, but laid over it was peace. "Always come back to the children. To Tandy. To Amy." Danni was beyond surprise at this point, and thought that Amy's gift was seeing the dead, just like Alice's. But as Alice continued listing other children she'd helped, including Ioana and Katie in Cutchogue, she thought it was likely Alice's dead 'informers' whispering in her ear.

She laughed eventually, "Tell Sarah I will never turn my back on them."

"It's hard, but if you let bitterness in it will consume you." Alice turned a hard look on Danni, "And Sarah says to remind you that the wards you gave those children were created by you. If you lose your way, they'll lose your protection."

That was a sobering reminder.

"Do you… do you know who I am?" She forced herself to ask.

"From what little Sarah has told me, you had a harsh and unkind upbringing. You have chosen to not be harsh and unkind yourself. Who you are is good, that's all that matters."

Danni's eyes prickled at the unexpected kindness. Alice sat back with a weary sigh and an ancient black man appeared, Alice's great-grandfather, with coffee and biscuits. "Now, Alex is very taken with you, Danni. Could we tempt you to stay here another night? My visitors are patrolling my grounds and they say we're safe as can be in these troubled times."

Danni thought about it. The sun was now low in the sky again and she felt blissfully at peace, despite their conversation. Given the events of the last few days, she recognised that she desperately needed a reprieve.

"Are you sure I'm not putting you in danger?" She asked.

"I done told you I would not put my family in danger, Danni. Stay one more night, be at peace. We'll even wash all your clothes for you and see what we can add to your supplies. Who knows when you'll next get the chance?"

Danni stayed and that night went out to the bayou with Alex to have sex in the moonlight. They returned to his bed when the others were asleep and he woke her early the next morning before everyone else and made her breakfast before driving her to the airport. As he dropped her off he handed her a package from Alice, then she got the first flight out, to LA.

On the flight she carefully opened the package, which contained a charm bracelet far superior to anything she'd crafted. Also a note telling her to keep adapting her wards *"The secret is to be unpredictable."* Read the note, and she realised that is exactly what the Fallen had done at their last ritual. Next time she had to re-do her tattoos, she determined to create new designs.

She put on the charm bracelet and folded up the note, but when the plane touched down in LA, both had vanished, leaving her with just the memory.

Consequences

Harry and Sam sat in their car on the green, outside the Old House which was still cordoned off with crime scene tape. They had been grilled by the FBI, all the notes left by 'Emma' had been confiscated, and a shitstorm of procedure and jurisdiction had landed on their heads, but they were briefly celebrities, which was enough for them to keep their jobs. There was even talk of an award.

They were officially, 'officially' off the case, but they still had a lot of questions. Keeping to a policy of honesty, they had canvassed the little town, advising that they were not supposed to be there, but that it had been them who'd pretty much single-handedly saved those children. So far everyone had been helpful. The 4 people keeping watch on the house had been identified as part-time residents of Cutchogue, 2 couples. They had been on the heritage society, and had manipulated access to the Old House that fateful night. They had also vanished that night along with another couple from the town, and a search of their houses had revealed black magic paraphernalia in all the homes, but was otherwise a dead end.

"Cupboards full of black candles, little creepy shrines or whatever you call them, black robes." Shivered Sam, recounting the gossip they'd picked up. The houses were sealed as crime scenes and they'd considered breaking in for a look, but the whole of Cutchogue was on high alert and they reckoned they'd be spotted – and saving kids wouldn't be enough to let that slide.

"No news from Emma?"

Harry shook his head, "And after the shit we been through, I hope she stays away."

"Yeah, the FBI were real interested in her. Especially that Marbas guy, he gave me the creeps, Harry."

"They clammed up when I asked them about the monks." Stated Harry thoughtfully, "Seemed real pissed that we'd spoken to them."

"And here I thought we were all on the same team." Sam shook his head sadly.

"Emma said they got people inside the FBI," Harry eyed the Old House thoughtfully, "And their accomplices here in Cutchogue all have, *had,* top jobs. If they hadn't run off, they'd have walked without charges, Sam, claimed they didn't know what was happening."

Sam nodded, "Makes you wonder why they broke cover."

Harry started the car. "I think we should go the scenic route home, via that monastery."

The sun was low in the sky when the huge wall of the monastery grounds came into view. They followed it for miles to the gate, again marvelling at its size. They had to buzz repeatedly for a response, and were initially denied entry.

"It's not a very friendly place for a monastery is it?" Asked Sam, as Harry buzzed again.

"Can you tell Brother Ailwyn that I want to talk to him about Emma?" He said into the intercom, and was rewarded by the gates opening.

They were taken up back stairs to Ailwyn's office this time, and in a corridor they passed a young man in jeans, who Harry recognised from the café near his house, just after Danni left.

Harry nudged Sam and put a hand on the man's arm.

"I know you." He stated. "You were in Brooklyn."

Harry had time to feel a solid bicep before the man yanked his arm free and stomped off. Their guide, ahead, shot them an annoyed look and hurried them on to Ailwyn's office.

Ailwyn did not seem pleased to see them. He was polite but frosty as they settled into seat before his desk.

"What do you want, Detectives? Your case is closed, unless you're here to talk about your young visitor?" He asked.

"We'll get around to Emma, but we have some general questions."

Ailwyn made a show of checking his watch, "I have 20 minutes before Vespers."

"We'll get right to it then, starting with why you didn't mention that previous crime scenes held the location to the next crime scene?" Asked Harry, both of them with notebooks, poised for Ailwyn's response.

"That information was relayed to the FBI." Replied Ailwyn.

"How come they failed to stop those kids getting murdered in Brooklyn then?" Asked Sam, his voice raising as he got angrier by the second. "12 children who'd had shitty lives were rounded up like so much trash and slaughtered in a shitty factory in the heart of one of the richest cities in the world."

Harry cast Sam a look that calmed him, as Ailwyn considered, crestfallen. "Sorry, I should have been clearer. We told them about the coded messages in their rites, I couldn't work it out in time."

"You had 5 *years* to work out a set of coordinates and you failed? Emma did it. She says that she told the FBI,"

"Really?" Ailwyn looked genuinely surprised. "No, that doesn't make any sense, they would have acted. How did she tell them? I mean, who? And why didn't she tell us?"

"Well, her father passed on the information to the FBI

and then died shortly afterwards." Stated Harry. "I can understand why she doesn't trust anyone very much."

"You can't be right. Why would anyone allow children to be killed?"

"You tell me? You failed with Cutchogue. Without Emma those children would be dead, all of them. She worked out the date, time and location in around 12 hours. *She* saved the lives of 25 children. Single-handed." Added Sam.

"Which implies you're not much of an expert." Added Harry. "Or you don't care."

Ailwyn opened a drawer and pulled out Emma's notes, taken from Harry's house by the FBI.

"Do you understand what she did? *Really* understand? The Fallen change the codes, they create new associations between long dead languages. *Emma*, who we know as Danni, is truly exceptional, she's... she's a genius. I would dearly love to meet her."

"I noticed that when you bugged my phone so you could stalk her." Ailwyn flushed, "Yeah, I recognised one your *brethren* when we came in, he burst into the coffee shop just after Emma left."

Harry and then waited a moment, but Ailwyn didn't respond.

"Even if I wasn't a police officer, that's still a crime by

the way." Added Harry.

"Were those kids ever a priority for you?" Asked Sam.

"I'm not sure what you mean?"

"I mean, you never asked who betrayed her father at the FBI, and you seem more interested in capturing Emma than saving children's lives."

Ailwyn couldn't meet Harry's gaze. "I am a man of God, I am bound to look after all souls and protect children… I failed in that duty."

"Yes you did." Said Sam.

"Are they going to perform another ritual? Somewhere else, maybe, in less than 5 years? Seeing as Sam, Emma and I interrupted this one?" Asked Harry.

Ailwyn blew out a long breath. "We're working on it, but they didn't have the chance to complete the ritual so we don't have much to go on."

Both men tensed and Ailwyn met their gazes, "Thanks be to God, and to you two."

Harry and Sam got to their feet.

"There's a lot here that bothers me, Ailwyn." Said Harry, deliberately dropping the 'brother', "A lot of people are dead, a lot of innocent children, and I'm not convinced your religious order particularly cares."

He placed his card on the table, “I would be only too happy for you to prove me wrong.”

The so-called Fallen were in a richly furnished room in a large house belonging to one of their many followers. They’d moved out of the city to the Hamptons, to a secluded house in Sagaponack. A nervous Doctor Baker, one of their followers who never asked questions, bandaged Belial’s hand, watched by Tarel, who giggled whenever Belial cried out in pain.

“Fucking bitch! That fucking cow led them right to us.” Spat Lilith.

“Fuck her, I want the men who shot my hand!” Shouted Belial, and the doctor flinched.

Lilith paced but Abaddon and Armers sat at the table, both focused on the other man at the far end of the table, a living corpse - Beleth. 20’s, tall, muscular and black, but his complexion is an unhealthy shade of grey in his eyes rheumy with cataracts. He was tied to a portable metal frame, manacles around his ankles and wrists.

“It is unfortunate we could not wake Beleth.”

“Fuck Beleth!” Shouted Belial, and Beleth turned his dead gaze on him. He moved his hands, which rattled the chains. “And fuck those two pathetic policemen. I want them dead.”

Belial’s face twisted with rage and the doctor backed away from him.

“Danni’s the one we need to catch.” Shouted Lilith, overriding whatever Belial else was going to say “How many followers are here?”

“Lilith-.”

“How many?”

Abaddon puffed a breath through fleshy lips. “30, but 10 more are coming.”

“40 is enough. Tarel, find the newcomers and introduce everyone, get them comfortable.”

Tarel pouted, “You get them, I’m busy.”

“Get the fucking followers, Tarel.” Lilith stared at the younger woman, who radiated fury but stomped to the door and slammed it closed behind her.

“It doesn’t matter,” Said Armers, “Beleth only has a limited shelf life. As I told you before, he burns through his bodies too quickly.”

“So we don’t summon him until we need him.” Finished

Abaddon.

Belial cast a hard look at the doctor, who resumed bandaging his hand, then looked at the others.

"Are you ever going to tell me the plan? I am part of this." He pouted. "And I am the only one who's been fucking wounded!"

"Because you're a child, Belial, a stupid child." She leant forward and parted her red lips - not a smile. A shark bearing its teeth. "Useful to the cause... or useful fuel for Beleth. "

Belial eyed everyone as he processed.

"Finish up, Doctor, then join the others." Lilith's smile broadened as she focused on the doctor, but still contained no warmth. "It is time for you to get your reward. Make them happy, Belial. It's important they are ecstatic." Her gaze remained fixed on the doctor.

A huge ostentatious room designed for large parties. Tables had been pushed back against the walls, replaced by beds and low couches. Flimsy, sheer fabric was draped artistically, creating the impression of a decadent harem. Thirty followers lay entwined on the beds and on cushions on the floor, including the 6 people from Long Island - the 4 'security guards' and another younger couple. All were nude, surrounded by scattered cups and goblets of wine, most dozing. Tarel and Belial entered with the doctor and a very ordinary, dumpy couple, Alice and John Kent. These 2 had rounded up homeless children for them in Brooklyn with offers of a warm bed and hot food, their wholesome faces hiding their depraved souls.

"Doctor Baker, Alice and John, you're a little late to the party, but not too late. And later you will receive your reward for your years of service."

The others in the room woke and studied them, most with distaste. Beautiful figures who spent many hours at the gym, or in surgery, defying age that crept up on many of them. Belial stood behind Alice and reached round, under her top, to caress her breasts, as Tarel lead John and the Dr towards the bed.

"These two helped us in Brooklyn." Added Belial, "At the moment, Alice and John are our most favoured." He directed the comments at the people who'd failed them in Cutchogue.

"But, we are very appreciative of your service to the Fallen." Added Tarel, dropping to her knees before John's crotch and unzipping him, her other hand on Baker's crotch.

Thompson shot a hateful glare at his wife, as if somehow blaming her – and she returned the look.

“Is it nearly time? When’s the ceremony?” Demanded Mrs Thompson.

“Tonight! We are waiting on a few more followers who also earned their place here.” Replied Tarel.

The crowd woke up as cheers and laughter sounded, everyone giddy with proximity to the Fallen. Mr Thompson and Dr Baker were shrewd enough to have some doubts. They had met a very other few followers in the past, their activities always secret, and always their rewards had been swift – money into an offshore account, a promotion, or, in Baker’s case, a witness of malpractice disappearing. He’d never met any real Fallen in person before, and to be honest they terrified him. But like the others he was carried away by the pheromones of the Fallen. The subtle scents they used to entice and bewilder, easing any doubts he had. Horney again, the followers swarmed Tarel and Belial. Around the room, others woke and began caressing each other. Distant screams carried and the new couple tensed.

“What’s that?” Asked Alice.

“Sacrifices. Our gods are ever hungry, Alice.” Whispered Belial.

He moved one hand down, into the waistband of her stretchy, a-line skirts, and began to massage between her legs, one hand still working on her breasts.

"Unbelievers, Alice."

Worried, Alice looked to John, but his eyes are closed in ecstasy. A quick scan of the bed – nobody cared, everyone oblivious, kissing each other, caressing each other, and Belial's persistent fingers. He trailed kisses down her neck and she too closed her eyes as she pulled off her skirt.

The screams continued in ragged, agonised bursts, ignored by everyone, even though they knew they belonged to children.

Danni picked up an ID from a locker in Los Angeles and changed her appearance again, keenly aware that she was burning through ID's and money rapidly, with no obvious way of replacing them. She needed to get back under the radar of the Fallen and the Order, urgently.

She booked herself onto the first available flight out of LA, slept and ate on the plane, availing herself of all the food she could get to build up her strength. She was halfway to Bangkok when the ritual woke her from her sleep.

The Fallen had kidnapped more children as they'd travelled north, leaving a trail of death and devastated families. They had sacrificed the children quickly, saving their blood for the boldest ritual yet, one that would change things forever. Now they were ready, and each Fallen had taken a group of their followers aside to prepare them.

Lilith was in a large, darkened room with fat candles strategically placed. She stood before a table at the front, used as an altar. A thick book was in the centre of the table, Aleister Crowley's grimoire. Dr Baker, the Thompsons and another couple from Cutchogue, a lone woman, Alice and John stood before Lilith. Eight of them, all dressed in long black robes.

"I have selected you, our most faithful." Stated Lilith, and the group preened. "For you I have a special service, as your final test."

Black shadows formed at the edge of the room and Alice gripped John's hand, but he shook her off, focused on Lilith. Having partaken in so many succulent, nubile men and women, his fat old wife no longer held any attraction.

"Some of our followers, who you have cavorted with, they have betrayed us." Stated Lilith and the room grew silent. "When we called out for their help, they did not come to our aid." She looked to the Thompsons, "That is why we failed in Cutchogue."

She sauntered to Alice first, hips swaying seductively. "There is no room for disobedience in our new world."

Alice blanched and Lilith moved on, pausing before each of them, "No room for the weak."

"What do you want us to do?" Asked a worried John.

"There are too many of them for us to subdue!" Added a worried Mr Thompson, who'd paled at the thought of actual violence herself.

"But you are not alone, we are here with you!" Lilith laughed, "And I don't want you to kill them. They are mine to sacrifice, and you have the honour of holding them for us."

She returned to her place at the front. "In a moment the others will join us here, and I will welcome them. I will say the words 'prove your loyalty', and you will secure the people I indicate. You will help us cleanse our followers, until you alone remain."

The group eyed each other apprehensively, especially Dr Baker. It was one thing to patch up wounded criminals and supply illegal drugs, but quite another to actually take part in a human sacrifice.

"Doctor, you must look after them, make sure they don't stay dead." He shuffled and the others looked nervous.

"Have I chosen wrongly?" Asked Lilith, the threat

tangible in her tone.

The followers hastily agreed and bowed their heads, and she clapped her hands.

Tarel, Armers, Belial and Marbel led in 4 other groups of 8, all dressed in black robes, followed by Abaddon. When they were lined up, the Fallen began chanting. The mist at the edges of the room grew thicker and shapes swirled, until Lilith raised her hands and silenced them.

Beside the table was a bucket and she hefted it and poured blood over the grimoire, soaking the book, spilling over the edge and dripping onto the floor. Another bucket of blood, and the followers noticed that the grimoire wasn't wet – it had soaked up the bloody offering. Lilith's group of followers had left Cutchogue with the Fallen, had been with them when they captured the children, and they all knew it was these innocent children's blood that fed the book. None of them protested however.

"You chose the path of the Fallen." Lilith stated. "Each of you signed a contract with us, to progress our cause, in return for wealth and power."

The 40 people in the room all had vivid flashbacks, projected into their heads by the Fallen assembled before them. An offer, of a life of ease and wealth and power and privilege. Armers had approached the Thompsons shortly after their marriage, 15 years before. An unexpected heart attack would kill a rival, they would both get promotions, and all they needed to do was provide a drop of their blood. Of course they would be called upon to perform services for other Fallen over the years, but they were so morally compromised that they had never minded what was asked of them.

Alice recalled a beating she'd received as a social worker, when a young offender had objected to her getting him sacked from his first job after prison. The young man, whose life she'd ruined, had cornered her and lashed out – and Tarel had been there, offering retribution. The young man, and all the scum she'd been forced to pander to, would suffer. And they had. For 10 years she'd been the scourge of young delinquents who tried to turn their lives around... Another remembered the pending court case for that threatened a long prison sentence, which vanished after he'd signed his contract with the bewitching Lilith. Another remembered when Abaddon had appeared in his house, with photos of him with children. He hadn't really had a choice but to sign, but his life had got better since – and much more satisfying.

40 memories, and each follower felt their skin prickle where the Fallen had cut them and taken their blood.

Lilith waited while they each recalled their pledges. Surrounded as they were by Fallen, emitting their heady stench of power, each of them grew excited. She wanted them eager to please and hungry, to make her ritual even more powerful. When she thought they were ready, she opened the grimoire and held it in her arms as she faced them.

"Tonight we begin the mass awakening of our brethren."

The Fallen's chants grew louder.

"We no longer call individuals, we call *all* my brothers and sisters and awaken them!" Lilith stopped before 16 people and laid a gentle hand on their heads, and they turned smug smiles on the others.

Lilith read a passage from the book, in an ugly guttural language that caused the candles to flicker and the fog to thicken. The followers pressed closer together as the temperature dropped and red eyes appeared in the mist around them.

"Now. Prove your loyalty." Said Lilith.

24 followers moved forward to grab the 16 people Lilith had touched, each of them briefed by a Fallen in their own groups. They grabbed their arms, trapping them, barging each other in an effort to be more useful, none of them realising that each group had received similar orders. Thompson moved first, grabbing the woman next to him, holding her arms as Armers approached her.

“What are you doing?” She demanded.

“Awake, Danyal, your time is here!” Lilith shouted.

“No! I’m one of you! I’m a follower?”

“Awake Sorath, whose number is 666.” Replied Lilith, as Armers put his hands around the woman’s throat and started to choke her. “Vapula, with the Sight.”

She bucked and writhed, held fast by Thompson, and Marbers approached the next man.

“Get off me!” He shouted, struggling against his captors.

“Xaphan, who feeds the fires of hell.” Marbers began to choke the him, and Tarel stepped up to the next captive as Lilith continued her summons, “Qemuel, who was destroyed.”

Belial and Abaddon began choking their victims, Lilith calling out 16 names as she took a man around the throat, “Vapula, Ronobe, Orobas!” She yelled.

Armers’ victim died and he grabbed the Doctor to perform CPR while he moved swiftly onto the next. “Procel, who tempts with sacred knowledge.”

The first woman bucked and her eyes snapped open, pitch black. Dr Baker jumped back, but Marbas grabbed him and he started CPR on the second person.

“I call Ose, president of hell! Orobas, Paimon,

Penemuel, Morax, Caim, Dantanian, Naamah, Decarabia, Lix Tetrax." Dr Baker hurried to keep up, running between bodies, performing CPR as the corpses woke with jet-black eyes, and all around them, the black fog thickened and dark shapes writhed and twisted hands reached out towards them.

The original 16 were dead, and they subdivided them again. Tarel and Belial had each prepared their groups of 8, and these 16 now turned on 8 others, grabbing them and holding them, including Lilith's group – who had failed at Cutchogue.

"Wait! What are you doing? We're faithful! We've proved it!" Shouted Thompson.

"I got you those children in Brooklyn!" Shouted Alice, outraged.

They struggled as the Fallen choked the life from them and the doctor brought them back, Lilith chanting all the while, summoning her kin to new, host bodies.

"Imamiah, Naberius, Ipos, Forneus, Eligor, Enepsigos, Flauros, Focalor."

Doctor Baker was exhausted. He kept himself fit but was running out of energy to keep up CPR, but fear and adrenalin drove him on. Not everyone had been resuscitated, but he recognised those that had were no longer people, and still the list went on, until the final 16 turned on each other, each of them told that the last people standing would join the ranks of the Fallen.

"Gaap, Lahash, Glasyalabolas, Gamory, Gusion…" Continued Lilith, calling out to her brethren. She did not know who was near enough to hear her call, and who already inhabited a human body, but she would wake every single of one of them. "Hagenti, Halpas, Gadreel, Gamygyn, Lerajie, Leviathon!

"Awake my brothers and sisters! All of you, awake!"

Four followers were left standing in the middle of a swirling sea of fog, surrounded by the Fallen. Lilith, Tarel, Belial and Armers turned on them, and they finally realised their stupidity. Their acts of betrayal had fed Lilith's ritual, every bit as much as the blood of innocents, and their self-serving pity and terror continued to feed it. Like the others before them, they wailed about their 'contract' as the life was squeezed out of them.

The doctor was the last human left in the room, and he realised fully that he would never leave it. Of the 40 followers, he'd brought back 22 and a further 15 had found their own way into the human hosts without his help. Exhausted, he felt himself lifted onto his feet.

"You did well, Doctor Baker." Said Lilith, staring deep into his eyes.

He had a moment of hope that he might not die, he might still be useful, but Abaddon led in Beleth and undid his chains. The other Fallen left without a backward glance, and locked Beleth in the room with the doctor.

Later, as the 37 'new' Fallen headed off to shower and change, a weaselly looking approached, eyeing them with curiosity.

"Lilith?" He asked. "You called me?"

She laughed in delight. "Soras, you're awake."

Danni was sleeping when her head exploded in pain, and she had to wake the passenger beside her to hurry to the toilet and vomit, her head splitting and her skin burning. She pulled up her sleeve and watched as her tattoos lifted once again from under her skin. She grabbed an air steward and asked them to fetch her bag, with an excuse of morning sickness, then with shaking hands, desperately reapplied her tattoos.

The onslaught was relentless, the ink lifting as quickly as she drew it. She gave up and insulated herself instead, drawing wards and sticking them to the walls, floor and ceiling of the cubicle.

She waited out the flight, telling the stewards that she was too sick to move - terrified *they* would trace her, terrified the cabin crew would call in her sickness and the message would get intercepted, terrified the Fallen would be waiting when she landed. Whatever they were doing was powerful so it obviously involved the taking of human life. Her anger simmered and she shoved it aside. She wasn't sure how long she could evade their sustained attacks on her magic, and she was definitely weaker without Father Richard. Unlike her, he had no innate magic, but he could create protection runes, linked to the tattoos on her body.

When the plane landed in Bangkok, Danni reapplied basic tattoos in the wash room at the airport, relieved when they stayed on. Whatever onslaught they'd organised during her flight seemed to be over for now. She lost herself quickly in the crowds and checked into a cheap, tourist hostel where she re-tattooed her body – again – except her hands, feet, face and neck. Supple and ambidextrous, she contorted to tattoo her legs, torso and arms, leaving only her back and upper legs. As she dressed, she could feel the absence of protection as if she had painted a large target on her back. Her priority was to hide, and to do that she needed to tattoo herself fully, and hope it lasted longer.

She headed to the Train Night Market, easily navigating tourists, touts, stallholders and locals. Light fingered, she bought some things and stole many more – hats, long-sleeved tops and light trousers. She started in a bouncy blond wig, with pink linen trousers and a long-sleeve, floaty top, mingling with the tourists. With almost magical ability, as she pilfered clothing from under the noses of the keen eyed stallholders, and metamorphosized. One minute a floaty American with a California drawl, the next a grungy Brit, the next a hard accented South African. She progressed through the market, eagle-eyed for CCTV and camera phones, constantly changing and listening to her senses.

They remained quiet, but she covertly scanned the crowd for familiar faces, anyone who might be following her. She noted a young man studying her, but discounted his interest as amorous, and she soon lost him in the crowd.

Satisfied that she'd topped up her supplies, she left the market and jumped on the first bus she found. She switched buses, making a circuitous route through Bangkok to the Banglamphu area as night fell, when she began her hunt for a tattoo shop. She hailed a tuk-tuk at random and asked if he could recommend a tattoo shop, which he was only too happy to do.

"I know best tattoo. Secret from tourists. Very best" He assured her.

He took her out to a backwater, to his cousin's shop, an unprepossessing building in a patch of wasteland, that he promised held a world-renowned artists. He escorted Danni inside and she over-tipped him, in front of the male owner of the shop.

Intervention

With big, blue eyes, Danni eyed the tattoo shop, pretending to be impressed by the thousands of images, clearly cut out from magazines. All that mattered was that it was far enough off the beaten track to be perfect.

"Oh my, this is the real thing, huh?" Her American accent was flawless, though she doubted they'd notice.

As she took in her surroundings, she noted the lack of any obvious CCTV. There were 2 Thai women, Naiyana and Achara, at the back, finishing a tattoo on a heavily muscled Thai man, and one wall had a large mirror for customers to examine their body art.

"Are you up to hygiene standards? I don't wanna be catching AIDS or whatnot." She refocused on the owner, who was eyeing her figure lasciviously.

"We very clean. Please, come." He took her arm and guided her towards a chair.

"I need my back done," Danni disentangled herself and crossed to the mirror, "but I wanna see what y'all doing. Can you get me a mirror?"

The man struggled to understand her, but Naiyana handed her a mirror.

"You, hold up."

Danni grinned at the woman. "Well alright then."

Danni then asked to use the bathroom. The shop owners were alarmed by her request and Naiyana said maybe they shouldn't tattoo her, with the kids about the back. Danni kept her expression blank, but hopped from foot to foot.

"I'm sorry, y'all, but I got a touch of the runs." She winced, and mimed needing the bathroom.

"We need the money, and it's just the bathroom. We'll be fine." He insisted to Naiyana, who grudgingly conceded.

The other woman, Achara, escorted Danni to a corridor along the outer edge of the building, that ran alongside the road. There were 3 doors on the left, the first open on a room with a little stove and mattresses on the floor. A baby lay asleep in a cot and Danni shared a smile with Achara as she peered in on it. Along the corridor, the next door led to a bathroom – a loo, basin and grubby shower with a window onto the backyard with metal grills over it. At the end a metal backdoor stood propped open, with an inner mesh door against insects. In the yard, chickens scratched at the ground, then another building with solid metal doors and a gate into the yard.

Danni's companion guided her into the bathroom and stood with her back to the yard, to block Danni's view.

Inside the bathroom, Danni tried the bars over the window, which were solidly attached. She heard a vehicle pull up outside and doors open. Using an overturned bucket, she climbed up and peeked out, in time to see a battered blue van was now in the yard, it's back doors open. 2 armed men stood back as a dozen children climbed out. Aged between maybe 9 and 15, one kid fell and the guard yanked her to her feet and shoved her.

The door to the building opposite was now open and Danni could see more children at the door, huddled and miserable.

Danni's heartbeat accelerate, as Achara tapped at the door, and Danni stepped down to flush the toilet. Her wards detected no sign of the Fallen, but she was well aware that they weren't the only evil in this world. Something bad was occurring in the back, and the sensible thing would be to get far away. Danni threw water on her face, trying to think. If these children were in danger, which they were, how could she leave them? She vividly remembered the sickening feeling of being too late in New York, on the train... and then there was New Orleans, where she had ... where she had saved a little girl's life, and met Muma Alice. And yet she couldn't fix all the badness in the world.

She re-joined Achara in the hall, noting that she'd closed the back door onto the yard. Achara looked on the brink of saying something to Danni, but the man from the front came out to see what was taking so long, and the woman held her tongue.

Danni went back to the shop, thinking furiously, and straddled a couch then pulled up her top, to hide the tattoos on the rest of her body as best she could. She then drew a large eye on a piece of paper and instructed Naiyana on where to place it on her lower back.

“I want these exact dimensions. You just draw around what I’ve done and copy these.”

The woman took the paper while the man produced a booklet of designs.

“You get pretty tattoos?” He tried to hand her the book, but Danni shook her head with a smile.

“I like these ones. Can y’all do them?”

“I’ll do her.” Said the man in Thai.

“Idiot man, go back to the front of shop.” Snapped the woman as she grabbed a trolley with tattoo guns and ink.

The pair argued in Thai but Naiyana won and sent the man packing. Danni eyed the room casually, hearing the sound of the baby from behind the door, who Achara hurried off to tend to. The other man had gone, she noticed, leaving just her in the shop.

Still unsure what to do, she decided to continue with her tattoos. She watched carefully in the mirror as Naiyana tattooed the large, central eye of protection on her back. It was called different things in different cultures, but most civilisations had some form of it – a Hamsa, a Nazar, the Eye of Miriam – or Fatima, l-għajn... Danni kept a careful eye on the progress of the tattoo, correcting the tiniest error in symmetry, while listening to the chatter between the Naiyana and the man, who seemed to be her husband.

When she'd finished the eye, Danni produced more hand-drawn designs for her shoulders and lower back. If the woman was surprised, she kept it to herself.

Danni's thoughts kept returning to the children in the back, and she heard Naiyana discussing them, protesting it was not right to keep them here, in their premises. Her husband was more prosaic, stating they had no choice. Choice... we all have choices. Even Danni, made the 'choice' to run... or not. Now she had a precedent to do more than hide in the shadows.

Which is when the creeping sensation began at the nape of her neck, the still exposed part of her skin. Then the phone rang and the man spoke quietly into it, and cast a long look at Danni. Her back was nearly finished and the other woman had joined Naiyana to speed things up

"Hurry up." Called the man, in Thai. "They're collecting

the children in an hour and she needs to be gone."

"Run!" warned her 6th sense. The people coming for the kids were working directly or indirectly for the Fallen.

"We should not help them with these children, Naiyana." Stated Achara, unaware that Danni could understand her.

"What would you have me do?" Snapped Naiyana, "If we do anything, we die."

"We have blood on our hands."

"We cannot stand up to them, Achara! Or would you like them to take baby Boonsri too?" Achara cast a worried look at the door to the back, to her baby. "Do you want to face their anger?"

Achara resumed work, but when she reached up her t-shirt lifted and Danni saw a small tattoo on her stomach. A simple outline of a devil's head. Shit.

"Nice tattoo, what's it of?" She pointed to it, big smile on her face.

The woman hastily pulled down her top Naiyana glared at her.

"Have you got one too?"

Naiyana smiled and pretended to not understand. Meanwhile the man at the front seemed nervous, his hand hidden under the counter where Danni suspected he had a gun. Her internal alarm was clamouring for her to get out of there.

Danni hummed a tune and kept her expression bland as she thought furiously. Her encyclopaedic knowledge had traced the tattoo to a gang in Bangkok, and the gangs always led back to the Fallen, directly or indirectly. She should run, right now.... But she wasn't sure she could abandon those children. *"You should fight."* That was what Amy had told her. And, she admitted, she had liked it.

Father Richard had told her she must never be caught, but in her heart she knew she was not leaving without trying. In all her years apart from her Father, she'd encountered many children touched by shades of evil, and she'd always helped – without exposing herself. All of that was for nothing if she abandoned them now.

Naiyana didn't betray any emotion continued her work – and then the customer from earlier returned with another man, both armed.

"Finish. You pay. You go now." Naiyana couldn't meet Danni's eyes as she put down her needle gun and fled to the back of the shop. The owner at the front greeted them with false cheer, talking quickly until they shouted at him to shut up.

"Nice ass on that one." Stated on of the gunmen to the shop keeper, looking at Danni.

"She's a tourist, it would be bad is she went missing." Said the shopkeeper, "I heard her talking to her boyfriend, telling him she was in my shop."

Danni pulled down her top and rummaged in her bag while she thought.

"Oh you suddenly speak English do you?" Queried the gunman, and the owner blushed.

"Naiyana heard." He mumbled.

Danni wandered over the join them, eyeing the gun without fear.

"It's like being home in Texas" She said, eyeing the guns. "How much do I owe y'all?"

The gunman hesitated a moment, then shrugged.

"I can have some fun with the girls before I pass them on, this one's hardly fresh!" He laughed, dismissing Danni.

And that did it - Danni snapped. For the second time in her life. For the second time since Father Richard had died. Rage erupted from a well deep inside her. Her blue contact lenses shattered as her eyes blazed amber. She grabbed the man's arm and used her momentum to pull him over her shoulder and slam into the ground, stunning him. Before the second man could react, she stomped on the wrist of the fallen man and grabbed his gun, then spun and fired. A perfect shot in his temple, then she turned her gun on the second man on the floor.

"Let those children go." She stated, in perfect Thai.

The man who owned the shop had produced a gun, which he levelled at he, though his hand wobbled with nerves.

"Drop gun!" He shouted in English.

"Don't make me shoot you." Replied Danni in fluent Thai, though she kept her gun trained on the other man.

"Kill her or I will kill your entire family!" Shouted the armed man.

Time slowed. Every possible scenario flashed through Danni's mind as she spotted another gunman outside, the man in front of her, the owner of the shop... Then she shot the gunman in the head.

A moment of silence while the shop owner stared at her in terror, but Danni was already diving for cover as a hail of bullets rained through the window, almost cutting him in half. He was punched backwards and collapsed on the floor where his arm flopped, close to where Danni lay.

"I killed him." She thought, *"My actions killed him."*

Her gaze flicked to the two other dead men as she cowered behind the counter, glass and wood splinters flying, until the bullets stopped. She quickly checked the ammunition in her gun, then covered her gun-hand with a towel and played dead.

What was left of the door opened and the third man came in, scanning the room. He called out two names, then kicked the corpse of the owner. He stomped through the wreckage and spotted her body, and she prayed he wouldn't fire first and check later. He didn't. He walked over and kicked her, which is when she opened her eyes and shot him in the chest.

He flew back with the force of the bullet and she got up. Her instincts cautiously told her there was no one else outside, not yet. Wincing from the multiple ricochet wounds, she got to her feet and ran to the back of the shop, scooping up her bag on the way. She erupted into the corridor, pausing at the back room, where the women and baby sobbed quietly.

"We need to get out." She told them in fluent Thai. "Now."

They remained frozen for a moment, taking in her ability to speak Thai – and the blood that oozed from multiple wounds, but Danni ran on, to the back of the building. A truck was parked in the yard and another gunman waited there, unsure what to do. Before he could react, Danni threw open the door shot him between the eyes, then she erupted into the yard and dived under the truck.

Silence, loud after the shooting, and she detected no other presence. She checked the cab of the truck, then the back, then ran to the other building in the yard, shooting off the lock. She pulled open the door, to a room full of about 20 children.

"Get into the truck. Quick!" She shouted in Thai.

The children were frozen, eyeing her with fear. She belatedly remembered that children, well, children and animals, were always scared of her, and her gun-toting, gore splattered appearance made her terrifying.

"This is a rescue but you must hurry." She eyed the stunned and frightened children and found an older girl of around 15.

"We don't have long before more men come." She told her, and the girl nodded, but another girl of around 14 shook her head.

"They paid my parents. They will punish them if I leave." Said the girl, and Danni felt another bolt of rage and the children whimpered as her eyes blazed. She bit back her instinctive response.

"Well, they're gonna be pissed now either way, so..."

Danni directed a hard look at the 15 year old, who started herding the children out, then ran back to the women in the shop. There was a gas cooker and Danni shook the bottle to check it how full it was.

“I have spilled my blood here. I need to burn this place down. Have you got petrol? Anything flammable?”

“Is my husband dead?” asked Naiyana.

Danni paused, then nodded. She should be feeling guilty, but instead she felt exhilarated. She would examine that later, when they were safe, but she supposed it was worrying.

“I did not kill him.” She replied.

“Yes, you did. You have killed us all today.” Spat Naiyana.

“Then do what I do and run.”

“There is no running from these people! They are everywhere, they own Thailand.” Spat Naiyana.

“Change your names. Hide!”

“There is no hiding. They always find the ones who run.” Danni didn’t like the expression on Naiyana’s face as she eyed the baby.

Bleeding, in shock and in pain, Danni’s anger was fading, replaced by sickening fear that news would reach the Fallen very quickly, and the people they sent here would be much, much worse than the men she had killed. Danni remembered their tattoos.

She grabbed the baby, who wailed in surprise.

“Please don’t hurt her!” Cried Achara.

Danni placed her hand – still holding the gun – on the baby’s head and whispered a calming spell. The baby instantly quietened, and she ran her free hand over her body, feeling for a cold, dark spot. On her belly she found it, and pulled up his t-shirt on a tattoo of a devil.

“It’s the gang tattoo.” Said Naiyana, daring Danni to condemn her.

“This is *not* a tattoo.” Replied Danni.

Pushing aside her pain, she touched the tattoo and focused – on the ink under the skin, and the spells woven into the brand. The baby yelped once in pain and the women screamed, then she gurgled and fell asleep. She lifted the baby to show the women her belly as she brushed dust off, the tattoo completely gone.

“This is the devil’s brand. They poison you through this, and use them to trace you. They *own* you while you wear this. I can remove them from you too.” Stated Danni, “But not here. We have to get those children and leave.”

“Magic?” Asked Naiyana.

“The very blackest magic.” Danni was running out of time. “I can remove them or just leave you, but either way I must burn all traces of my blood. Have you got petrol?”

Naiyana nodded and Achara ran off for petrol, while Danni handed the baby back to Naiyana and ran to the back.

The kids were climbing into the truck and Danni took the pistol from the fallen man and checked the ammunition. Then she lifted a small child into the back, who flinched away from her.

"I'm gonna take you to a monastery. You can hide there for as long as you need, you'll be safe."

Naiyana and Achara came out, carrying the baby and a meagre bundle of possessions, and Danni ran past them back into the shop. She turned the gas on in the stove then shut the door and threw a match onto the petrol Achara had sprayed around the shop, then ran back to the truck and demanded that they threw away their mobile phones as she got it and drove away. Achara sat in the back with the kids, Naiyana up front with Danni, radiating pain, confusion and hatred, mostly directed at Danni.

They'd been on the road for an hour as Danni tried to work out a route with Naiyana sobbing quietly beside her. Then she felt a familiar itch on her forearm as Naiyana and Achara doubled over in pain. Danni leant over and yanked up Naiyana's top to see her tattoo wriggling.

"They're hunting." She said. "Do you know the forest of Rayong?"

Naiyana gritted her teeth against the pain, and wails came from the back, but she nodded. Danni drove them out of town to a large bridge, then took a side road that led downwards, and parked up underneath, out of sight.

"We have to remove your tattoos, and do something about this truck," She stated, jumping out to examine it. "is too recognisable."

It was an ex- army transport truck, with a bed on the back with a metal frame with canvas over the top, old and cobbled together. Frightened children climbed down from the truck and Naiyana came to join her as she tested bolts that held the frame on, which rattled loosely.

"Kids, gather round." Shouted Danni, turning to Naiyana. "Show them your tattoo."

Naiyana studied her feet, but nodded, and Danni lifted up her top to show the children.

"This marks you as the property of the Fallen and their foot soldiers." She stated, "Does anyone else have it?"

Most of the kids shook their heads, but the 14 and 15 year olds came forward with Achara, with identical tattoos on their stomachs.

"Do you want to be someone's property?" Asked Danni, and they shook their heads. "If you do, you stay here."

Danni got the other children to rummage in the truck for tools – anything to undo the metal frame on the flatbed at the back. Then she removed the brands from the children, digging deep on her reserves of strength as she untangled the magic and withdrew the tattoos. Hands shaking, Danni moved onto Achara then Naiyana who screamed in pain. Dizzy now, Danni thudded to the ground but instructed them to remove the metal frame, urgently, and they began hammering at the bolts.

She must have nodded off because when she woke is was broad daylight. Naiyana offered her a bowl of soup. They'd managed to get most of the frame off and someone had started a small fire to cook up food.

"Will the monks protect us?" Asked Naiyana.

"Not if we bring the Fallen to their door." Replied Danni, too tired to be patient. She saw the children's frightened looks and changed her tone. "That's why we need to disguise their truck. We'll go to Wat Marp Jan monastery. In Rayong. I'll make sure they don't find the truck, and it's far enough away for you to be safe."

Danni ate quickly, then went to the truck and loosened the final bolts that were stuck, unaware of the curious glances between Naiyana and Achara, at Danni's surprising strength. She then hurled the metal into the river and reluctantly, turned to Naiyana.

"I'm too tired to drive, and..." She watched Naiyana's reaction keenly, "a western woman driving a truck is too obvious."

Naiyana nodded. "I will drive to Rayong."

"You might be tempted to go back to Bangkok and hand me over, with all these children." Danni now looked to Achara. "And think you can get back your life."

Both women flushed, the thought had clearly crossed their minds. The children watched on in silence.

"That doesn't just mean your continued collusion with slavery and rape of children." Stated Danni, as Achara started to cry. "The gangs will never accept you back, they won't be allowed to."

"What can we do? We've lost everything." She sobbed. "The gangs-."

Danni's eyed her with utter contempt. "You think the gangs are bad? They are nothing compared to the ones who are hunting you now."

"Because of you." Spat Naiyana.

"No!" Shouted Danni, her rage swelling, her voice echoing under the bridge so the children flinched. "Because of *you*! You dealt with them. You allowed them into your home." She pointed to the children, "*You* put your lives over children's, and now the Fallen are coming."

She looked on at the frightened children, dismissing the

women, "Is anyone here tempted to go back to Bangkok? Or back to your families?"

The children quivered.

"I don't know why your parents sold you, but even if they didn't, even if you were kidnapped off the street and want nothing more than to go home, none of you can, ever again. Because now you are hunted."

She allowed time for her words to sink in.

"You were branded by the Fallen, and they will hunt you forever." Younger children started to cry, but Danni continued.

"If they catch you, they will pull out their insides while you watch, and make you eat them." Despite the bright sunshine outside, under the bridge seemed to go dark, "They will torture you to betray everyone you've ever loved," Continued Danni relentlessly, "and finally, they will pull your soul from your body and feast on it."

Danni eyed everyone in turn.

"Does anyone doubt me?"

Nobody replied.

"They are waiting in Bangkok, hoping to catch our trail, and if they get your scent they will chase you forever, as they do me. Think about that when you think about going home."

Danni was too tired to argue any more. She climbed into the back of the truck and pulled the tarp up.

"Kids, we'll sleep in the back, under the tarp. Naiyana drives, Achara beside her, with the baby. It might remind you of your priorities, and if it doesn't, I will kill you both myself. Slowly."

Danni lay down and fell asleep instantly. Not a deep, restful sleep, but a slumber full of nightmares and things reaching out for her. She woke as they bounced along an uneven road through forest, which clipped the sides of the truck. She pushed aside the tarp as the truck emerged from a lane in the forest to a clearing before a beautiful white temple.

"Everyone out! Off the truck." She woke the children, saddened as always when they flinched from her touch. "I will take the truck and get rid of it."

A monk with a shaved head, in a long, saffron gown had come out of the temple and was eyeing the truck.

Danni looked beyond him, at the beautiful building, and wished she could go in there and find some peace, but the Order *and* the Fallen were both after her, and the monastery's loyalty was to the Order. They would call them, then they would catch her – if the Fallen didn't find them first. However old the monastery was, she doubted they could withstand the Fallen. It would be a massacre.

Danni scrabbled in the glove box and found a scrap of paper and a pen, and drew symbols – the names of the Fallen, written in Thai.

"Give this to the Abbot, tell him they are hunting you." She held onto it when Naiyana grabbed it. "Never speak these names aloud."

Naiyana nodded and took the paper, as Danni slid over to the driver's side.

"Tell the Abbot everything, tell him all about me, but tell no one else. Trust nobody else with this."

Danni waited impatiently for Naiyana to unload the children. The monk came over, casting a puzzled look at Danni, but then he was handed the baby and he lead them inside.

Danni turned the truck around as more monks came out, and drove away through the forest, heading for Cambodia. She stopped near the border and waited for full dark, eating some old rice cakes and changing into the clothes she'd brought in the market, with a wig of jet black. She had no prosthetics, and not enough time to alter here appearance fully, but managed to slip over the border undetected. She left the truck in Phnom Penh the next day and got on a train heading to Vietnam, where she got a flight from Ho Chi Minh to Manila, using yet another precious ID she'd now have to burn.

An elderly Abbot eyed Naiyana and Achara, before looking back to the piece of paper they'd handed to him.

"I can offer you sanctuary here, for as long as you need, but you must enrol as novices and follow our ways."

Naiyana grimaced and the old man smiled. "You don't need to join our order, Naiyana, just agree to follow our rules while you live here."

"Thank you, Abbot." Said Achara.

"You bring great danger to our quiet monastery." The 2 women nodded understanding, "You must not speak of this," He gestured to the paper, "Not amongst yourselves, not even to my monks, never. To say these names it to invite them in."

"She warned us, Abbot." Replied Naiyana, "We have some idea of the danger."

"I don't think you do." His kindly old face went hard. "In your worst nightmares you cannot truly imagine what is on your trail."

The women paled, but he continued, relentless, "You must avoid all pilgrims and visitors, and you cannot leave the grounds, not until I say that it is safe. If you leave, even to the village, I will not let you back in."

The women nodded again. The old man relaxed and gave them both a blessing and watched them leave. As soon as they were gone, he burnt the piece of paper they'd given him, then picked up a telephone and called the Order.

"Danyal's in Thailand."

Manila

Danni was fully healed within a couple of days, but the down side was she needed lots of sleep and food. Her metabolism had kicked into overdrive and she desperately needed a place to lay low for a couple of days to recuperate. Aware she was running out of IDs, clothes and money, she headed to Divisoria Market. She stole more clothes and used the last of her cash to buy food, gorging herself and buying supplies. Then she began to change her appearance, ducking into an alley to pull a skirt over her leggings, then changing her top and adding a stolen big floppy hat. She zig zagged, then another quick change – this time black trousers, black top with her black wig.

She found and internet café full of tourists and students and got out her computer. She was careful about using the internet, even on the dark web, but now she looked up news from her recent trail. Scotland first, searching for Amy, and was relieved to find no news. She then browsed for news in Germany, Switzerland and France, where she found a photo of a smiling Charlie, posted by friends after his body was found in the Seine, beaten and burnt. Murdered. Because of her.

Danni pushed her food aside, her apatite suddenly gone. *She* had killed Charlie. And Naiyana's husband as surely as if she'd pulled the trigger herself. She had killed the cult members in New Orleans, and she had shown natural expertise with the gun, killing with clean shots.

"I killed again." It didn't matter that they were child traffickers... now the whole family were on the run. She reflected on her constant running since her father's death, aware that she could not keep it up. She had saved the children in Long Island, but the deaths of the homeless children in Brooklyn weighed heavily on her. There were too many of them and only one of her, and she couldn't keep up with this war.

Danni had no idea how she would replenish her tattoos next time, but she determined to not risk anyone else. She forced herself to finish her food, and checked back onto social media to looked up Charlie, and found images of her tattoos in a homage to his work. The idiot hadn't listened and had posted Danni's tattoos – and brought them straight to his door. She didn't feel any less guilty, but she did feel a little relieved.

Danni was exhausted, emotionally and physically. Tired of the chaos that followed her, tired of constantly moving, literally drifting like flotsam. Helping children had seemed like enough to her, and if she ever felt the desire to settle, that instinct had kicked her in the teeth and forced her to flee. But it had felt good to fight back, if she was honest.

"I have killed." She told herself again, *"And if had felt good."*

Danni stopped the train of thought, telling herself that she needed rest. Somehow.

She emerged from Divisoria Market in a shapeless dress and large straw hat. She changed her gait, hunched her shoulders and rounded her back to appear much older, and heaved herself onto a bus to Beundia Bus Terminal. A quick change there, and now she was an skinny, haggard housewife with a headscarf who boarded another, random bus. She managed to get a seat after an hour and fell asleep against the window. She woke with a start when a heavy man sat next to her, and decided to get off.

She was at Nasugbu Bay. Night had descended and she made her way down to the sea, sticking to the shadows and avoiding everyone. She found a small marina with fishing boats as she ran out of energy. She climbed onto an ancient boat called Little Fish, and crawled under a large tarpaulin where she fell asleep. She half woke at dawn as someone climbed onto a boat and a dog barked excitedly. She considered moving, but her internal alarm didn't seem bothered so she decided to sleep again and see where the boat would take her.

She woke again as the sun was setting, a full day later, all her wounds healed but her stomach cramping with hunger as the smell of something cooking wafted through the air. An old man, Koy, had spent the day at sea before lowering the anchor and tending a stew over a small stove, his dog, Gamon, beside him.

"I have never had a stowaway before." Called the man in Tagalog. "Come. I made food."

Danni was still under the tarpaulin at the front of the boat, hidden, she thought, from view by the tarp and a small cabin. She climbed around the cabin to see him stir a rice and fish mix, then set out 3 bowls. Gamon stuck close to him, low to the ground, cowed by Danni.

"Oh, I was not expecting a Western girl." He said in Tagalog, before attempting English. "No hurt. Eat." He shushed Gamon, resuming in Tagalog. "Hush Gamon, you big coward."

Dogs didn't like Danni - no animals did, they crossed the street to avoid her, ears flat on their heads, tails tight between their legs. Children were scared of her too of course, unless she helped them, and Danni presumed that then they decided that whatever frightened them but was on their side was to their benefit. As Danni approached the old man, the dog pressed herself to the deck.

"I'm not the one who needs to be worried." She said in fluent Tagalog, in the man's regional accent. If he was surprised by her accent he hid it well, and chuckled at her.

"I am an old, old man, I have no fear of death."

"There are worse things than dying." She repeated the words she'd said to Achara.

The man's smile faded and nodded in agreement, "Last night I dreamt that demons were coming to the

Philippines. But when I woke I realised it was not a dream, so I came to my boat."

Danni took a bowl of food and she sat on an upturned crate, considering his words. He had the Sight, which is perhaps what had drawn her to his boat, and the elderly clung to superstitions that youths scorned, especially fishermen. She was not surprised by his dream either, the Hunters were catching up with her so quickly since her father's. Ravenous as usual, she scooped up the food, deciding to ignore his comment.

"Thank you," Said Danni between mouthfuls. "I will swim to the shore and leave you in peace. I mean you no harm."

The old man picked up his own bowl and ate slowly as he also watched the coastline.

"Then where will you go?" He asked, and Danni didn't have an answer. "Stay tonight, tomorrow help me fish, enjoy the peace of the sea. She is not always this kind to us fishermen."

Danni debated for a moment, then agreed. What else did she have to do, other than hide? She rinsed her bowl then curled again to sleep, waking at dawn when he threw nets into the water.

"Good morning, Westerner. My name is Koy. And you've met Gamon." He patted the dog and smiled a beautiful smile.

The day passed peacefully and Danni felt the tension gradually leave her body. Koy obviously realised that she was in trouble, but he didn't pry. When the sun was directly overhead, she helped him erect an awning over the deck, then stripped to her underwear and dived into the sea. If he was surprised by her tattoos he didn't show it, but Danni suspected that very little surprised him.

She sank under the waves and let the quiet wash over her, holding her breath as long as she could. She wasn't worried about sharks, like all animals they avoided her. She swam to the surface, then swam laps around the boat, relishing the feel of the water and the freedom from the world. When she was tired, she nimbly hauled herself back onboard via the anchor rope, to Koy's amazement.

She then curled up on the deck and fell into a deep, relaxing sleep. Until she dreamed.

A cliff face hurtled passed and the sky receded, a circle of rapidly contracting daylight.

Heat shimmered in waves and over the roar of the wind, something else - a distant wail of misery. The rock-face, passing at such speed, grew darker until the light above was nothing but a pin-prick.

A single white feather floated upward, hovered, in air that shimmered with waves of heat, then caught fire...

Koy watched Danni twitch and moan in her sleep and Gamon stayed as far away as the boat would allow, whimpering.

"Silly dog!" Said Koy, petting her.

His voice may have reached Danni because her moaning stopped and she seemed to grow calm. As the setting sun washed the sea in a red glow, Koy gutted fish and prepared an evening meal. He coughed intermittently and spat into a hanky, careful not to wake Danni, as Gamon inched closer and closer, puzzled by her. When Koy called her for food, she yipped excitedly, waking Danni. Instead of retreating from her, Gamon inched forward, tail half wagging.

"Gamon wants to be your friend." Laughed Koy.

Danni eyed the dog in surprise and put out a tentative hand, which caused Gamon to back away. Koy chided the dog and told her to be brave and Gamon sniffed at her hand. The dog's tail thumped on the deck and she pushed her wet nose into Danni's hand, to her delight.

Danni stroked Gamon's head, relishing the texture. "Animals never like me."

"Animals see into our souls." He passed her a bowl of food and Gamon trotted back to his side. "Gamon sees your soul is good, though it took her a while to decide. Not all animals are so clever."

Silence settled again, broken only by the lapping of waves against the hull. Two islands of peace in her turbulent life – first in Louisiana, and now here on the ocean. Both since her father's death. Danni eyed the old man who'd given her this breathing space.

"Do you have family, Koy? Should you not have your children helping you?"

"I have 6 children, 28 grandchildren, and 7 great grandchildren." He passed Danni his wallet – empty of money but full of photos. "None of them liked to fish. They all moved to Manilla for city work."

Danni detected his resignation and understanding. Fishing was a hard life, the big money taken by the large enterprises who plundered the ocean with their trawling nets, leaving very little fish or income for the smaller folk. Scanning the photos, she paused on a picture of a young Koy with a woman, his wife.

"When my wife died, they all tried to bring me to Manilla, to live with them, but what kind of a life is that for a man of the sea?"

Koy flicked through more photos and stopped again on a middle-aged man.

"My youngest son," Said Koy, "the only one who inherited the Sight, to his disgust. He works in banking, whatever that means."

"People today do not want the Sight, and I can't say I blame them." Replied Danni.

"Making ourselves blind to gods and devils does not mean they no longer exist, nor that they stop seeing us." It didn't need Sight to see the arguments Koy had had with his son, many years ago. But the flash of anger faded. In his heart, Koy wanted the best for his children and accepted their decisions.

"The demon in my dreams." He said after a while, watching the sunset. "It's hunting you."

Danni could have denied it. But she keenly missed Father Richard's insights that, while not compassionate, had her best interests at heart. Her 6th sense reassured her that Koy was a good man, with a well of earthly and spiritual wisdom, and talking with Alice had already unburdened her. It was a novel feeling, sharing her load with strangers.

"Not it, Koy, *they*. They are legion." She shivered and pulled on her clothes.

Koy eyed her keenly, then he blinked and shielded his eyes and had to look away.

"I can see why. You are very powerful, Westerner, and you have one foot in the Otherworld."

Danni snorted. She didn't feel powerful, she felt like a mouse, always hiding from predatory owls.

He sensed her response, "You are so dazzling that you almost blind my Sight."

Danni eyed him with concern, and gestured to her tattoos. "These are supposed to hide me."

He chuckled, "They hid you from me all day! I should have known I had a stowaway as I walked up to Little Fish. But not now we are talking, up close." His smile faded, replaced by sadness. "I am sorry, you carry a great burden."

Danni's eyes prickled unexpectedly at his compassion.

"It – they – were here many years ago, and the Buddhist Monks repelled them. Why do you not go to them for help?" He asked.

Danni considered the question carefully. Her father had told her to stay away from the Order, and all religious paths led to the Order. The Hunters wanted to use her, but the Order saw the harm in her – they wanted to put her down like a diseased animal.

"Like animals, I'm not sure what monks would make of my soul, Koy." She replied.

"So you run from God as well as the Devil."

Danni turned a startled look on him. She had never thought of it that way… could it be true? Father Richard had also implied that there was something inside her, something bad she had to resist. Alice had detected it.

"I run from the *agents* of God." She replied carefully, "I have tried to help people, help children who get caught up in their battles." Her self-defence sounded hollow in her ears. 'Tried to help' had meant murder and chaos in New Orleans and Bangkok, and she had as good as killed Charlie in Paris. "But I seem to harm everyone I come into contact with."

Danni slumped, defeated.

"You do not control the actions of others, Westerner," Said Koy, remembering the news he'd watched recently, the deaths in New York, that had given him a creeping feeling of dread.

"Devils hurt and kill, regardless of you or I. It is their nature to destroy." He cast a speculative look at Danni, before continuing. "Though they seem to be getting worse again. Ten years ago in Mexica, five years ago in Russia, those little innocents in America."

Koy's kindly features twisted in an unaccustomed expression of hatred, as Danni eyed him in surprise. But his rage quickly faded and she found herself crying with him, for the children. She thought of Amy again, who'd begged her to fight.

"Fight them! You can fight them. You've got magic, just fight them." And for a moment she wished they were here, that she could finally confront them. She remembered what it felt like to kill those who'd hurt children. "They will catch me eventually."

“And you must be ready.” Something must have shown on her expression because Koy nodded, his expression worried. “When you meet them, they will appeal to your best and worst instincts. Be particularly wary of the first one, for good intentions pave the road to hell. Like Gamon, I can see you have the capacity for great good, but you must be wary of the darkness in your nature.”

Danni felt anger crackle. If the trade for letting people in was personal comments, she should maybe keep her mouth shut.

“I’m not like them.” She kept her voice level but Gamon skittered away from her.

“In some ways you are.” Koy replied truthfully.

“You think I would hurt ever children?” She jumped to her feet and her eyes flashed amber.

“Not deliberately, or at least not at first.”

“Never! Never, old man. I would never hurt anyone!” Danni remembered the people she killed. She mentally amended that she’d never hurt children... except she hadn’t helped the children in Brooklyn, and she had made an entire family homeless in Bangkok. How many others had she inadvertently hurt, while planting tiny gardens around the world for miniscule pockets of ‘peace and love’.

Gamon now quivered with fear, flat on the deck, but Koy was unperturbed.

"You have something inside you, you can feel it, which is why you are angry at me. One day, you will be a powerful and unpredictable weapon, and you're not sure if that's good or bad."

Koy stroked Gamon to calm her.

"I know they won't taint me, I KNOW that! But why can't they just leave me alone? I just want to stop running. I didn't ask for this."

"What makes you different to those dead children around the world, young lady? They did not ask to be sucked into this storm either." He chided gently, an echo of Alice's words. "They did not ask to be sacrificed to cold gods before their lives even began."

Danni had been searching for answers she supposed, and 'fate' had provided her with some. Fate or something else, she amended with a shiver. 2 wise people had found her with the same message. Be careful of who you are, and don't get caught. Danni suddenly felt tired and she sat back down. She released a long, weary sigh.

"What then? What should I do? I don't know anymore, they're catching up with me so quickly... People are hurting because of me."

Koy coughed, discretely, and spat into a handkerchief.

"You must learn more of your nature and your power, and pick your side. God or the Devil." He managed, before spluttering again. "This is something everyone must do, Danni..."

He dissolved into a coughing fit and Gamon nosed the his leg, picking up on his distress. This old man had been nothing but kind to her, and she no right to vent her frustration on him. Feeling ashamed, Danni suddenly noticed how painfully thin he was, his skin yellow under his tan, and she hurried to fetch him some water.

"You're dying." She stated, and he nodded.

She released a long sigh, letting go of her tension, and Gamon came back to her and pressed herself against her leg.

"Do your children know?"

"No. I left a note telling them I had cancer and that I was going home to die."

"Home?" Asked Danni, then realised he meant the sea.

"This is my last ever voyage."

Then sun had set during their conversation, abruptly, as it did in the tropics, so they sat in darkness.

"I think this is the lull before the storm for you,

Westerner. Savour it." Koy reached out and patted Danni's hand. "But then again, what do I know? I'm a just silly old fisherman."

He dragged himself to his feet and lit a small lamp. "Now, we don't have fuel and Little Fish," He patted his boat fondly, "is far older than me, and may not survive a storm. But, we have a sail! Pick a destination and we will take you."

Danni eyed him in surprise, followed by delight.

"Really?" He grinned, and she saw blood on his teeth.

"I would like to just keep sailing with you, out to sea, but I expect they'd find me there too... so, can you take me to another country?"

Koy pointed out to sea. "South is Indonesia," He turned again, "that way is Malaysia, or Borneo. I think it is safest for Little Fish to skirt Palawan Island for Borneo."

"Borneo it is." Gamon barked approval.

"Help me stow away, my last adventure on this earth could be rough sailing."

Ambulong Island

They didn't make it to Borneo. The wind was against them and Koy's condition got rapidly worse and he apologetically told her he would have to drop her off early. She had tried to get him to a doctor, but he refused, happy that his time on earth was up. Danni had given him a glimpse of the incoming war, and he was pleased that he wouldn't be part of it. He worried about his family, and wanted time with the sea to pray for them, and for this strange young woman. As night abruptly descended, he set her on the shores of Ambulong Island, advising that he would set off a beacon for someone to find Gamon. He predicted fair weather for the next week, and thought the faithful dog would be safe enough with him until the end.

Danni had changed into tie-dyed tourist clothes and joined various drunken parties spilling onto the beach, listening for any local news that might be a concern for her. As she progressed along the beach, she eyed the hotels until she'd found an old hostel with little huts on the sand. She'd checked in as a loud French woman, claiming she'd fallen out with her roommate who kept screwing men in their shared bedroom.

Her room, a hut on the beach, had a double bed with a mosquito net, a battered drawer unit and a rug on the floor, a door to a small shower room. Danni shed her clothes and stood under tepid water, her eyes closed, washing away the saltwater from the sea and her sweat. Then her eyes flew open in alarm and she stared down at her body as tattoos slid off again and ran in dark rivulets down the drain.

“No, no, no!” She slammed the water off, and the sound of a storm carried in the silence.

Danni dried her hands and ran to her bag, as torrential rain lashed against the windows, and trees creaked outside, battered by fierce winds that had sprung up from nowhere. She rolled back the rug from the floor and pushed it against a wall as she opened her backpack. Moving quickly, she withdraw chalk and hurriedly drew a circle around herself, then added the points of a pentagram.

Another sound carried, over the wind, a scraping at the door. Frantic, Danni rummaged in her bag and pulled out a handgun, which she pointed at the door, but over the wind, the unmistakable whine of an animal.

“Gamon?” A bark, then more scratches at the door.

Danni hesitated, then crossed to the door, which flew open in her hand, blown by the wind. Gamon ran into the room, to the centre of the pentagon, and pressed herself to the floor, whimpering. Danni scanned outside, then battled to shut the door again, the floor already drenched.

She eyed the dog and her scrawled chalk drawing. “You’re a stupid dog.”

She half-smiled, then crossed back to the circle and again, beside Gamon.

Outside, over the wind, screams carried and she thought of the revellers caught out by the sudden storm. The hairs on the back of her neck stood up but she'd known the second her tattoos washed away that this wasn't a natural storm. They were coming and she was cornered.

She stroked Gamon, happy that she wasn't alone, but also worried for her. As the roof of her hut strained, threatening to lift off, she rummaged in her bag for an ancient mobile phone which she powered up.

She had several numbers memorised and her first message was a text to Harry.

"I'm going to the Order. Danni." She hesitated, then resumed typing, "AKA Emma."

Then she dialled a number she thought she'd never ring.

A young man in a cassock sat at a bank of computers. A red light blinked and a low, persistent alarm sounded. He eyed the alarm and blinked in surprise, before grabbing a handset.

"Subject A's mobile phone is active?" He switched on a speaker and Danni's voice carried over the intercom.

"I'm on Ambulong Island if you want me, but you don't have very long to get here."

"She's calling in?" Said the young monk, then repeated it, shouting. "She's calling in!"

A call went through to Anders who was at Wat Marp Jan monastery with the abbot, having just interviewed Naiyama and Achara.

"Brother Anders, remember that she saved these children." Said the abbot.

Anders didn't acknowledge him as he ran from the room to a waiting helicopter.

Danni had added runes around her pentagram, dressed herself, and sat in a meditative trance. She had nowhere to go, no way off the island, though she appeared to be in the eye of the storm for now. She'd passed hours expecting the roof to lift off before the storm had quietened, but her little hut was stood firm and was now quiet. A peak out of the door showed it raged still in the sea around them, and Danni hoped Koy had got far enough out before it hit. She had the very strong feeling this storm was localised around her.

A 'tap-tap' at the door, and then it opened slowly.

"Danni?" Anders poked his head around the door and Danni raised her gun, while Gamon growled.

"My name is Anders. I'm from the Order... thank you calling us, I've waited a very long time to meet you."

The door flew open in a stray gust of wind and Anders stood there, soaked, his hands raised in a calming gesture. Danni started to get to her feet, but then toppled forward, unconscious. Gamon turned to growl at the back window, as Ailwyn pushed open the blinds with a rifle. He eyed the dog in surprise, then looked at Anders, who shrugged.

"I didn't know either... bring it."

Ailwyn shrugged, then fired a sedative at Gamon, who yelped then collapsed.

Rescued

Danni woke up to pitch darkness. Utter darkness and total silence. And a strange, unsettling rocking motion.

She inhaled deeply and her eyes flared amber, for just a second. Gamon whimpered and her tail 'thump thumped', and floor, and the amber light in her eyes dimmed then winked out.

A soft light came on to illuminate a small, neat bedroom. A wardrobe and bedside table, and Danni, sprawled on a double bed against a wall. Beside her, Gamon nudged her hand as her tail thumped against the floor.

"What the...?" Disorientated, she looked around. "Where the fuck am I?"

Anders leant against a wall, watching her. He wore a monk's cassock, his hands hidden in the sleeves. He rolled with the room, that tipped gently from side to side.

"We are in a shipping container on the deck of a large cargo ship, somewhere in the Pacific Ocean." His tone was gentle, reassuring.

"You kidnapped me!" Danni felt the spot on her back where she'd been tranquilised.

"You called us for help."

"And you fucking kidnapped me!"

"You are hunted, and it has your scent. We sedated you, just to stop it tracking you. It was in the Philippines, Danni, racing towards you, we only just got out in time."

Anders allowed a moment for this to sink in, and Danni shuddered, then he gestured to the container walls around them.

"This container is covered in wards of protection, heavily painted over to camouflage us, and hidden among hundreds of other containers. It was all we had at short notice."

Danni eyed the room, then turned a venomous glare on Anders, who maintained a bland smile.

"It has a shower, a kitchen-."

"I want to leave." Gamon nudged her hand and she absently stroked her ear.

"Neither of us can get off until we dock and are un-loaded-."

"So I'm your prisoner!"

"We're both prisoners until docking, Danni, but then you are free to go if you choose." He shrugged, "You called us, remember? This is the best we could do."

Danni eyed him with distrust.

"Get freshened up while I cook dinner."

With that he's gone, leaving a confused Danni staring after him.

"How long am I imprisoned here?" She shouted.

"A couple of weeks! Not too long."

Danni eyed the room, still stroking Gamon. She had her bag, with her computer, and clothes, though when she checked the cupboards they were stocked with generic 'lounge wear' in various sizes. She then followed Anders into a corridor, Gamon beside her. She passed a door into a bathroom with a walk-in shower, then continued, passing a door to another bedroom. The last door opened onto a large kitchen-diner-living area.

Anders cooked at a stove, deftly holding implements in place as the ship undulated.

"There's red and white wine, or beer." He held up a glass of white wine for a sip. "There should be spirits and mixers too." He returned his attention to the food. "I'm making lemon and salmon pasta, I hope that's alright?"

Danni examined the room, noting suction pads on the table to stop things sliding, a large TV on one wall, comfy-looking sofas before it.

"There is no internet, no external connections, but we have a library of films."

She paced the room to explore it, Gamon at her heels,

and she noticed that he stuck beside her, ears flat, to give Anders a wide berth. Danni tapped the wall, a plasterboard cover over the metal behind.

"I can't stay in this small space, I need to be outside."

Anders turned to face her, expression kind. "Danni, you have lived a nomadic life, even with Father Richard. Why not enjoy a few days where you are not hunted?"

Danni ignored the reference to her father, eyes wide as she scanned the room, and Gamon nudged her hand.

"I am sorry about Father Richard. Over dinner, I thought I could tell you about him, before he left the Order." Anders set the table, and looked pointedly at the dog. "But maybe you should see to your hound first. We haven't housed a dog before, but I have put newspaper down in the shower tray."

Danni glared at his back, her senses struggling to wake up after being drugged. They were wary, but not clanging in her head. And as he'd pointed out, she had made the phone call.

Danni showered and examined her naked body, odd without its tattoos. Then she took off her wig and decided to leave it off. She couldn't remember the last time she gone without it, or contact lenses. She stared at her fully natural reflection – the stubble of her red hair in a halo around her head. Her strange, amber eyes.

She returned to her room and repeatedly held her nose while breathing out, to relieve the pressure in her head, until she realised that the deafening silence was the complete and utter absence of magic around her. She sat on the floor and breathed deeply to calm her mind, and discovered that her connection with Otherworld was missing. For the first time in her life, she was 'normal'.

She deepened her breathing and tried to go into a trance, but her stomach grumbled and she felt light-headed, perhaps as a result of the drugs. She joined Anders, who didn't comment on her appearance and they ate in silence, until the final course, cheese, fruit and biscuits, each with a glass of wine, Gamon curled at Danni's feet.

"How did you get me off the island?" She asked.

"Helicopter. It was hairy flying in, but the storm abated as soon as you were unconscious." Anders replied, and Danni eyed him sharply, wondering what he thought about that. He was of the feared Order, who she had avoided all her life. She only had her father's perspective on what they wanted from her.

"You went to a lot of effort to come and get me. Why? And don't say it was because of Richard."

"You asked us to."

"Right, and you do this," She gestured to the container, "for everyone in trouble?"

Anders' shoulders sagged. "No. I wish we could, but no... you're important."

"Father... Richard, he told me not to trust you."

"Yet you rang us."

"Because I had no choice."

"There's always a choice." Anders studied Danni. "Why did Father Richard tell you to avoid us?"

"He said you wanted to kill me."

"Kill you?" Anders replied, shocked. "We're a holy order, Danni, we don't kill children!"

Danni eyed him with suspicion, unsure if her instincts were right about the Order, or if she was biased by years of her father's relentless efforts to avoid them. She'd felt the pull to run away, even as a baby, but even her phenomenal memory couldn't place her first couple of years of life.

"Why did you hunt us then?"

"We never *hunted* you! We always knew where you were, more or less, and could have 'taken' you at any stage in your life. We thought it would be good for him, good for both of you." Anders shook his head, "I will be honest and say that I argued against Richard raising you, I think you had an unnecessarily tough upbringing and would have been much happier with a family. And we hoped that Father Richard would come back to us one day, perhaps when you'd grown up."

"So why did Father tell me that you wanted to kill me? And why did he run from you then? I mean at times, we really needed help, why didn't he reach out to you?"

Anders applied thought to the question.

"He was also running from the Fallen, who as you know are relentless in their quest. Sadly, he painted a target on your back too." He shrugged, "I suppose we are also a lifetime order. Normally, it is not an option to leave us, we sign up to death and beyond. Ultimately, I think that Father Richard was unstable and paranoid."

Anders allowed a moment for that to sink in, and it had more than a ring of truth, Richard had been both.

"Danni, you can't have believed that we want to kill you, not in your heart? You would never have rung us if you did... You took those children to Wat Marp Jan monastery, because you trusted them. You knew they reported in to us, and your instinct guided you there." Anders shrugged, looking pained.

Danni considered. What he was saying made sense, and she had turned to them when her back was to the wall.

"We have approximately 20 days on this vessel," Danni gaped, shocked at the prospect – that was way more than a couple of weeks. "I would like to use that time to get to know you, and reassure you about the Order, and perhaps get your help on the way. When we arrive, as I said, you will be free go if you still want to."

Her brain mapped possible routes, and realised they must be heading for the US, West Coast, likely LA. She was stuck here – and they hadn't, after all, killed her on sight.

"Let me tell you about the man who raised you. Richard joined the Order in his middle age, after his family died." Danni blinked in surprise and Anders nodded, but looked sombre.

"A wife and two children, all killed by... demons." He emphasized the word, intent on Danni.

"Demons?" Queried Danni.

"The Fallen."

Danni pondered that, and Anders gave her time. Koy had referred to demons, but she wasn't entirely sure what that meant. She had seen the work of the Fallen and she supposed that was as good a description as any. And since Richard's death her world had opened somewhat. She had met Koy and Muma Alice, who had offered her pieces of a puzzle about her own identity, but she wasn't much closer to working it out.

“Why did he leave the Order?”

“Because of you.”

Danni gestured for him to continue. “The Order’s location is secret, but on the outside we look like a small monastery. You were left at our gates.”

“I was a foundling?” Danni scoffed, but Anders laughed, amused.

“Yes, a foundling!” Danni didn’t look convinced. “People have left babies at religious houses from time immemorial.”

Danni remained sceptical. Her father had never given her details but this didn’t feel right. She’d had the impression that he’d kidnapped her from her parents, though she couldn’t place where that thought came from. Her excellent memory trawled her conversations with Richard and he’d never mentioned it specifically. A name hovered in the corner of her memory, but it vanished when she probed, and she had a feeling she didn’t want to know it anyway. Asmo…

“Richard tended to you personally,” Continued Anders, a welcome interruption, “until you could be placed in an orphanage or with a home, but, well he grew very close to you. Possessive, so he wouldn’t let the others care for you. We think you reminded him of his own children.”

Danni had very clear memories of her childhood, and this didn't fit. He'd never been demonstrative or 'caring', in fact most of her life she'd felt that he viewed her as an unwelcome burden. And their limited conversations about the Order hadn't included the option of her adoption.

"We could do with your help. *You* saved those children in Cutchogue, we weren't able to do what you did. But we'll talk more tomorrow."

Danni opened her mouth to protest, but Anders yawned.

"I haven't slept for twenty-four hours." He gestured to the table. "I'll leave you to clean up. Help yourself to anything you want."

Danni watched him go, then collected together the dinner items and filled a small dishwasher. She felt strangely dislocated from the world. The charms on the shipping container insulated all the background noise and muffled her sixth sense, and the silence disorientated her. Still, she had craved peace and time to think, and that is exactly what she had now.

She saw to Gamon and then returned to her room and attempted meditation again. It was strange, without the constant background noise she hadn't even realised existed. She had a picture of their container on the deck of a large vessel, buried in and amongst hundreds of other containers. She imagined the ship, huge in itself but tiny in the Pacific Ocean as it made its steady progress through mostly calm seas.

She once again sorted through her memories – every detail of her conversations with Muma Alice and Koy. She was used to working out puzzles and she had several new pieces, she would meditate on this unexpected journey and see if she would finally work out what her place was in all this. The Fallen wanted her really badly, and since Father Richard's death she'd barely had time to breath their efforts had been so relentless. The storm on Ambulong had not been natural, and she shuddered to think what fuel they had used to unleash so much power.

To her surprise she slept deeply that night, and woke, refreshed, to find Anders already up, with coffee made and a stack of folders piled up on the table.

"What's this?" She gestured to the folders as Anders poured coffee into 2 cups.

"There is a television and films library, and I would encourage you to relax, but this." He gestured to the papers, "Think of it as your bill for this rescue. Richard was our primary expert in dead languages and we know he passed that knowledge on to you. The police showed us what you did to help them in Cutchogue, Professor Brewer was astounded by your grasp of ancient languages."

She opened the top folder showing crime scene photos

from a massacre.

"They're changing, Danni. Help us work out what they're up to?"

"Brooklyn?" She asked, pushing the gruesome images away that turned her stomach.

"Perth. Australia. Two nights ago when the storm hit Ambulong. The night we picked you up."

She spread out the photos, sickened. Dead bodies, drained of blood, brutally murdered. Runes and spells on the walls, and her eyes flashed amber with her anger. At least this sacrifice hadn't included children. This was a different sacrifice, yet another sacrifice, to the ritual that had targeted her on her flight to Bangkok.

"They're insatiable. They will never stop." Said Danni.

"Unless we stop them." Replied Anders. "Do you know what the Order does? Our purpose?"

"No." And she realised that she didn't. Her Father, Richard she mentally amended, he had never discussed them.

"We fight demons, Danni. Things that should not be on earth, but that have seeped through the cracks of hell." He turned to face her, his usually mild expression replaced with disgust. "And we send them back."

Something in Anders' tone made Danni shiver. He smacked his hand on the photos of the runes.

"This is our map to them. These are summoning spells. Spells that wake the evil in people." He studied Danni intently as he spoke. "If we can work them out, we can stop these... monsters."

Danni's eyes darted from his face to the file, to the grisly photos of bodies which she pushed underneath the runes, and Anders' intensity faded. It was alluring idea... could they really stop them?

"They have given us a map to them, if we can interpret it. They have given us their names..." He tapped on a highlighted section in a photo, "Aba-."

"Never speak their names!" Sweat broke out on her upper lip, but Anders was unphased. He shrugged and continued.

"You're the key, Danni! Give us your time on this journey, that's all we ask.

Danni's inner senses were waking up, warning her, though that could just be naming one of the Fallen aloud.. she decided that later on, she would reapply her tattoos, regardless of the protective wards on the ship.

"Help us to stop them, once and for all?"

Something didn't ring true in Danni's head. "Richard already tried to help. He told the FBI when I worked out the location for Brooklyn, but they did nothing."

"You're not telling the police this time. The Order have a fragile relationship with the authorities. We're asked in sometimes to assist, but usually we get this far too late to help." Anders' expression turned passionate. "With you on board, we could maybe translate this last ritual in Perth. We could get ahead of them for a change."

The idea was alluring, but... she didn't trust Anders or the Order, but what if she could help? Could they be stopped? Ultimately she supposed that was why she had called them, and not sailed into the sunset with Koy. She absently rubbed Gamon's ear, and the dog gave a 'whuff' that seemed to agree with her thoughts. Still, why had Richard left them?

"When we get wherever we're going, I'm free to leave?" She asked.

"The Abbot wishes to meet you, but after that, yes. You'll be free to go, Danni. Please, just give us these days and help us."

Danni considered. "Are we safe?"

"They have no way to find us."

"Okay." Danni released a long sigh.

She eyed the pile of folders and nodded to herself. It was what it was and 20 days was a lot of time to think, and maybe even help...

She went to the bottom of the pile, to the older records from the Order which contained copies of Egyptian hieroglyphics. She ran her finger under a line of symbols, reading ancient words of death and destruction. She shuddered and closed the file, moving onto the next, with more hieroglyphics, which she quickly scanned. The next was Mayan, with hand drawn diagrams of ritual sacrifice, and she quickly scanned the runes. She stepped forward through time, categorising by century, culture and language, by specific naming of fallen angels, mentally comparing each ritual for similarities and differences. Muma Alice had stated that Crowley had somehow learnt how to awake the Fallen, then his rituals were lost until 20+ years ago, and Danni checked for differences pre and post the Crowley grimoire, from the point of his death in 1947.

She wasn't sure what she was looking for, but her interpretation of older rituals seemed to change as she accessed more data. She was familiar with most of them from Richard's copies, but there was much more information here. The more recent files contained police reports and autopsies, in Russian, Chinese, Spanish.. multiple languages in addition to the ancient languages of the rituals.

Danni was beginning to suspect that the runes were fluid, influenced by events and knowledge, so interpreting them would never be fully complete. It was daunting but also heartening she supposed. The Fallen were changing their rituals, but there could be brand new clues in the archives of their atrocities.

She tried sorting the files according to religion and found a folder relating to a massacre in France, in the 8th century. Belsanc Monastery had housed dozens of monks, most of whom had been slaughtered in their beds. 12 of them, including the abbot, had warranted special treatment and she winced as she saw a print of the 12 monks in chains, suspended upside down, blood draining from wounds in their bodies. Something about this story made her shiver, and she quickly moved on.

Danni spent the day focusing on the older files, spreading out documents on the floor, sorting them into different groups as she tried to make sense of them. She had to admit that she was intrigued, her brain seeking a solution to the puzzles.

Back in the Order's HQ, monks watched Danni read the folders, then watched as she walked Gamon to the bathroom, before switching to a camera feed of Danni in the bedroom. Cameras tracked her every move, from showering, using the toilet, to going to her bedroom and painstakingly reapplying her tattoos. They recorded the shapes and symbols she used and then traced them, mapping to them to their own records, adding any variations. They recorded her all night as she fell asleep – and thrashed wildly when she entered a nightmare.

Belsanc Monastery. Moonlight filtered through a massive hole in the roof of a stone room. Around the room, tonsured monks were chained, naked, upside down. Their bodies were punctured all over, soaked in their own blood which dripped down and pooled at their feet.

One monk still lived. He moaned pitifully and a slender, dark haired woman approached. Lilith. She ran a long nailed hand along his torso until she reached a puncture wound, then she dug her nail in and he screamed.

"You did this, Danni." She said. "And you enjoyed it! Come back to us."

The room was lit by a low light. Danni writhed on a bed, moaning in her sleep. She came awake with a start and sat bolt-upright, her eyes flashing amber. She eyed the room in panic, then pushed aside the covers and jumped to her feet.

Gamon barked once and she calmed down, dropping to her knees to pet the dog.

Danni rolled her shoulders and then performed her exercises, a series of moves loosely based on multiple martial arts. From his bedroom, Anders watched her a laptop screen, focused on the dog.

"You're a puzzle, dog... Why aren't you scared of her?"

A message appeared on the screen from Ailwyn.

"Brother Marco has vanished."

Anders read the message as he watched, then typed his response.

"The monk who helped us in Manila? I shall pray for him."

Ailwyn's reply came quickly, "You were careless, Anders. He didn't need to know we have her."

"He was our contact for the shipping container, Ailwyn, I had to communicate with him. Besides, he didn't know our route."

"But he did know that you're on a ship in a shipping container!"

The curser flashed, awaiting Anders' response, but instead he watched Danni leave her bedroom, Gamon in tow, as Ailwyn continued typing.

"It won't take a genius to find your ship, and it will bring too much attention to intercept you before California."

"Have Faith, Brother Ailwyn."

Ailwyn started to type his response, "We can't risk..."

Anders typed, overriding Ailwyn, "Have a welcome

party ready for us, Brother."

He shut the lid of the laptop, cutting off Ailwyn, and unplugged it, locked it away and then left his room.

Hunting

The Fallen had moved again, from Australia to Thailand, hurried over to the Philippines, then back into Thailand, following Danni's trail. Members (and leaders) of different Thai gangs were dead before them, as was Brother Marco, who had died most painfully. He had been resilient, refusing to tell them what he knew for a long time, but nobody could withstand the Fallen forever.

He had advised that Danni had been sedated and then collected from Ambulong Island and taken to a shipping container. The monk revealed that the container had been loaded onto a huge cargo vessel, and the crew had no idea what they were transporting. He didn't know the ship's departure port, its name, destination or the route, and as a novice he had never been to the Order's headquarters.

The Fallen began tracking all ships from all ports in the region within the last 5 days. They would find the ship, either at sea or after it docked, and then they would trace the cargo. The Order would take Danni to their headquarters, their safest base and the only place capable of holding her.

And they would let them, because they would follow. They had argued about the ritual in Perth, as it shattered their occult pattern, but Lilith had been adamant – and it had nearly worked! Danni had been trapped on Ambulong Island and they had been on the way when the Order got to her, so very, very close! Lilith had stepped foot on the island as Danni's presence vanished.

But this might well be better, she had to concede. The Order were a problem the Fallen would have to tackle eventually, and the number of Fallen at her disposal was growing. Since the ritual in America and then again in Australia, more and more of her brethren were waking and making their way to join them. The problem was, they didn't yet know where to go.

Tarel and Belial sat at the end of a long table in yet another affluent property, formerly the home of more of their followers, whose remains Beleth ate. They watched him with amusement, both liberally splattered in blood.

Armers, Lilith and Abaddon sat at the other end of table, Marbas connected remotely.

"No more, Lilith." Abaddon droned on.

He had argued most strongly against Perth, worried they would upset the occult balance, but Armers had sided with her, as had Marbas, who was still in the US with the FBI who were liaising with international police forces, all hunting the 'Ritual Killers'. Marbas had argued that they needed to divert attention from the US, while Tarel and Belial had, of course, had nothing useful to say. The others, the newly awakened, were still too dizzy on their memories and were more a hindrance than a help as they needed to be restrained from their basest desires. Restrained enough to not get caught or expose the others anyway.

They argued back and forth over their next course of action, as Lilith was struck by a memory of Medieval England, former incarnations of herself with Marbas after they'd met and recognised each other. They'd been trapped in a squalid house, raging peasants outside the door.

"You cannot keep playing with the occult, we are bound by its rules and they could backfire on us." Abaddon droned on, for the hundredth time.

Marbas had snuck out and caught the mayor's daughter, and brought her screaming back to the house, and he'd been seen.

"Our cycle is changing, Abaddon." Replied Armers, who was the best of all of them at interpreting the runes. "The five years are no longer necessary. We have created a new pattern."

Lilith and Marbas had both burned to death in the house, which was the last time she'd seen him. Marbas felt her gaze and looked up. He smiled at her, but her gaze remained frosty. It had taken her many lifetimes to come back fully to herself. She would find a way to make Marbas pay.

"We have performed too many ceremonies! I don't just

mean drawing too much attention," Snapped Abaddon. "We must consider the consequences if our spells backfire. We could be expelled from this world. We risk too much!"

"We unleashed the storm in Perth!" Snapped back an increasingly annoyed Armers, "With power we've not seen since we had willing followers and blood sacrifices. There is a momentum, Abaddon."

"But to what purpose? We don't have Beleth or Danyal-."

"But we do have plenty of our brethren." Interjected Tarel, enjoying the dispute.

Everything had changed when she'd found Crowley's grimoire, Lilith reflected, that told her how to summon her brethren. The Fallen were selfish and bitter, which made them solitary by nature, and they all had their own agendas. Marbas was greedy and unreliable, given to rash, public violence that brought attention to him. She wondered what acts he'd committed during his time in the FBI, and wondered if they were a threat to his brethren. Besides, they were all greedy, she conceded... although, she mused, Belial was by far the stupidest. They were all arrogant, Lilith more so than all of them, she reflected, but Abaddon and Armers were also cunning... and Tarel. She was cunning too, though she hid it well. And only herself and Abaddon seemed to understand that Danyal was the key to unlocking this world and, ultimately, finding their master.

"Enough. Abaddon is right, we must respect the occult patterns. But Armers is also right, the patterns have changed. We must study our last rituals and see what they reveal to us." She said, bored of the argument. Bored of her brethren that she was forced to spend so much time with. She had to keep them close until they had Danyal, and then... then they could all do what they liked. All of them could in the newly shaped world.

What the Order didn't realise is that they did not write their own instructions when they sacrificed. They recorded instructions as their rituals revealed them. Perth had been a huge risk, and Lilith had allowed her rage to overcome her. The results had been magnificent – even if their target had slipped away. But she wasn't too worried about it. They could work on interpreting the results, but she would focus on tracking the ship that carried Danni across the sea. Now the Order had captured her she was out of their reach as she'd be locked away, but she suspected she'd found a chink in their armour.

Modern day technology, which would do the work for her.

The Order

Anders joined Danni, who was reading the file from the Belsanc Monastery massacre, that felt eerily like her dream.

"Can't sleep either?" Danni closed the file abruptly and he put the kettle on. "Nightmares ruin my sleep."

Without looking at her he started making coffee, and Danni shivered. Last night's nightmare had felt so... real. She pushed the thought aside and got to work. She organised and re-organised the papers as Anders brought her coffee.

"Those are all old files, surely you've read them?"

"Richard's copies were incomplete." Danni said, setting aside papers she hadn't seen before. "And besides, each new ritual links back and reveals new meanings in the old rituals. It's all about associations."

Her hand moved to the folder on the monastery murders, more than a thousand years before. The one that had haunted her dreams.

"How do you get these?"

"We teams of followers dedicated to unearthing records of the Fallen. They scour bookshops, markets, auctions and of course the vaults of old churches and monasteries."

“Back to Uruk? Five thousand years ago?”

Anders flicked through the folders and pulled one out. “I believe that’s the earliest written record, though there’s a record of folk tales back at the monastery. Tribal stories handed down in that region, they likely predate Uruk.”

She sorted all the spells into piles, and then began recording the locations, cross checking with her own memory. The Fallen had changed their pattern drastically for their last three rituals, from Cutchogue to Perth, breaking an ancient cycle that she was sure would have repercussions, but she wasn’t sure what they might be.

She sorted the names of the Fallen; Lilith was the first, always listed topmost in the rituals, and she had awoken Abaddon in Louisiana twenty years before.

She scribbled down references to dates and created a pile of spells. Together they had woken Armers in China, then Tarel in Mexico, then Belial in Russia, with Marbas. She didn’t know who they’d woken most recently, but the names listed in Perth were frightening. Scores of Fallen, their names repeated in multiple variations – Balberith, Caim, Mephistopheles, Sabnack, Semyaza, Vassago, Wormwood … the list went on, including one she refused to write.

She came back to another repeated name. Beleth, who sent a shudder through her body. It wasn’t clear if they had him as they kept summoning him and there was confusion over how his name was recorded….

"Do you ever wonder how you can speak every language on the planet? Even dead languages?" Anders asked, interrupting her.

Gamon growled and Danni petted her to quieten her as her senses jangled.

"Richard was… thorough in my education." She replied, terse.

"You alone worked out the Cutchogue location, date and time, something we couldn't do."

"Maybe you're not as good as you think." She snapped, "Richard taught me from dawn 'til dusk, for 16 years. No holidays, no breaks, just studying."

"And you have a natural aptitude, Danyal."

Danni's skin prickled, "That's not my name!" She spat. "If you want my help, I need to concentrate."

Anders nodded but did not leave.

"Aren't you tired of being constantly on the run? Why don't you join us?"

Danni tried to summon her 6th sense, but the quiet of the protective runes on the container seemed to shut it off. The thought of no longer being alone was enticing, as was the idea that she could stop running - but she didn't trust Anders. Or the Order.

"I'm not joining your Order, Anders. I'll meet your Abbot and then I'm gone." She turned a feral glare on him and he put his hands up in surrender.

"If you could discover what they're planning next, that would be very helpful." He said, and left her in peace.

She worked her way through the files, making new piles as she sorted them with different associations, constantly writing on a notepad. She stopped only to snack and 'exercise' Gamon. She'd found a ball which she bounced along the corridor which the dog ran after excitedly, although she had to admit that the annoyance this caused Anders was part of the fun. After hours of sitting hunched on the floor, Anders insisted that she stop to eat at night – although inside the container, day and night was just a concept.

"Was Richard always serious?" She asked as he served spaghetti bolognaise, to her and to Gamon.

"He was by the time he joined us, but I suspect that he'd been very different as a young man." Answered Anders, "Though the person to ask is Brother Ailwyn, they were close friends while Richard was at the Order. You'll meet him at the monastery... if you like, before you leave."

"How did Richard learn about languages? I presume he

studied them before he joined you, but I could never find him on any internet searches?"

"He changed his name when he joined the Order, as we all do." Anders mulled over his response. "I don't know what his name was before, just that he came to us with an interest and expanded on his knowledge once he'd joined us… though many think that exposure to demons opens the door on knowledge."

He picked up a pile of papers that Danni was avoiding. Satanic occult markings that left her feeling contaminated. He pushed them aside and wiped his fingers on his leg, as if to remove a taint.

Anders then eyed her. "Was he cruel to you?"

"Never!" She replied quickly – too quickly.

Anders raised an eyebrow. "He was a driven man when I knew him. A hard man."

"And you're not?" She snapped back, and he shrugged.

"I have never raised a child."

Danni reflected. Anders had known Richard, presumably knew his faults, and she wasn't sure why she was defending him.

"He was never… loving. He was fair, always fair and just, but justice is seldom kind I think. I wonder what he was like with his own children."

"I once saw a photo album that he kept. Pictures of him with his wife and children, on holiday or just out together." Anders watched her side-on, interested in her reaction but striving for casual. "Swimming, playing sports, the usual. He smiled in every picture, which is something he rarely did when I knew him."

Danni felt a pang of sadness, noticed by Anders.

"You don't believe he loved you, do you?" He asked, and Danni wondered if Anders wanted that to be true.

"I never felt he did when he was alive. But he sacrificed a great deal for me, why would he do that if he didn't love me?"

"Because you gave him a chance at a second family?" He replied, then seemed to think about it, "But raising you the way he did was entirely selfish. Why would he not allow you to be raised by a normal family if he'd cared for you? It seems like he put you through hell, Danni, which suggests his mind was unbalanced."

Danni didn't know how to respond, so she said nothing.

"I am sorry, it seems as if the Order should have intervened." There is was again, the idea that they'd always known where they'd been. But then why had her Father kept them on the move? Why *had* he left the Order if what Anders said was true? And, if it was all true, why hadn't they intervened? Her entire upbringing had been brutal in many ways. Unless...

"Unless..." Said Anders, seeming to read her thoughts, "He was hiding you from the Fallen. Do you think they hunt you because of the knowledge he taught you, or because of *who* you are? Have you ever asked why are they after you, Danni?"

He hesitated over her name, and Gamon growled. Danni was aware that she was in dangerous territory.

"Like you say, Father Richard taught me too well. As I showed with Cutchogue, I am a real threat to them." Danni replied.

"Yes, that must be it." Anders stood up abruptly and cleared the plates.

"I'll clean up dinner, let you get back to work. How far have you got?"

Danni relaxed, relieved to change the subject.

"They've changed their entire pattern, which is a huge risk with the occult. I have Brooklyn to Cutchogue, then nothing so far, but there will be a pattern. They performed a ritual 7 days ago, while I was travelling to Thailand, before this one in Perth which summoned the storm."

Anders looked at her with interest. "A ceremony 7 days ago? We have no record of that?"

"Well, you need to search harder!" She snapped, "And the ritual in Perth doesn't seem to be a summoning as such, or at least not to a particular location that I can find. I mean, they used it to power that storm but it's more than that. It's a… they're calling out to dozens of their kind. I'm making a note of names as I decipher them, but it would be good to have the internet."

"Dozens? Dear God, what are they planning?"

Danni gave a weary shake of her head. "I don't know. I don't even know if it'll work, they've thrown the occult rule book out from what I'm seeing."

Days passed and each day Danni uncovered more and more names - and every night her dreams became more vivid. She seemed to travel through time, vividly recounting events in ancient Rome or Greece or Egypt, flashes of which stayed with her when she woke up. Flashes that appeared as she read historical records of innumerable atrocities. She wondered if Anders was right, if prolonged exposure to the Fallen was somehow rubbing off on her. Tainting her.

And as Danni added more names to her list, her disquiet grew as she read and re-read the material, trying to piece together a modus or reason behind their change. The Order also frantically tried to work out what the Fallen were planning, verifying Danni's decoding. It seemed that the Fallen were issuing a mass, general call to arms, which made no sense. The Fallen operated alone, out of the spotlight. However many they were, they were outnumbered by humanity and could never agree on a common goal.

While she worked, the Order watched her, awake and asleep. They covertly monitored their contacts and scanned dark web traffic for any indication that the Fallen were tracking the ship carrying Danni and Anders, acutely aware of how vulnerable they both were.

Over dinner one night, in the habit now of conversing with Anders in much the same way she'd spoken with Richard, she broached the subject of the summoning spells.

"I can't find a location hidden in the photos taken in Perth. I've cross referenced back with all the previous rituals and I can't find anything." Stated Danni.

"What are they writing then?"

"Names. I'm still deciphering them, but there are just lots of names. There must be a location hidden somewhere, but maybe we need more to unpick it."

Danni shoved aside her food and pulled over her notes.

"See, they're repeated, in slightly different ways. This hieroglyph is in the US, China, Mexico, Russia and again the US last month. Repeated, always with a vessel of some description. A goblet, here an amphora, a chalice... variations of the same thing, in the same position, then in Russia linked to blood. A knife, an sword, a snake meaning poison when taken in this context, but the snake in later rituals is linked to betrayal *and* poison. It's all contextual." She rummaged through her notes from Brooklyn, "These symbols together led me to Cutchogue, but *only* because of their previous use in other rituals."

She sat back, frustrated.

"But the snake is *also* the name for..." She refused to speak them aloud, ever, so she wrote 'BOTIS', "whose appears as a viper. Or here, a cat," and again she wrote a name 'FLAUROS', "but until Cutchogue they focused on a single name and laid a trail to a location." She shook her head, frustrated.

"There are elements missing. Are there any more rituals you may not have the crime scenes from? We know they've performed at least one without any authorities discovering it," Said Danni, thinking of the assault on her flight – a powerful enough assault to melt through her tattoos, which the Order seemingly knew nothing about, "I mean, those homeless kids in Brooklyn, if they hadn't picked such a public place, would anyone have ever asked where they went?"

Anders eyed her notes, "We monitor global news, but I guess there are many places with homeless or refugee children. When we get back to the Order, we'll double check for disappearances."

"A large number. These sacrifices need a lot of blood to feed them."

"We'll look into it as soon as I get back in touch with them."

Danni got to her feet and resumed her work, her appetite gone.

"Perth worries me, Anders. I can't see a pattern, but there is always a pattern."

Anders cleaned up and retreated to his bedroom. With the Order, they watched her work – and recorded everything she did. She began the next day with her morning exercises, then exercises for Gamon, followed by breakfast. Anders received notice that they were heading into El Segundo, California, but when he joined her for breakfast he didn't mention it.

Later that day, their crate was lifted from the ship. It swung wildly, throwing them both to the floor, causing the dog to scrabble and yelp in panic.

"What's happening?" Asked Danni, grabbing the frightened Gamon. "Are we sinking?"

"No." They stood up tentatively as the container swayed from side to side. "We must be in port."

They had a sensation of movement and the container titled, then, eventually, a shudder and heavy clang that reverberated through the soundproofing as they were placed on dry land. The stillness was disorientating after days at sea with constant rolling.

“I believe we have landed!” Smiled Anders.

“When do we get out?”

“They’ll load us onto a lorry and transport us away from the port before they let us out.” Replied Anders. “A good few hours, maybe another day.”

“Okay.” Danni recovered first, tidying up the scattered papers, “I don’t know if what I have is helpful, Anders. I don’t think I can tell you anything new, but I’ll be ready to meet your Abbot.”

Anders left her then and returned to his room. He was satisfied that she had given them all she could voluntarily.

“Come and get us.” He typed Anders on-screen.

He sealed his door shut as gas was released in the rest of the shipping container which would knock out Danni and Gamon.

Awakenings

Wormwood woke to a strange tugging sensation in his chest. He was in a homeless shelter in Central London, a shared dorm in a hostel, and at first he thought someone was trying to steal his things.

He sat up with a shout and flailing of fists – but nobody was near him. He pulled aside his filthy shirt and eyed his chest, before pain exploded behind his eyes. He was transported to his recurring dream, of falling away from the light into unbearable pain. Anguish, burning, remorse, rage... the dream usually faded before he woke, but now he remembered it fully. He relived it, and his rage returned.

He was Wormwood.

He took in the men sleeping in the dormitory and his rage encompassed them, puny, feeble humans. He stopped flailing and reached into his bag for a large kitchen knife, then he jumped on the nearest man and slashed up and down in a frenzy. 6 other men shared his room and they woke to the man's screams. In a panic they ran to the door but Wormwood was too fast. In a whirl he slashed and hacked until the room resembled an abattoir coated in the blood of the dying.

Wornwood's rage didn't abate but a cold rationale settled and he hurried to the night manager's bedroom and killed him, quickly. Then he took his time showering, shaving, helping himself to new clothes and making himself presentable. When he was ready, he let himself out of the hostel. He had somewhere to be.

A shack just outside of Capetown in South Africa. The man of the house came home, drunk, and grabbed his wife with clumsy hands that pawed her for sex. He'd already given her HIV – not that she realised. She was beautiful but strangely vacant. She vaguely remembered having children with this man but couldn't recall what had happened to them. She'd spent every living moment at a remove from the real world, completely cut off from reality.

A few moments before her husband came home, her stomach cramped and a burning spread through her chest. She felt herself falling and flames rising up to meet her, but they only consumed her flesh, leaving the entity of herself intact. The man had walked in and wobbled over to her, pulling up her skirt to take her from behind, but she batted him aside. Angry, he hit her, sending her sprawling onto their bed – and Zepar remembered.

She tasted blood on her lip and allowed the lump of a man to climb on beside her, fumbling with his trousers. She reached her hand to hold his throat and through his drunken haze he eyed her in surprise, seeing an alien intelligence behind her eyes. Her hand gripped tighter on his windpipe and panic set in.

He tried to bat her off as he felt her nails sink into his skin, deeper and deeper until her fingers closed around his windpipe, which she ripped from his body. She pushed him off onto the floor and licked her fingers as she got to her feet. He was still thrashing and wheezing as she stepped over him. She had somewhere else to be.

Sabnack was on guard duty in a supposedly friendly Afghani town, stationed with a small group of UN soldiers. A child later questioned would say that he was peering out of his window and saw Sabnack approach a fellow soldier. The other man glanced at Sabnack before turning his attention back to the desert, which is when Sabnack had slit his throat. The child had watched Sabnack disappear into the town, at which stage he'd roused his parents. Terrified, they had fled to an underground cellar and locked themselves in as screams erupted from outside, with the recognisable rat-a-tat of recurring gunfire.

Sabnack worked his way through the town, killing through stealth, at first those who'd pissed him off, then, as every fresh drop of blood brought him back to life, he killed indiscriminately, from his fellow soldiers then onto the townsfolk. He cut his way through them before abandoning the town and heading out into the desert. The child's family, worried about fire, stepped out of their cellar and crept up to their roof, further horrified to see insurgents around their town. Then they watched Sabnack walk calmly up to them.... And the insurgents melt away. If anyone had asked them, they would have said that they saw pure evil that day. The not-man who approached them carried the stench of hell, and they fled.

All over the world the Fallen woke.

Over in Russia, Botis was, by anyone's reckoning, a complete waste of space. He lived in squalor in a run-down trailer which boiled in summer and froze in winter, and stank – of discarded, mouldy food and of his repulsive, putrid body odour. His parents, strict Russian Orthodox devotees, had died when he was young, and people half-joked that he'd broken their hearts with his general vileness. He was considered to have severe learning difficulties and largely written off by society, which suited him. Especially when his one and only talent had led to his dream job in a small zoo. He never interacted with the public, but he cared for the snakes. He had no fear of them, even the deadliest, and had never been bitten, and if you watched him closely, you could almost imagine he was able to communicate with them.

He had been cleaning out a cage, surrounded by hissing, venomous snakes. Then he'd felt flames rising up around him, and had turned circles in a panic for his beloved snakes... only to find there were no flames. Entwined around his legs and arms, curled around his neck, the snakes came to him and worshipped. Botis remembered.

Not everyone was successful though – in a prison yard in the USA, Balberith woke in an exercise, taken over by a terrible rage. He attacked the man nearest him, who was part of a gang and whose fellows fell on Balberith and killed him before the guards even knew what was happening. In Romania, Semyaza experienced terrible pain in an aging body that promptly died of heart failure. In France, a beggar outside Notre Dame awoke and launched an attack on tourists. He killed 4 people in a mindless rage before the police shot him dead. Another Fallen was driving a truck full of drugs through the mountains of Columbia when the pain and shock of his awakening distracted him, and he drove off a cliff to a fiery death.

But many more Fallen survived those few minutes of disorientation. Wormwood, Sabnack, Zepar, Caim, Mephistopheles, Botis, Vassago, ... around the world, the Fallen woke up. There was a change coming.

Two of a Kind

Danni was woken by Gamon licking her face. They were no longer in the container but now in a box, around 6 foot square, the interior (and she guessed the exterior) covered in runes. It rolled and bounced, feeling very different to the roll of the sea – harder and faster, so mostly likely an unpaved road. Gamon had messed the container, more than once, which caused her to wonder how long she'd been out. Her bag was gone, with all her possessions, and she was starving, a feeling that she'd not had for the last three weeks, and poor Gamon looked dehydrated.

"Come here, girl." She pulled the dog close, "You'll be alright."

The car or whatever she was on moved onto a flat, paved surface, and all the while Danni stewed. The Fallen were building up to something – something new and something huge. The clues were in the documents she'd read, but she couldn't place it. She tried not to think what it meant that she was now captive in a container, and hoped it meant that they were taking extra precautions while moving her.

She suspected not though and hugged Gamon close as she felt the vehicle slow, then heard the hiss of gas and tried to hold her breath, but before long she collapsed with Gamon.

The next time Danni woke she on a bed in a small room,

absolutely furious. Gamon, lying on the bed and peering intently into her face, went mad with joy. She jumped on Danni, jumped off the bed and ran in circles, then jumped back on again, yapping all the while, which did something to ease her mood, until she inspected her surroundings.

The walls were of stone and she instinctively realised she was underground. The muffled, heavy silence indicated she was in another heavily warded room, even before she noticed the wards painted onto the walls, some of which were her own design, which could only mean that they had seen her body – spied on her naked. Her anger returned and she got out of bed, weak and stiff. Food had been left on a tray, and she saw an empty food bowl and water had been left for Gamon, but it didn't reassure her – or lessen her anger.

She strode to the heavy wooden door which, surprise-surprise, was locked. Then she turned her attention to the walls and ceilings again, but couldn't see any cameras. Even so, she knew they were there. They must have recorded her on the ship, and now she wondered if they'd had internet access the whole time.

She ate breakfast and as soon as she'd finished the door opened, reinforcing her feeling that she was being monitored. Ruby came in, covered head to toe in a hijab and niqab, her hands gloved.

"I thought this was a Christian monastery?" Queried

Danni.

"We are multi-discipline in our search for the Fallen." Replied the woman, and Danni got the distinct feeling that she was not happy to be here.

"Where are my things?" Asked Danni, but woman either didn't know or wouldn't be drawn.

"I'm to take you to the bathroom, you can showers or bathe."

"Then I see the abbot and get to leave, right?"

Ruby didn't say anything as she stood back to let Danni out. Later, Ruby was waiting outside the bathroom when Danni came out, showered and dressed, to find Gamon missing.

"A member of the Order has taken her for a walk. She was reluctant to leave your side while you slept, but she has been well cared for." Stated Ruby, before Danni could ask.

"While I slept?" Queried Danni, "That's one way to describe being drugged."

But again Ruby refused to be drawn and just walked off. Danni didn't need to see her face to realise that Ruby didn't like her, and she kept Danni firmly in view as she took her through a series of corridors and finally up 3 flights of curving, stone steps to reach the ground floor, then another set of steps to the first floor, then along to

Ailwyn's office.

The big window threw Danni for a moment, and she realised she hadn't seen daylight for maybe a month, since Ambulong. Confused by the brightness, then almost instantly overwhelmed by her Sight as it flooded back, no longer blocked by wards or charms. She'd lived too long in silence, and the input was a harsh, loud and clamouring. Her fear returned – the Fallen were planning something big and a confrontation was inevitable. Her best hope was to remove herself from the Order when the battle occurred. Or should she? Should she instead make a stand and fight them? Maybe, but she wasn't about to pitch in with the Order.

Ailwyn watched from behind his desk as a dazed Danni strode to the window with its bright sunlight. When her eyes adjusted she soaked up the sun, relishing the feel on her face. The noise from the waterfall drew her however, and she looked down at the roaring, ugly waterfall in the centre of the courtyard. As usual, monks of different religions were prostrate before the water, though several turned to look up at her, as if disturbed by her presence.

"Impressive isn't it?" Said Ailwyn, joining her at the window, interrupting her thoughts.

"Ugly." Replied Danni. "So, are you the abbot I'm supposed to meet before I head off?"

“I’m Brother Ailwyn. Richard was once one of my closest friends, I was sorry to hear of his death.”

“Richard was a brutal, bitter old man.” Danni found herself saying.

Ailwyn snorted a laugh. “Aye that he was.. but not always. He was once the best of us.”

“He remained the best of you. Even when he was beating me when I was just a small child, which apparently you were fully aware of, he was only trying to protect me. From you. See, I don’t believe you did know where I was, which is why you’ve also kidnapped me.”

“Not kidnapped.” Ailwyn’s expression turned sad, “I am sorry for your treatment. We were trying to keep you from the Fallen.”

“Good.” Danni stated. “In that case, where is your abbot? ‘Cos I’m about done here.”

“I’m sorry, our abbot was called away I’m afraid. As you know, the Fallen are gathering in large numbers, or at least attempting to until they fall out.”

“Look, I’m grateful for you coming to get me but I can’t do any more for you. I’ve looked through everything, there is no pattern to detect.”

“So you just want to leave?” He asked.

"Yes. As agreed."

Ailwyn looked out at the fountain as he seemed to carefully pick his words.

"Do you know what the Fallen are?" He asked finally.

Danni retreated from the window – from Ailwyn. She sat on the sofa and poured coffee from a jug.

"Monsters, devils, demons." She replied, thinking of the shadows left on the souls of all the children she'd met, and he nodded.

"Aye, we have many names for all the devils." He said. "But the Fallen are a particular breed. We believe they are the angels who rebelled against God, who He cast out of His presence."

A great sadness washed over Danni with his words. His voice faded as her recurring dream intruded – *Danni fell. Light and goodness faded bringing a terrible, aching sense of sadness.*

"Every religion mentions them," Continued Ailwyn, "in various guises with their own multiple, different names."

Screams surrounded her and the temperate rose.

"We, as His agents, and we are duty bound to act against them...".

Her skin melted and her bones crackled.

"Just as they seem bound to fight against us..."

A single white feather floated up in the heat-shimmer.

"...They have blighted the existence of mankind since our very first days."

He turned to face her and she snapped out of her daydream, "They did the ultimate wrong, and they take their hate out of us, His chosen. Humanity."

Danni drank coffee she didn't want as her tattoos prickled her skin in warning. They were on dangerous territory here, literally and metaphorically.

"Do you know how the Fallen inhabit human bodies?" He asked, returning to his desk so he could study her.

Danni swallowed her coffee with difficulty as a lump filled her throat.

"We believe that *generally* it's pure luck. They can inhabit babies most easily, but they must be in proximity of a stillborn at the moment of death. Luckily for them, many babies die every day, most still in the womb, and the mother is forced to carry an abomination full term. Although, of course they can kill a human themselves, if they are powerful enough. Or if they are invited in."

Danni's stomach rolled.

"Their 'host' body must die and its soul depart, but our research tells that inhabiting adults is less successful than babies. It seems something of the host's personality remains after death. Perhaps at a cellular level."

He seemed to wait for a response, but Danni had nothing to say. She doubted she could talk even if she wanted to.

"Even inhabiting babies has its problems. Fortunately for humanity, these demon spawn don't always realise who they are and require an event to remind them of their true selves... An act of violence or depravity, either witnessed or initiated by them."

He waited again for her to speak, and continued when she didn't.

"Until Aleister Cowley changed that. He worked out, or was told, how to wake them. His work was destroyed, but then re-learnt 2 decades ago. These are the rituals carried out by the Fallen."

Danni instantly thought of Sarah's whispered words, so clear to her that she wondered if the ghost child was here. This Order was supposed to have destroyed that book which the Fallen were now using, but she wasn't about to volunteer her knowledge.

Ailwyn produced a stack of pictures, photographs of people and paintings. He selected one, a remarkably detailed print found in a monastery in England from the 3rd century. A hugely overweight man – a good likeness of Abaddon, made before the man was burnt at the stake. He then produced a photo of a portrait found in the Neverlands, of the same man. Next he showed her a photograph of him taken in the early 20th century.

"We believe this is Aba-."

"Don't speak their names!" Shouted Danni, before continuing more quietly "*Never* say their names aloud."

Ailwyn got another stack of photos, ignoring her outburst.

"It doesn't matter what the colour of the baby is that they inhabit, they always revert to their own look. Ab... This one," He held up Abaddon's photo, "is always pale skinned, like a corpse, with black, greasy hair and is always hugely overweight.

"This one," He held up images of Lilith, "once appeared in Africa and it was remarked that her curly black hair fell out, replaced with straight hair as her skin paled. The same has happened in reverse, with dark skinned babies born to Caucasian families. They always revert to their own look, Danni."

Something in the way he said her name sent shivers down her spine, but he got to his feet.

"There's someone I'd like you to meet."

"I want to leave, Brother Ailwyn. Anders said I would be free to go."

"Just a bit more of your time. Please, come with me."

Ailwyn went to the door of his office and held it open for her, and she reluctantly followed. She'd been dazed by information overload, but she caught a whiff of something, a very faint scent. Harry! He'd been here at some point, which meant she *was* in the US, most likely the East Coast. She suspected her route on the ship had been direct over the Pacific, offloaded on the West Coast then driven over land. Her eyes strayed to Ailwyn's desk, to a phone sitting there, which might help if she could find a way to reach it.

Ailwyn coughed, for her attention, and she followed him out. He took her down again, three flights, then into a large chamber.

The room was huge, lit by candles, with bare stone walls covered in symbols from different religions: A Christian Cross; The Buddhist Wheel of Dharma; a Taiji, the Yin and Yang of Toaists; The Torii Gate of Shinto; a Star of David; The Star and Cresent of Islam; a Hindu, Sanskrit Aum; a Sikh Khanda. And under each symbol was an armed guard.

A chair was bolted to the ground, which made Danni shiver, and a long table faced it. 8 robed men and woman sat at the table with Anders, with 2 empty seats at the end. Alwyn sat in one and gestured for Danni to take the other.

As they sat, a second door opened. A young woman was dragged in by 2 guards, with another 2 behind with guns trained on the captive. Her hands were tied behind her back and she was forced to kneel in front of the table.

"Identify yourself." Said Anders.

Danni suddenly grew conscious of her own scruffy appearance as she noted the woman was stunningly beautiful. She ran a hand over her stubbly hair... then looked into the woman's eyes and recoiled. They were dazzling green eyes, but underneath... Danni thought her eyes were like a stagnant pond with something putrid swimming under the surface.

The woman noticed her reaction and laughed, then stared intently at Danni as if puzzled.

"Do I know you?" The woman asked Danni in an upper class, English accent.

Danni's stomach flipped. She had no illusions that this was one of the Fallen, she could feel the rankness radiating from the woman. This was the closest she'd ever been... she turned her head and barely stopped herself from vomiting, to the woman's amusement.

"Tell us your name, Demon." Repeated a woman on the panel of judges, her accent Parisian French.

"Fuck off." Replied the woman.

"We believe you to be Gom-."

"Don't speak their names!" said Danni urgently to Ailwyn.

"It's already here, we cannot summon it?" Asked Ailwyn.

"Gomory." Finished the judge, and Danni winced, watched by a confused Ailwyn.

Gomory laughed, a beautiful, tinkling sound. "Your arrogance, it is astounding." She said, mimicking the French woman's accent exactly.

"Do you deny who you are?"

Gomory let out a long, bored sigh.

The panel opened folders that each had before them, and inside were copies of a Dutch portrait from the 1600's.

"Jacob van Ruisdael painted this portrait in 1682, the year of his death."

Ailwyn passed a photo of the portrait over to Danni – it was Gomory, without a doubt. The thing in her body laughed and preened at seeing her beauty.

"He only ever painted landscapes, I believe that is the only portrait he did." She said. "Nowadays they might have a better understanding of his real cause of death."

Her eyes glowed putrid green, and the panel continued.

"So you vanished for nearly 400 years. Where did you go?"

Gomory pouted, and shrugged.

"How came you to inhabit this body?" Asked someone else.

Gomory raised a slender, middle finger at the panel, and a guard slapped her across the face. Hard. She poked her tongue out to lick blood off her lip.

"What was it doing when you found it?" Asked another of the panel.

"She – *it* - had entered a summer camp in Texas, where she likely seduced four teenage boys before taking them into the woods. Each one of them was tied to a tree and... castrated. A warden found them and called the police, who caught her driving away from the camp site in a stolen car."

"The trouble with having such beauty is that it's impossible not to stand out from the boring, ugly masses of humanity." Gomory laughed again and Danni felt the urge to vomit again. Anders opened a file.

"We've tracked your route from Nicaragua, from the trail of bodies." Gomory laughed harder, "In three weeks you've travelled through southern and central America-."

"Did you like my present to your little brothers in La Mia?" Asked Gomory.

Ailwyn clenched his jaw and held up a folder, "This thing killed 6 elderly monks in La Mia, a small monastery in Nicaragua."

"And have you heard from the brothers near Santa Rita in Honduras?" Asked Gomory, met by silence. She laughed again when Ailwyn nodded to a guard, who left the room to investigate.

"Into Guatemala then Mexico, leaving a trail of dead men."

"All castrated and forced to watch themselves bleed to death, though I hoped some of them might survive. I wondered what life for a man might be like without a penis." Added Gomory.

Danni wondered briefly why this woman was confessing so freely, and her confusion must have shown.

"When we catch them, they always want to show off their crimes." Stated Ailwyn.

"They also know that we see through their guises. They cannot hide their true, corrupted forms from us." Stated Anders.

"Where were you going?" Asked someone else.

Gomory pouted again, and got another hard slap.

That was when the torture started. She was hauled into the chair, her wrists and ankles bound with iron, which hissed and sizzled as it burnt her skin.

"Their kind can never stand iron." Stated Anders.

Danni vomited into her hands and dashed to the door, which was barred as a guard stepped into her way, as she tried to close her ears to the screams.

"It doesn't matter what you do, humans, we'll all be free soon enough." Gomory raged through her screams.

Ailwyn joined Danni and they let her out, and he escorted her to a bathroom, where she emptied the contents of her stomach.

"You don't have to go back and witness that." He said through the door, his tone almost kindly.

She washed her mouth out, and her tears away, and repeated Alice's words.

"Be careful that anger, however justified, doesn't turn you into a monster."

"What's that?" Asked Ailwyn from behind the door.

Danni left the bathroom, determined to get away from this.

"What do you need me to do to get out of here?" She asked him.

"Things are moving fast now, forces are gathering. I think you are the key, Danni. You can help us to end the Fallen's time on earth." Responded Ailwyn.

"So you're not going to let me go?"

"Please! Help us?"

Danni slumped, realising there was no easy way out of here. She would go along with it and wait for an opening – what choice did she have? Oddly, she heard the sound of the waterfall again – the torrential rush of gallons of water, with something underneath it, a whispering, like the quiet rustle of leaves. Underneath the whispers, she thought she detected screams.

"Continue to translate the texts and give us a full list of names, and try to discern what they are planning."

Danni shook her head and the sounds receded. She very nearly asked Ailwyn for the truth – would they ever let her go? But she didn't think he'd lie to her. Anders, yes, but Ailwyn seemed different and she didn't want that question answered. So she agreed and he led her to another room underground, heavily warded and full of whiteboards and all the papers, books and images the Order had collected relating to the Fallen.

She began re-working her research, methodically, trying to detect a pattern as she added to her list of Fallen who were being summoned. As her list grew, her heart sunk as it soon numbered hundreds. Hundreds like that monster Gomory.

She was offered the use of the monastery garden to walk Gamon, as long as she had a shadow of guards, but she couldn't bear to be near the waterfall and only went outside a few times to get the layout of the buildings and surrounds. A huge perimeter wall surrounded the lands, visible in the distance. Fields were cultivated, growing various crops, and there was even a large vineyard, but always in the background was the rush of water and the underlying whispering that haunted Danni.

As soon as she'd got the lay of the land, she stopped going outside, and reinforced her own wards on the room she worked in, where she contented herself with doing her own exercises and allowing others to walk to dog.

She sorted and re-sorted the Order's research, going back thousands of years, and focused on the pattern. There was only one source she refused to read – the Satanic cuneiform. When her hand strayed too near it, or if she accidentally brushed against, she was assailed with violent images that left her stricken with a migraine.

Prisoner

The Fallen had left the Philippines and crossed to the US, led both by Armers and Lilith's research. As they travelled they searched for others who had awoken, all over the world, and then sent out Fallen to fetch them – willing or unwilling – by following their tell-tale pattern of mayhem. Money was not a problem, they had been manipulating economies since society began, and they had more than enough humans in positions of power to ease their transit through borders.

The problem was that the Fallen seldom agreed on anything and generally, their hatred and insatiable hunger for pain and torment kept them on fixed, independent paths, but Lilith had awoken Abaddon 20 years before for a single, specific purpose – to find and release the Morning Star. The others generally agreed, once she'd had a chance to explain, but it was a fragile alliance. She wouldn't have long to yield results before it fell apart.

Lilith was certain she had found the cargo ship that carried Danni, and it had docked in LA. She was utilising contacts for haulage companies and independent drivers who might have transported Danni from the ship, and had a few promising leads. She had dispatched trusted Fallen and human disciples to follow those leads, even as she kept the others close. The house they now resided in was a Hollywood mansion, high above LA in large, secure grounds, that once belonged to an ardent supporter, who had been fed to Beleth not long after they arrived.

The surviving members of his family, along with various homeless people from LA that Tarel and Belial had discretely collected, were now huddled in a corner, bound by their hands and feet, sacrifices for Armers. While Lilith followed clues left in the human world, Armers worked in the occult, interpreting the messages revealed in their sacrifices. Unlike Danni, the Fallen – or those who managed to occupy human bodies - were unable to cross into Otherworld, and their memories of their time spent without a host were unreliable, so they relied on their rituals for their plans.

Lilith was too impatient and Abaddon was too brutal, while the others were too stupid or too self-centred to focus for long on anything outside of their own pleasures. Armers was the only one with the skill, patience and intelligence to sit down and work through the codes they'd received, and he focused on the Satanic cuneiform that Danni avoided.

Armers wrote symbol after symbol on a table – using his finger, dipped in fresh blood. Abaddon watched him, as usual eating, while Beleth was chained to a wall, prodded by Tarel, who giggled every time he roared and lunged for her.

Lilith joined them. She was bored, waiting for her contacts, Fallen and human, to report back.

"Beleth has a long memory, Tarel, and we will release him at some point." Noted Lilith, but Tarel shrugged.

"I'm the one who feeds him, and he's always loved me."

"Wanting to fuck and devour you isn't love." Replied Lilith.

Beleth strained again, his piggy eyes fixed on Tarel, who wandered to the captives. They screamed and cringed away, but Armers turned a poison glare on her.

"I need them."

"I got them!"

"Then get some more." He replied.

"Be discrete, Tarel. We can't risk the police following you here, not yet."

Tarel looked like she'd rebel, for a just a moment, but then she went off to find Belial. She was also bored – bored of waiting around, chafing at Lilith's restrictions. She had been woken 10 years before, and had joined them for rituals in the intervening years but mostly chose to live on her own, in her own way. She'd been with the other Fallen full time for weeks now, and was ready to break away again.

Lilith watched her, then turned to Armed as he wrote a fresh rune in blood.

"Well?"

He ignored her.

"Are we even on the right continent?" She asked.

"You fucked up the patterns with your insistence we sacrifice at completely the wrong time." Spat Armers.

"It's a simple question, Armers."

"Nothing is simple about these instructions. Except you perhaps." He snapped back.

Armers dipped his finger in the blood and copied another rune – and this time, the wood sizzled and the rune burned into the table.

They peered at it, but Armers didn't comment.

"Armers! What does it mean?"

With a weary sigh to emphasize how much they tried his patience, Armers looked at Lilith.

"We are being called to this continent." He replied.

"Where exactly?"

He ignored her and went back to work.

"I could have told you that." Said Abaddon. "The Fallen that we awake are all heading here. We can all feel the pull."

"But where? The US? Canada? Mexico?"

"Somewhere in the US." Stated Armers. "I need fresh blood."

Lilith yanked another prisoner to his feet, this one a young man in his late teens. He sobbed and begged for his life as Lilith tipped a bowl of drying blood onto the floor, then slit his wrist and poured his spurting blood into the bowl. Despite her slender frame, the young man was no match for her strength, and she easily held him as his lifeblood drained away.

Armers dipped his finger into the fresh blood and wrote another rune, which sizzled and burnt into the wood.

"Armers?" Asked Lilith.

"East of here is all I can say at the moment." He stated, refusing to be drawn. "Now all of you fuck off and leave me in peace."

Lilith went off in a huff, to spur on her own search, but Abaddon remained, still eating, focused on Armers.

A week passed, with Danni's list of names growing ever longer, but no idea what they were planning – except chaos and devastation. And as time passed, Danni felt a growing urgency to get away from the Order. She noticed that her guards were more relaxed, happy to leave her alone as she worked now she'd shown no sign of trying to escape. One afternoon, while Gamon was being walked, she unpicked the lock on her room and found the post outside deserted. Grabbing her chance, she ran from the chamber and headed towards the entrance to the monastery, which she knew was near Ailwyn's office.

She kept to the shadows, but had to duck back when she heard multiple footsteps running towards her. She backtracked, but as more people joined the hunt for her, she was forced into a part of the monastery she didn't know. With the guards ever nearer, she backed into a stairwell that led down.

Hoping she might find tunnels under the monastery, Danni ran swiftly down the stairs. She lost count of the steps before she emerged into a vast room, well-lit near the staircase but then fading into pockets of light from oil lamps spaced regularly, that faded into the distance. The cavern was vast.

Under foot was a flagstone floor surrounded by inky channels of darkness - water. Holy, blessed water too. Wary, Danni set off into the darkness, passing giant shapes either side - Sarcophagus. Despite her hurry, Danni stopped to read them as she passed – multiple faiths, she realised this was the cemetery of the Order, where its dead were interred.

"My predecessors." Anders' voice carried, he was in the cellar with her, "The Order have fought the Fallen since the dawn of time."

Accompanied by a huge man, Agamjit, he stepped into the light at the bottom of the stairs.

"You mean since humans evolved from apes?" Replied Danni, before darting deeper into the darkness.

In reply, Anders snorted a laugh. "Since God granted us knowledge of them."

He progressed further into the crypt. "There is no escape from this chamber, you'll have to come out eventually."

Danni was distracted by movement on top of a sarcophagus. "When are you going to let me go, Brother?"

More movement, a young, ghostly woman who opened her mouth in a silent scream.

"I think it's time we stopped playing games, isn't it?" Their eyes scanned the chamber, searching for Danni. "The Fallen are gathering, never so many at one time."

"And why haven't you stopped them? I thought that was your job?"

Danni wasn't accustomed to seeing ghosts in this world, but she had seen plenty in Otherworld. Another figure appeared before her, the outline of a man. A young, handsome man, tethered to the sarcophagus. He dropped to his knees before Danni, hands together in supplication, begging.

“We will stop them, with our last breath. And that includes you, Danyal. We will not let you join the Fallen.”

“I’m not one of them.” Replied Danni, but her attention was on row upon row of tombs, all with figures attached, all silently screaming, crying and begging.

She turned in a horrified circle as ghosts appeared everywhere.

“What have you done?” She forgot her urgent need to flee, caught in their anguish.

Agamjit and Anders followed the sound of her voice, and spotted her, staring in horror at what they could not see. They only witnessed her mesmerised by their ancestor’s graves, while Danni saw the ghosts of the dead, begging her silently for help.

Sickened and horrified, she turned on them. “What evil have you done here?”

A distant scream, an echo carried from far away. The rustling of whispers started, and the ghosts grew more desperate, tugging against their ties to their bodies. Danni covered her ears and backed away, straight into

Agamjit. She bounced back and slipped, towards the water, which splashed upwards.

"Don't let her touch the water yet!"

As Danni fell, and the water rose up to meet her, but Agamjit scooped her up and chucked her over his shoulder.

"Get her out of here." Spat Anders.

The water churned now and the ghosts tugged at their invisible tethers, frantic, as thousands of voices whispered. Anders cast a puzzled look at the water, then the emptiness above it, unable to See. Agamjit carried Danni back up the stairs and behind them the whispers died and the water calmed into ripples that slapped against stone until they died out.

At the top of the stairs, Ailwyn stood with 2 more monks, including a female 'monk' warrior in saffron, Buddhist robes.

"Don't touch me!" Shouted Danni.

The group emerged from the stairwell, Danni still over Agamjit's shoulder. Danni pushed upright and her hands raked Agamjit's eyes, and he dropped her to the floor, then felled her with a brutal slap.

"Our ancestors rejected her very presence."

Danni leapt to her feet, her cheek red from the blow, which faded instantly. Furious, she pointed at Anders.

"You are abominations!"

He studied her with disdain, and her eyes turned totally black then amber again in the blink of an eye.

"You are unspeakably cruel." She pointed a finger at them in turn, lingering on Anders and finishing on Ailwyn. Her irises now sparkled, like they erre full of miniature galaxies. Fat tears welled as her anger receded, replaced by intense sorrow for all those trapped below.

"It's time to wake her up." Said Anders, unmoved.

Danni was returned to the chamber full of books with Ailwyn and Anders, who handed her more papers.

"I'm not reading these. I don't want to do anything to help you." She spat.

They eyed her coldly and her gaze flicked to the now-guarded door. With reluctance, Danni pulled over the documents and started to read.

The first papers related to Father Richard, a dossier on his life. It was true that he'd been a scholar of the occult, a professor at Oxford University with a wife and children, until the day the monsters came. He'd been visited by... Danni's stomach did a flip and her heart nearly jumped from her chest as she read a name.

Asmodeus. The name resonated deep inside her and filled her with terror.

Father Richard, then called Professor John Appleby, had been investigating the Fallen Angels for a paper he hoped to publish, and had stayed late at his college when Asmodeus came for his family. His wife and children hadn't let the demon in willingly, as the destroyed back door testified. When the professor finally got home, he'd followed a trail of havoc to the upstairs bedroom they'd desperately locked themselves in, which is where he found their bodies. Or the remains of their bodies.

Tears slid down Danni's cheek as she read John Appleby's progress from teacher to warrior monk, as the Order found and recruited him. Ailwyn then handed her the next bunch of papers, these from 22 years ago, and her stomach did a flip. Asmodeus again.

The Order was perpetually on his trail, following clues over the years but always too late, driven by Father Richard's obsession as he immersed himself deeper and deeper in occult languages. They didn't realise that when Asmodeus sacked a small convent in Italy, he'd taken a young nun and locked her away. They didn't initially know that he had then selected his most devoted followers to... Danni tasted bile and had to swallow vomit as she read.. to gang rape the nun until she became pregnant.

Asmodeus had kept her alive until her baby was born, which is when the Order caught up with him. They found him performing a ritual to 'bring into being'. A twist on the awakening ritual the Fallen were now carrying out – or so they believed.

The Order had arrived to find the nun dead, cast aside once her purpose was accomplished. The baby… again Danni choked back bile as she read. The baby was dead, blue from cyanosis, empty of its human vessel., until Asmodeus summoned Danyal to inhabit its tiny body, when it woke up and started crying.

Murder. Infanticide. Rape. The bloody and violent conception, birth, death and rebirth of a monster. The folder was one that Richard had never shown Danni.

The Order had stormed the stronghold and captured Asmodeus, killing his followers. The decision had been made to kill the baby too, but Richard had intervened. He'd taken her and vanished, and then spent the next 22 years trying to keep her safe from the Order.

Ailwyn watched Danni read. Emotions ranged over her face as she flicked back through her earliest memories. Pain, death, loss, fear… mostly fear.

"This isn't me." She said.

"You are that baby, Danyal. You know this."

She shook her head. "No! No. And… why would he take

me if I was?"

"We think Father Richard, who you admit never loved you, chose to believe a baby was blameless, whatever its origins" Replied Anders.

"When we discovered what Asmodeous was planning, he had argued for mercy, for raising the child within the confines of the Order, but he had been overruled." Added Ailwyn.

"Because you never were a baby!" Shouted Anders, suddenly angry. "Richard went against us, his new family, out of some misplaced recollection of his own, human children."

Ailwyn placed a calming hand on Anders's arm. "Despite his personal tragedies, he chose to save you from us."

"That's because I am human!" Shouted Danni.

Ailwyn produced more papers, these a stack of photographs, the first a portrait from the Renaissance that was undeniably of Danni.

"This was painted in Florence in the 15th century."

Danni picked up the portrait, which looked exactly like her, and was assailed by... memories? A masked ball, laughter.

Ailwyn picked up an old piece of vellum and read from a Latin text.

"'Justina had fiery red hair and strange, ambers eyes.... That glowed when she was angry'."

Another vision, this one of a villa outside of Rome. Some sort of party with senators and their wives, generals, concubines, musicians, gladiators and slaves. Some reclined on low couches, others were on the floor. Every single one of them dead or dying. Danni shook her head to clear it.

"Justina was covered in tar and set fire to in AD 300." He added, handing her the text.

Dazed, she began to read, but was swept up in another vision, of a Roman senator making a speech. Another vision, of gladiators in an arena, fighting to the death...

"Throughout history you appear, and you have always been a wildcard. You are linked to the worst atrocities, but you have also sabotaged your own kind many occasions."

Anders examined her, puzzled, but then shrugged and sighed.

"But then the Fallen only help each other if their interests coincide, and when they do meet, they generally fall out and kill each other. Which brings us to the question of why they are waking so many of their kind? And why they do seem to be working together now."

Ailwyn got to his feet with effort, suddenly feeling very old.

"Your punishment will be delayed if you help us." Anders shot Ailwyn a dark look.

"No!"

"You will be fed, you can see your dog, then we'll be back with more questions. I don't want to hurt you, but we will do anything to stop your kin, Danyal."

"No, Ailwyn! We must wake it. It has failed to dredge more from its memory, we must force the transformation."

"Give her more time."

"We don't have time. I'm taking this up with the High Council, we must force *it* to awaken. It is time, Brother."

Their voices receded as Danni dreamed of falling.

Anders swept from the room leaving Ailwyn, who watched as Danni fell off her chair into a dead faint.

Of light and goodness fading, with a terrible, aching sense of sadness. Screams surrounded her as the heat increased, melting her skin and crackling her bones, as a single white feather floated up in the heat-shimmer.

She felt death approach, but then was back in the old monastery, hundreds of years ago, with monks suspended by hooks on the wall, crying in agony.

"You did this, Danyal." Said Lilith.

"Danni?" Asked Ailwyn.

Danni was back in the villa outside Rome. She stood on a balcony, Rome spread out below her in the distance. In the room behind, blood spouted in arcs that splattered against the walls until it filled the air, churned up by a great, swinging sword.

A woman materialised inside the bloody fountain. She moved with lethal grace and lightning speed, until time slowed. Her blade swung in final swirling an arc over her head, then she dropped it and walked towards the window. Blood rained slowly on her, thinning from a torrent to a mist as she emerged like a spectre.

"It seems I've made a mess of your house." Lilith said, joining Danni on the balcony and taking a goblet of wine from her hand.

"They will kill me for this." Stated Danni.

Lilith saluted with the wine, "Perhaps you'll stay dead this time."

Ailwyn picked up the fallen Latin document, outlining the charges against Justina. He remembered there was an addendum, some sort of testimony, that had become detached from record. He had ordered it while he collected evidence against Danni, then had forgotten about it. He left Danni on the floor and went downstairs to the library where a clerk retrieved it for him – the original document was, worryingly, missing, and this copy had been misfiled.

Ailwyn ordered the monk to find it, then read the addendum. After the slaughter in a Roman villa, Justina had been tried. A single slave, a young girl, had survived and testified on Justina's behalf – she had not killed her household, she had been a kind master. The evidence was admitted to the record, then overruled.

Allies

Harry had received an envelope a few days after Emma left. Inside were 30 sheets of paper, each with complex patterns drawn on them, and they made Harry's fingers tingle when he touched them. Danni had drawn them on the flight from New Orleans to LA, and the envelope requested that Harry distribute them to the victims of the Fallen, the children who had been rescued. She was aware that 2 adults had also survived, and included pictures for them, and also noted that 5 of the children were most badly affected, and requested that he give 5 additional sheets to them.

Danni, or Emma as he knew her, was right. Five of the children were still in hospital, plagued by nightmares and near catatonic. Harry wasn't sure he'd get to see them, and doubted he could explain the 'gifts' he bore them, but he was determined to try, as his own hand kept straying to the charm Danni had dropped in his pocket. He'd been touching it when he'd noticed that the people outside the Old House were missing shadows. He retained some of his Catholic upbringing, but not much, and had no interest in the supernatural… but the events of the last few weeks had made his far less cynical.

He arrived at the secure hospital mid-afternoon, and bargained his way through to the Dr in charge of the children.

"I have been given pictures from a child who was taken

by the same people." Said Harry, the best idea he'd been able to come up with. "She became convinced that they were magic, and it, er, helped her recovery."

"Magic! These children have had quite enough 'magic'."

"It really helped her."

"Who was the child?" Asked Dr Rachid.

"Olga." Harry said spontaneously, and nearly winced. "Over in Russia. I'm afraid I can't tell you anything else."

"Did your department send you to Russia? That's quite some budget they have."

"No, a, er policewoman over there got in touch. Through Skype." Harry was aware he was floundering and showed the Dr the pictures, but he dismissed them.

"I don't want to risk it, Detective. They are severely traumatised and these look too much like the... the markings those evil people made at Cutchogue."

"Are they getting any better?" Asked Harry, desperate.

The Dr looked stubborn, and Harry started clutching at straws. "How about we ask their parents?"

"They are under my care, Detective. I decide what's best for them."

"I spoke with this kid. Olga. It really helped her. She asked these be given to the children. Please." Harry was aware he was perilously close to begging, but he'd been with those children after they were rescued, and he'd never seen such desolation. "Please."

The Dr hesitated, then picked up a piece of paper, which seemed to thrum between his fingers.

"I'll ask the parents..."

An alarm went off, interrupting him. Dr Rachid jumped to his feet and hurried from the room.

"I'll get back to you, just leave them here."

Harry didn't even debate as he followed the man, who rushed to the room of Simon. His terrified parents stood aside, helpless and sobbing, as Simon appeared to have a seizure. Harry instantly recognised him as a child he'd rescued, and he literally barged Rachid out of the way to reach him.

"Simon, it's Harry." He took the child's hands and placed them on top of one of Danni's drawings.

The shudders stopped instantly, and Simon relaxed.

"What the hell?" Asked Rachid, as Simon opened his eyes.

"Do you remember me, Simon?" Asked Harry. "I got you, and I told you you're safe."

The boy looked at the picture, and Harry handed him a

second one. "You're safe, Buddy, and I think these might help you realise that."

Simon's parents eyed Rachid with concern.

"It... it blocks out the bad people!" Exclaimed Simon.

"Yeah?"

Harry detached his hand from Simon's, but Simon grabbed him again.

"Was this from Danni?"

Harry's smile faltered, wondering who Danni was? Emma? And how had she 'spoken' the them?

"She told us she would help. And she told us we could trust you."

The adults in the room looked blank, including Harry.

"How did she tell you, Honey? Was she... with them?" Asked Simon's mother.

"No. No, she was a long way away, but she spoke to us." Simon looked confused, "I dunno how... but I'm not making it up. She told us she'd help!"

"It's alright, Simon. I believe you." Said his mother quickly, "And you are safe now, baby. Nobody will ever get you again."

Simon's dad stepped up.

"That's right, Son. We've got you."

Simon smiled at them, but held up the papers.

"No, *these* will protect me. You don't need to worry, these will keep the baddies away."

With that Simon subsided back on his pillows. "Tell Danni to watch for the FBI man, he's one of them." He said, before falling asleep, a slight smile curving his lips.

"Who is?" Asked Harry, alarmed. "Simon?"

"Don't wake him, he hasn't slept properly for days." Interjected Rachid.

"Did he speak to you about the FBI before?" Harry asked his parents, who looked blank.

"I'll ask him when he wakes up." Said Simon's mother, before eyeing the remaining papers in his hands. "Are those for the other children?"

Harry had been going to hand them to her to give out, but now he held onto them.

"I don't pretend to know how they work," Harry said to Rachid and Simon's parents, "But somehow they do. Can I *please* give these to the other children?"

Simon's mother stepped forward to override Dr Rachid.

"I'll speak to their parents. Introduce you." She said, beaming at Simon.

"And thank you again, Detective. Thank you for bringing these. Will you thank whoever Danni is, if she's real?"

Harry said he would, and hurried to the other children, a stunned Dr Rachid in tow. He asked each of them about the FBI, once they safely had the wards and relaxed, and 3 others didn't know but 1 child, Katie, confirmed that she'd visited them in the factory where their teaching assistant had died.

All of them responded to Danni's wards, much to Harry and especially Rachid's confusion.

Harry left the hospital before Rachid could waylay him. He took the remaining pictures to the other children, in person, and had a quiet word with each child. Every single one of them reacted to the wards, several by throwing their arms around Harry's neck and crying into his shoulder as they thanked him, which was an entirely novel experience for Harry. None of the other children confirmed that the FBI had been involved.

He went back to work, determined to mine every scrap of information he could about the murderers who'd taken the children, who'd killed *his* homeless children, and who were still at large. Still, he didn't have much to go on and had his own cases to work. It was nearly 2 weeks later that he got the text from Emma, now Danni, advising that she was with the 'Order'.

Nearly another month passed before Harry got two very strange phone calls.

"Detective," Said a voice with a deep, Southern drawl. "I'm calling about Danni."

"How did you get my number?"

"Oh don't you worry none about that, Sugar, I can get all sorts of things if I want to." She replied. "I'm calling about Danni. She's in trouble and could do with your help."

"Danni?"

"Yessir, that girl who helped you find those children."

"I know exactly who she is, but who are you?"

"You can call me Muma Alice. I met with Danni and she troubled my heart. Things are moving fast and a storm is gathering. You have no reason to believe me on this, but I feel that you care for Danni. Now I believe she got in touch with you."

It wasn't a question so Harry didn't respond.

"And I think she's being held not too far from you, and she's being held against her will."

Harry debated answering, but his life had veered into the weird the minute Danni had turned up at his door.

"She says she's with the Order."

"Yessir, that's what I believe too, but they don't mean her no good."

"Well, I don't know who that is? I mean, where would I start looking, if I wanted to?"

"You already been to see them! You met their priests and saw their waterfall."

Harry didn't respond – again at a loss.

"Danni's the key to stopping those evil vermin who had those children, but she needs your help right now, Harry, you hear?"

Before Harry could reply the line went dead. Oddly, he could find no trace of the call in his call history – the number wasn't just withheld, it was as if the call had never happened.

Almost as soon as Alice disconnected, he got another call. He answered a line heavy with static and the sound of... lowing cattle in the background.

"Detective Boswell?" Asked a heavily accented, European woman – an elderly one from the sound of it.

"I am Kezia of the Romani. I have information." She continued, as Harry struggled to interpret her English. "On Danni."

"Of course you do." Harry thought.

"There is big battle coming, Danni in middle. You must help."

"How did you get my... never mind. I already know, thank you."

"The Order is not as it seems." Replied Kezia, before disconnecting.

Harry eyed his phone and considered turning it off, relieved when he received no more odd phone calls that day. Meanwhile, in Long Island, the Order recorded the conversation and a note was sent to Anders.

Harry invited Sam to his house when their shift finished, and they cleared an empty patch of wall to restart their investigation. The first item added was a photo of Emma/Danni, picked up from a street camera outside the coffee shop.

"I'm still not sure what we can do, Harry. The might of the FBI, Interpol, Europol, pretty much everyone is on this and they've found diddly-squat." Said Sam.

"Well, apparently the FBI has been infiltrated," Replied Harry, fully aware of how paranoid he sounded, "And they aren't looking for Emma, or Danni, or whatever she calls herself. She said that warrior monks *and* the murdering assholes want her, and now the monks have her."

"She said the *order* have her, Harry. We don't know it's the same monks on Long Island."

"It's them." Harry didn't feel comfortable telling his

partner about the phone calls. In truth he didn't feel comfortable thinking about it – Muma Alice hadn't threatened him, but he'd felt ill at ease ever since the call. Almost as if someone was watching him...

"Her message also didn't say she was a prisoner? Seems she went there of her own accord."

"That's true but, if she did, I think she's in trouble now. Look, Sam, *she* saved those kids."

Sam nodded agreement. "The authorities and those monks did sweet FA."

"So, Emma or Danni, who is she really? " Asked Harry.

"Best guess, she got caught up in this cult, then escaped. Been on the run ever since."

"Maybe, but she said a man, Father Richard, taught her everything. Seems he made it his life's work to bring down the cult."

They eyed the photo of Danni, both thinking hard.

"The monks had the same data that Danni had, so they either lied to us, or they don't know shit." Said Sam finally.

"No, those bastards knew about those kids and did nothing." Replied Harry, angry.

Sam nodded and produced an aerial photo of the

monastery and grounds, which he pinned up beside Emma's photo. "I had to work real hard to get this photo, it's not on any public maps."

Harry grinned, "What, a dinner date?"

"A lot more than that." Sam wiped fake perspiration from his brow, "My FBI contact was very hard to persuade, Harry."

The moment of levity faded and Harry produced a map of Long Island.

"Cutchoque is mighty close to their monastery."

"Coincidence? I don't trust them, but I also don't think a bunch of monks would murder children." Said Sam.

Sam stepped forward to help stick the map up, and Harry added 2 circles, close together - one around Cutchoque, one around a nature reserve that surrounded the monastery.

"Harry, the case we never had is closed. The lieu made it really clear we'd have been canned if we weren't press darlings." Said Sam.

They both regarded the wall of 'evidence' - mostly empty. Harry sat on the side of a chair with a sigh. "I don't think Danni wants to be at the monastery."

Sam nodded.

"And I don't think she has any other friends, Sam."

Sam nodded again.

"I've a month of leave, maybe more..."

"No, Harry, you're not going off without me!"

"You just keep feeding me your FBI stuff."

"Not unless I come too." Replied Sam.

"Sam, there's a good chance I'll lose my job over this, but hell, I'm close to retiring anyway." Harry noted Sam's stubborn expression, "I need you on the inside, Sam. Find out everything you can about this Order for starters." Harry grinned, "Besides, I'm just gonna talk to them, ask them about someone called Richard."

Sam was still not happy. "I promise I'll call you if I need backup, okay?"

Sam finally nodded.

Harry pinned one more item on the wall. It was a letter to them both that he'd received with the wards for the children.

Harry and Sam,
Thank you for believing me. You put aside your doubts, put your careers on the line and <u>*you*</u> *saved those children.*
The very few people like you are the flashes of light

that help me carry on through this very dark world.
Danni

Alice

Alice called as many people as possible into the protective ring around her house, sending Alex to fetch their extended family and any nearby with Sight. She had felt the stirrings in Otherworld, and felt it when the Fallen awoke en masse, and anything she didn't feel herself was conveyed to her by hordes of terrified ghosts. She'd felt it when Gomory had passed close to her home, lingering in Louisianna on her way north, sniffing out people with Sight. The Fallen were always drawn to the gifted, aware that torture was felt more keenly. She'd hunkered down and Gamory had moved on.

Worse still was Otherworld. Alice watched as it filled up with the deformed shapes of demons. The twisted Fallen and their cousins from down below all prowled around her perimeter, sensing prey within their grasp. Fortunately they were distracted, and Alice stayed away. If they'd found her in Otherworld, she would have made a juicy morsel, but they scented change in the air. Doorways were being opened and they sniffed around the entrances to the human world.

On Trial

Danni was left in her chamber for what felt like hours. When they came for her she was bound and escorted by 4 guards, people she recognised who had previously been helpful to her. People she had no idea hated her so much.

Ailwyn joined them, his expression unreadable, and she stopped in front of him.

"You think I'm evil?" She asked.

Ailwyn eyed her, shoulders squared. "Yes."

"What about redemption?" She asked. "Do you believe in redeption?"

"Of course." He replied.

"What about for me?" She asked, not sure why she was even asking.

"You need a soul to be redeemed." Said Ruby, prodding her back to get her moving.

As they brought her through underground corridors, she detected a tension in the air. There were many more people about, moving around at speed, some excited, some nervous. The whole monastery had a bustling sense of 'expectancy' that sent a chill down her spine. Whatever they were planning didn't bode well for her. She was brought back to the chamber full of representatives of the different religions, only this time she was the one tied to the chair.

When she was secured they stepped back and took up positions around the walls. Danni turned her attention to the panel, who eyed her with disgust.

"I don't recognise your authority." She stated.

They continued to eye her, weighing up her future.

"I've done nothing wrong. I've only ever helped people, children, which is more than you've done. What gives you the right to treat me like this?"

She strained against her bounds and warrior monks, gathered against the wall, stepped forward in unison, slamming their feet onto the stone, each armed with different weapons.

Danni slumped back as she registered just how much trouble she was in.

"You have already been judged, we are here to carry out your sentence." Stated a woman.

"Judged? By you? This is a kangaroo court with no authority to judge me. Let me go!"

"*We* did not judge you, the Almighty did. We are merely seeing His justice done." Replied a man.

"And who gave you the right to speak for Him?"

Shouted Danni, getting angrier as she tried not to freak out. "Where's my dog?"

"Your dog is fine." Replied Ailwyn.

Danni calmed - a bit.

"You are no position to do anything on His behalf. You are cruel and deceptive. Those are not the tools of the side of the light." She directed her comments to Anders, but Ailwyn looked uncomfortable. "And *you* are a bare-faced liar. You lied to my face for weeks, wheedling and all the while plotting, that takes a special kind of nasty. No wonder Richard left you, you sacks of shit."

The panel eyed her coldly.

"Why did you bother? Why go to all that effort to befriend me? To pretend you're vaguely *human* and caring?"

"To see what you would tell us voluntarily." Replied Anders, completely unphased. "Do you still not accept what are, Danyal?"

"That is not my name!" Danni transferred her fiery gaze to Ailwyn as he held up the last folder she'd read – the ritual 22 years ago.

"We neutralised Asmodeus 22 years ago, but Richard took off with you before we could-."

"Before you could murder a baby?"

Ailwyn continued in his gentle, sing-song accent. He dropped the folder on the table, "Now we finally have you."

"My name is Danni. I'm not what you think."

"You are one of the Fallen." Stated a man.

An elderly woman leant forward over the table, spitting venom, "And we will send you back to hell, Danyal!"

"That's not my name." She repeated.

Ailwyn picked up the symbols of the religions, and approached her with them - a Christian Cross; The Buddhist Wheel of Dharma; a Taiji, the Yin and Yang of Toaists; The Torii Gate of Shinto; a Star of David; The Star and Cresent of Islam; a Hindu, Sanskrit Aum; a Sikh Khanda.

"Will you touch these, any of them, and swear before God that you are human?"

Danni's eyes flashed amber. "No."

Anders gestured to 2 guards, who approached with an iron bar. Over her fear, Danni had a a new feeling of dread – of impending doom. She had a feeling the scales were tipping and whole world was off-kilter.

"What are you planning?" She asked, but the thought was cut off as the man held the bar against her cheek while the woman held her down. A pain like nothing

Danni had ever felt raced from her face down through her body. She screamed as her skin blistered.

“Your type can never stand iron.” Stated Ailwyn.

They stepped back and removed the bar, but Danni’s whole face was ablaze with pain.

Danni gritted her teeth. “This is why you fail. This is why Richard turned his back on you. You have lost the moral high ground.”

“What are your kin planning?” Asked Anders.

“I have already told you what I know.”

Anders gestured the woman ripped Danni’s top and the man applied the metal to her torso, and Danni screamed again. She was panting when he finally stepped back, a livid burn on her stomach.

“Just tell us what the Fallen are planning?” Asked Ailwyn, who alone looked awkward at the torture.

“Something big, *Brother*. I don’t know what, but you’re not up to stopping them, you’re as evil as they are. You should let me go.”

“Why? Will you stop them?” He asked.

“Nobody can, but imprisoning and torturing me is bad for your soul.” Danni meant every word. “The Order has lost its way. I can see now that is why Richard left, you have become the monsters you seek."

Ailwyn looked pained. "We're not a sadists. We don't enjoy hurting anyone, even you."

"Maybe that was true when you joined, but you're enjoying this. I See you. You are corrupted, all of you."

Unable to make eye contact, Ailwyn didn't stop Anders when the iron was applied again until Danni passed out.

"We're killing her." He said as the guards tried to rouse her.

"We must complete her transformation, so she can commune with them."

"What if she's telling the truth?" Asked Ailwyn, which shocked the others. "Not about being one of them, though I don't think she knows, but that the message isn't there yet?"

Against their wishes, Ailwyn summoned Ruby to tend to Danni.

"Why must I help it?" Hissed Ruby.

"I thought your hypocritic oath applied to everyone?" Asked Ailwyn.

"Only humanity." She replied. Ruby hesitated, then crossed to Danni and knelt before the chair, then applied a salve to the deep burns on her face as Danni came round slowly.

“I advise you stay still.” Stated Ruby.

Danni yelled as Ruby rubbed cream into her stomach, overly rough as she dabbed the tender skin.

“Given how quickly its kind heal, this won’t be a problem.”

“I’m not one of them.” Replied Danni, exhausted.

“Iron doesn’t burn us.” Ruby’s face was hidden, her tone neutral.

“So a reaction to iron makes torture acceptable, does it? Like the others, you use your religion as a shield for your cruelty.”

Ruby answered in Arabic, “You can speak every language ever written, or spoken.”

Satisfied with her inspection, she got to her feet. “*People* have to learn, how do you just know?”

Danni had no answer and Ruby leaned forward to whisper. “You belong with the others, Abomination.”

“What others?” Asked Danni.

“Ruby, that’s enough!” Shouted Ailwyn, and Ruby left.

The whispering returned suddenly, drowning out all other sounds.

"Hello?" She asked, looking frantically around the room. "What is that?"

She recalled the ghosts tethered to their coffins, deep below her, but this was a different sound.

"Who is calling out?" She asked.

The panel eyed each other in alarm.

"Who is she speaking of?" One of them asked.

"It's nothing! She's stalling." Spat Anders. "This is your last chance, Danyal. Why are the Fallen gathering?"

Danni ignored him as the whispering grew in volume. Something was here, in the monastery. Close to her… close to getting out.

"This is getting nowhere, we must force her to transform."

"Not yet! We must try-."

"We've waited long enough, Brother Ailwyn. You may leave however, if this distresses you."

Anders gestured to the guards and they wheeled in a huge, metal device. An Iron Lady – a metal casket, straight from the middle ages. They stopped it behind Danni and heaved open a lid, to reveal metals spikes inside to impale her, but not deep enough to kill.

Outside in the grounds, Gamon tipped back her head

and howled.

It was hours later when Anders returned with guards to remove Danni from the casket.

She fell onto the floor, bleeding from her multiple wounds, and he allowed Ruby to give her a drink of water, but not to stop the bleeding. Danni had spent the time falling, the pain from the iron mingling with the pain from a fire that reached out for her but never quite consumed her.

She came around fully when Anders slapped her face. Her clothes were tattered with multiple holes ringed with blood and she could see that her tattoos had come off again. The Order's torture had removed her protective wards, leaving her wide open.

He held out the document she had created, listing the names of the Fallen.

"Read these out."

Danni swam towards unconsciousness again, but again Anders slapped her.

"Say these names."

"Never." She replied.

Anders applied a thin rod of iron to one of her puncture wounds, pushing into the skin.

In a corridor outside, Ailwyn paced. Head bowed, he clutched a rosary. He passed Aashif, dark skinned with a full heard in a green shirt with a Muslim star and crescent, and Agamjit in his turban. Ailwyn had time to reflect there weren't many places where so many religions worked together... then an agonised scream rent the air. The other monks walked on, but Ailwyn froze.

Back in the chamber, Danni screamed in agony as a the metal burnt, a blister spreading up her arm. Anders pulled out the metal and grabbed her chin. "Say the names, Danyal."

Danni shook her head and he pressed the metal back against her skin - which sizzled. "Noooo!" She screamed, her hair soaked with sweat, cheeks lined with tears as her skin crackled.

"You will say them, devil's spawn."

Danni sobbed and nodded, and her arms were released. Anders held up the paper in front of her, and had Ruby give her a sip of water.

"Saying their names summons them." She managed.

"And we'll be waiting."

Danni deep looked into his crazy eyes, then looked at the other guards, zealots all of them. And Ailwyn had run away.

“Tarel.” She croaked.

The whispers resumed in the room, and she shivered. “Abaddon... Armers... Belial... Sabnack, Allocen.”

The whispering intensified, along with her shivers. “Please?”

“Say them all!” Spat Anders.

“Andrealphus, Baal, Flauros, Penemuel, Gaap,” The whispers swell, a rustling that filled the room, “Gadreel, Rahab, Marchosias, Uzza, Naamah.” She sobbed, “Lilith, “Marbas.... Beleth.”

Anders smiled and had Danni been watching, his smile held an edge of insanity, as door slammed open and Ailwyn bursts into the room.

“Enough!”

Anders eyed Ailwyn, assessing his mood.

“Watch this, Brother Ailwyn.” Said Anders. He grabbed a crucifix from a chain on his neck and brought it up, close to her face, and she cringed away. “Say your name.”

Ailwyn eyed Danni’s bleeding, tortured body.

“Anders, stop.”

“Say it.” Anders brought the cross closer and the monks grabbed Danni again as she pulled away.

“Please!”

Ailwyn crossed the room and grabbed Anders. “It’s enough, Brother Anders!”

“Give her water.” He ordered, then grabbed Ailwyn and dragged him from the room.

He slammed the door behind him and eyed Ailwyn with fury. Then he took deep breaths and calmed himself.

“This is how Richard started. Don’t weaken, Ailwyn, not now.”

“She’s right. We’ve become the monsters we chase.”

Anders inspected Ailwyn, unhappy with what he saw. “She’s not human...”

“How do we know that? What, any means justifies the end?”

“We’re closer than we’ve ever been, keep your faith.” Anders turned back to the room. “And stay out of my way.”

Danni finished reading the list of names and 2 monks hoisted her to feet. The burning was fading slightly, or she was becoming more used to it, and the whispering returned. Her heart battered against her chest in an effort to flee her body, and if she'd had anything in her stomach she would have vomited.

She understood the voices. This time, she realised what it meant.

"He's here."

"The transformation is happening." Stated Anders, finally satisfied, but Danni wasn't listening to him.

"So are all the others you've captured." She looked at Anders in despair. "You've summoned the Fallen, here, where you hold *him*."

Anders packed up his things, finished with her.

"Put her back inside. She must be fully transformed when we bury her."

"You have condemned the whole world." Danni's voice was harsh and her lips cracked as she spoke, but the pain was minor compared to her burns. "You… you arrogant idiots. You deserve that the death that you have summoned."

Anders eyed the monks, who appeared nervous,

"We shall triumph, once and for all." He said, for their benefit rather than hers.

The Summons

The Fallen had made camp at a ranch in Nebraska. They'd called ahead to one of their disciples and told him it was time to receive his 'gift', and that he should dismiss all his staff and ready himself for their arrival.

The ranch covered hundreds of acres, well outside the nearest town, and a pretty family of five waited for them on the steps of a large house, neatly groomed, parents proudly showing off their three children. A battered van pulled up followed by two coaches with Fallen, all dishevelled and corrupted. While Armers, Lilith, Tarel and Belial manifested the lure of untold wealth and power, the other Fallen showed clearly the decay and decadent side once the flesh was corrupted.

The family's face fell, and their doubts didn't take long to get confirmed. Without ceremony the Fallen took over their house and grounds, to their extreme annoyance.

"This is not the reward you promised us!" Stated the man, as they rode roughshod over his land.

"You don't feel rewarded?" Asked Tarel. "You don't like your home? Or your fancy job title, Senator?"

She seemed genuinely puzzled by him.

"I like it fine." He replied.

The man, his family and remaining staff were in a huge

sitting room with a picture window that looked out over a huge deck then onto rolling meadows with cattle. At that moment one of the Fallen was chasing them with a chainsaw.

"And you're destroying it."

Timed to perfection, a crash from another room as something broke.

"I need to ask you to leave!"

The other Fallen ignored the man and his family but Tarel was fascinated.

"And how will you make that happen?"

"I own the local police."

"Uh-hu?"

The children sensed the scale of the problem before their parents, and tugged their arms, desperate to get away.

"We have friends in the CIA and the FBI!" Added his wife.

"Friends? Well, *they'll* understand the cause of your rapid rise to power, but there's still a bunch who might have a problem with it." Replied Tarel, mimicking their accents exactly. "Do you wanna call them?"

Lilith came in, followed 4 Fallen.

“Mum?” A teenager whispered, “I don’t like them.”

“Tarel, you and Belial need to fetch us some people. Go for the homeless, untraceable, and don’t get seen.” Ordered Lilith.

“You can’t bring homeless people here!” Said the man.

Lilith looked at her in surprise, then turned a questioning look on Tarel.

“The Senator doesn’t appreciate us being here.” She giggled.

“You signed a contract with us, Senator. You agreed to the price.” Stated Lilith. “Now, I need a car. What have you got?”

The Fallen crept nearer to the family, expressions hungry. So many Fallen together was a growing problem as few of them could restrain their appetites for long, and being together in such numbers was likely to draw attention from the authorities. Lilith didn’t know how long she could keep them together, and on a leash. More and more had turned up each day as they travelled across country, picking up the siren call to arms. Some found their own way, though they couldn’t have explained how, while others were tracked down by Abaddon.

Lilith swept a vase off a table to setup her laptop – she had work to do.

Tarel produced a knife, an expensive carving knife taken from their kitchen. The family huddled closer together, eyeing the dead eyes of the Fallen around Tarel.

"Hey, wait, listen, we've been loyal to you. We've earned what we have-."

"Well, technically those little illegal immigrants in your factories earned your wealth for you." Tarel replied, playing with the knife.

"Tarel, stop playing with them! Give them to Beleth then go and fetch more meat." Snapped Lilith.

Tarel pouted at being bossed around, but herded the family out.

"She's so bossy! You'd think she ruled us, but she's no better than us." She complained as she escorted them outside. "She's not more powerful than me, not really."

Tarel lowered her voice to a confiding whisper, "And the master threw her aside for Danyal."

"What do you want from us? Please. We've been loyal to you. We've done everything you've asked! We'll do anything! Please." The father was sweating while he wife started to beg as they approached the battered van. More Fallen were drawn to them until a crowd was gathered as they reached the van, encircling the family.

"Please!" Begged the woman.

“I don’t get it.” Said Tarel, genuinely puzzled by them – and annoyed at their whining. “You humans never read the small print, do you? Or you think someone else will pay your bill. It was all there in the contract, and this is collection time.” Replied Tarel, opening the door on Beleth, who was chained to the sides of the van.

“I mean, why would we care more about you than those Mexicans you had killed?” Tarel asked.

“I never killed anyone!” The family were terrified, clinging to Tarel’s engagement with them, desperately looking for a way out.

“Yes you did, Senator. Directly... indirectly...” Tarel picked up the youngest child and threw her into Beleth. The girl screamed, then her parents screamed as Beleth bit into her. “I mean, why ever would you think we’d treat you differently?”

The hysterical family couldn’t answer, so she shrugged and walked off, mystified by humanity.

“Let Beleth have them all.” She shouted over her shoulder, “I’ll be back with provisions for the rest of you.”

She headed to a brand new pickup, the family already forgotten, but stopped mid-stride.

“Hello?” She asked, looking around.

With the family still screaming behind her, Belial jogged

out of the house to join her.

"We've got pickup duty again..." His expression went blank as he listened. "Who's what?"

He looked at Tarel in surprise, who shrugged, equally bemused.

Inside the ranch, Marbas was next to hear Danni's call. He sat up and looked around the room in confusion. "Hello?"

Uzza burst into the room, dishevelled as always and belligerent.

"Who's calling me?" He demanded.

Lilith and Abaddon were close, examining the data trail from shipping containers, when their names were called. They looked at each other.

Tarel and Belial joined them, "What's happening? Someone's calling us?"

"It can't be?" Queried Lilith. "Danyal? She's calling from..."

"The Order headquarters?" Queried Abaddon.

"No! And surely they wouldn't keep Him there?"

Lilith, Abaddon, Armers – who was still deciphering the runes, Tarel and Belial shared stunned looks.

“It’s audacious, but makes perfect sense.” Replied Lilith. In a flash she had up the plans for the monastery and was grinning with delight.

“I don’t like it...” Abaddon huffed, breathless in his obesity. “Their headquarters? No, they’ve been careful all these centuries, this is too easy.”

“Arrogance, Abaddon. It was always their weakness.”

Abaddon shook his massive, jowly head. “No, Lilith, it makes no sense! They wouldn’t house him there, and they would never just tell us where He is. And why now? This is a summoning.”

“Danyal is summoning us. Perhaps she has finally picked us?” Said Tarel.

The other Fallen gave her a hard stare, and she shrugged.

“Or they do not understand what they are doing, not truly.” Said Armers.

“Who cares?” Belial said. “Feed one of the Fallen to Beleth before we go in there and we’ll easily overpower them.”

Abaddon had a map out and began plotting their route.

“There are more Fallen to collect and it’s a full day’s drive from here.”

They wanted as many Fallen as possible for the confrontation, and they wanted them fed, strong and angry – but balanced against that was that the Order might realise their mistake and move their master. Reluctantly they decided to spend a few more hours in mustering, before a rapid drive east to Long Island.

"Go and round up whatever people you can find. Don't bring the police here, but don't worry about who they are, grab however you can easily get. We need transport too, another coach."

Lilith took charge of planning how to enter the Order's headquarters. They would no doubt have called all their fighters home, ready for them, and she wondered if this was a trap. It didn't matter either way, they had unprecedented numbers of Fallen. She could still feel the echo of the call, and the pull of Morning Star. Lucifer would detect their presence when they arrived and overrun the Order. Giddy with excitement, she plotted the wards and protection around the monastery, and planned who she would sacrifice to gain entry. Their time had finally come!

Conscience

Ailwyn was at his desk, but unable to concentrate, haunted by dreams of Danni's tortured body. He had her file before him listing all the good she had performed, including Amy in Scotland at the moment of Richard's death. The Order relentlessly pursued Danni for years in their effort to catch her, and every single child they tracked down had nothing but praise for Danni. Her wards of protection were... unique but effective, and the Order had learned much from them. He wondered if they would fail once Danni was gone, exposing all those children again.

He re-read the notes about her time in Bangkok – the only reason she'd had to come to the Order was that she'd broken cover in Thailand. To save those trafficked children. He eyed her photo, then compared it with the portrait, trying to assuage his guilt. This was how Richard had started too. He'd confided his misgivings in the early days and Ailwyn had shut him out, then he'd gone on to save a little baby. His phone rang, cutting through his thoughts, to tell him that there was a detective to see him.

He didn't have time for this, but the monk on the phone said he was most persistent.

"He says he'll wait outside the gates until you see him. All night if necessary."

Ailwyn had to get rid of him, before the coming war.

Annoyed, he asked Harry be escorted up. He put away the file as a knock at his door proceeded Agamjit, who Ailwyn knew to be a zealot, all members of the Order were, but he was fair and honest.

"What is it, Brother? I am expecting company."

"Brother, I am troubled by what we just did."

"Torture you mean?" Asked Ailwyn, relieved he wasn't the only one. Anders was right, Richard had started to have problems with their brutality against the Fallen, a long time before he rescued Danni from their clutches.

"No! No, I am concerned that we have summoned the Fallen here."

Ailwyn and Anders had discussed staging a confrontation years before, then hatched the plan in Brooklyn, after their last sacrifice. Both of them were frustrated with the Order's lack of progress – and the body count they left behind. They had presented their idea to the leaders of each religion: a lure to the Order, then spring the trap and catch them, once and for all.

"Do not fear, Agamjit, this is our one and only task in life. To capture and carry out sentence the Fallen."

"But there are hundreds of them, Brother. We cannot win, and what if we lose?"

"The call to arms has been made. All of our numbers are joining us here for a decisive battle. Have no fear,

Brother."

A young monk escorted Harry in and Agamjit wasn't able to say more. He left, to prepare for the battle, but Ailwyn could still sense his misgivings. But he was in an army, and he would fight to the end. The Order's leaders made the decisions and the faithful did exactly as they were told – they knew they were soldiers when they joined. Ailwyn knew Agamjit had no fear of death, just of failure, and his concern unsettled Ailwyn. In truth, he'd also argued against the idea when the general awakening call went out, when he'd realised how many they were likely to face, but the Order overruled him.

"You having a party?" Harry interrupted his thoughts. He'd crossed instantly to the window and was looking out at the busy quadrangle below, full of people dashing back and forth. Many were heavily armed.

"There's a lot of you around today. Some sort of gathering?"

"What do you want, Detective? We're a closed order and the case is now firmly in the hands of the FBI."

Harry continued staring outside.

"Women too, which must make life interesting in a closed order. I must say I've never seen monks with weapons before? That's some heavy firepower out there." Harry grinned at Ailwyn, "You could say some hardcore fire and not so much brimstone."

"What do you want?"

To Ailwyn's annoyance, Harry wandered to the sofa and took a seat.

"Except those films with the warrior monks. They're Buddhists aren't they? Is that saffron robe Buddhist?"

"I see it was a mistake to let you in." Ailwyn reached for his intercom, but Harry finally got to the point.

"Are you aware that the Satanic cult has people within the FBI?" Asked Harry.

"What?"

"Several children confirmed it."

Ailwyn considered a moment, then nodded, "We don't know who, but yes, we realised they were compromised."

Harry nodded and moved on. "So, have you got anything else from the creepy scrawls yet?"

"I can give you a list of angels who rebelled against the Creator and were cast out. I don't see how that helps your investigation though, Detective."

Harry sat back, comfortable, and Ailwyn sighed and took a seat opposite him, ready to give a lecture. He was too distracted to work anyway, and Danni's words were echoing in his head.

"This coven believe the Fallen float, in a sort of limbo." Ailwyn searched for laymen's words. "The sacrifices and incantations awaken their kind, those other Fallen who have managed to inhabit human forms but don't realise what they are."

"And you believe this?" Asked Harry.

"Yes." Harry raised an eyebrow, and Ailwyn continued.

"I believe this coven is made up of Fallen angels, and that there are more of them now than ever before." Harry assessed Ailwyn, unsettled but hiding it. "Detective, they are searching for their leader, always searching, and they are very close to finding him."

"Lucifer?"

A shiver went through the air, like a ripple from distant explosion. Even Harry shivered but, a practical man, he shrugged it off.

"It is best to never say their names out loud, Harry." Ailwyn got to his feet. "But that is why there are so many of our Order here. And why I must ask you to leave now, there is much to do."

"Because you're going to fight angels?"

"*Fallen* angels, Detective."

Harry eyed him with a mixture of incredulity and concern, mostly for his sanity but also for law and order. He wondered if the FBI – scrub that, the army or government – had any real idea about this rogue band of armed monks.

"Who was Richard?"

Ailwyn barely hid his surprise. "We had a Richard here twenty years ago, but he left us."

"I think he left when he kidnapped a child." Harry produced the photo of 'Emma' from a street cam. "She's had a few names since then. She's the one who told us where to find the children the cult took."

A flicker of something crossed Ailwyn's face and Harry's fake humour vanished, replaced by anger. "She saved the lives of twenty five little children, not you. And I believe you are holding her here against her will."

The image of Danni's broken, bleeding body sprang into Ailwyn's mind. Then, a distant rumble of thunder, far off but threatening, like the growl of a monster.

"A drop in pressure... There's a storm coming."

Ailwyn swallowed while Harry worked his jaw, then put his fingers in his ears.

"You need to leave. Quickly."

Ailwyn crossed to Harry as he got to his feet.

"I'm not done with this order, Brother. I'll get a warrant."

To Harry's surprise, Ailwyn grabbed him in an embrace and leant to one ear to kiss his cheek, and whispered. "She is here, and she needs your help."

Ailwyn kissed the other side of Harry's face - a benediction. "There's a gate in the east wall, go there and wait, I will bring her there."

Ailwyn stepped back and made the sign of the cross. "God's blessing, Harry. Don't come into our monastery again, and keep that cross I gave you very close tonight."

The door to the office opened, and a hard-faced female monk entered. She shot Ailwyn a measured look, most likely listening in to their conversation.

"Remember, do *not* come back, Harry, however tempted you might be. You will not be readmitted into this monastery." Reiterated Ailwyn as Harry was escorted out, totally bewildered.

Wildwood State Park

The sun was low in the sky, casting long shadows through the trees. Outside a ramshackle old carriage house, hundreds of Fallen waited, silent and strangely patient. The door to the cottage was gone, ripped off its hinges and discarded, and candle light spilt through the doorway.

The Fallen were silent but nature made itself heard. Wind whipped through the trees, rubbing branches together and scattering leaves, while the nearby sea sent waves crashing onto the beach, growing fiercer and angrier, as if the sea itself objected to their presence. And in the distance, the low rumble of thunder.

Inside the cottage, more Fallen were crammed into the room, and though they were silent, their human bodies were struggling to contain them. In the candle light, their flesh and bones seemed to contort as the Fallens' real forms twisted under the skin, pulsing and writhing to get out. They cast strange shadows, distorted and unrelated to their human form. All their eyes were focused on the front of the room.

A table held Crowley's grimoire, and Lilith sat on it, one hand on the book, while Armers addressed them, outlining the plan they had put together. She surveyed their forms – some of them externally beautiful, many of them externally ugly, all of them utterly repugnant under their thin skins. All of them disposable. Most of the m were worse than animals, driven by rage and all-consuming hatred, who had forgotten their former glory as they tried to fill a gaping hole in their beings. The vast majority couldn't even find their way into this world without assistance, and then they had no idea what they were – and quickly lost the bodies they'd stumbled into while they were still young.

The exceptions were few. Asmodeous and Abaddon, of course, but their rivalry limited their time here. After her own period of floating without understanding, an encounter with Asmodeous had reminded her of herself. She had followed him and witnessed his confrontation with Abaddon 500 years before, who had then run away to lick his wounds, hiding in his filthy swamp, making no attempt to remember himself or find the master.

At that stage she'd realised that brutal ejection from the human host caused disorientation, and once she came back to her true self, she'd been careful to avoid the angry mob. It was better to move quickly between bodies after death, and she'd cultivated her own followers to assist her, but had always, frustratingly, failed to do so seamlessly. She'd partnered up with other Fallen through the ages, their rituals focused on switching or awakening their bodies, but all they had managed to do was open a temporary portal to Otherworld, which gave tantalising snippets but never revealed enough.

Asmodeous had managed it, but the Order had him now. They would free him – after pointing out his uselessness to the master. He was, she grudgingly conceded, the most powerful of them all, and he had worked out how to remind his brethren who they were, awakening heaven's rejects in their pitiful human shells. He had shared the information with Crowley, perhaps to enlist his cult into his service, but the Order had killed Crowley and taken the grimoire, and Asmodeous had never shared with anyone else. He could have done what she did, and united them to free Lucifer, but like all their kind, he was completely self-obsessed. She would make sure Lucifer understood his treachery.

She stroked the grimoire and eyed her closest accomplices. Abaddon, Armers, Tarel, Belial, Marbas and herself, all of them successful at waking themselves. But she was the strongest of all of them, the one who remembered most often. It was also she who had discovered Crowley's grimoire, but she discovered it too late to claim it from him. It was she who had then worked several lifetimes to find it again. It was she who had cultivated a young member of the Order to retrieve the book, though she realised he must have had help from within. She nearly laughed at the thought – all this time, her lover had been so close and she hadn't realised! She was the one who hunted for him in every lifetime, and she was the also one who hunted Danyal every life she lived, throughout the centuries, hating her for stealing the Morning Star from her.

She stood now, to take over from Armers, eying the assembled Fallen, relishing their mad, incoherent and exquisite rage.

"We are gathered in numbers not seen since the Fall."

The Fallen begin to chant, a whisper under their breath.

"And after an eternity of searching." She shouted, "We have found our master."

The sound of their voices mingled with the storm, adding an undertone of menace.

"And tonight we free him!"

Conscience

The monastery was a hive of activity. When it was founded in the new world, protective charms and holy relics were woven into the fabric of the building, built into the surrounding walls, even into the layout of the grounds, and all the religious disciplines checked and re-checked the protections and wards. The founders recognised the risks of discovery, but Ailwyn doubted that any of them could have predicted that their heirs would invite the Fallen in. Monks practised with their weapon of choice all over the grounds, while more prayed before the holy water in the quadrangle. They didn't doubt that the Fallen would break through their defences, but the plan was to stop as many as possible of them on the way, and stop them reaching their destination.

Ailwyn prepared his own weapons then did a tour of the main buildings, offering words of support where he thought they were needed. Then he made his way to Danni's prison cell. He relieved the guards at the door and went into the darkened room. The monstrous 'iron lady' stood upright in the middle of a pentagram. Rusty sides, it glowed a sinister red in the light of an otherwise empty room. Pure evil, Ailwyn thought.

He closed the door behind him and headed to the torture device, grimacing as he noted a pool of blood underneath.

"Danni?" He leant close to the casket, his ear to a vent.

“Danni, can you hear me?”

Danni answered with a moan of pain.

“I am sorry we did this to you.” Ailwyn reached for 2 latches locking the casket closed, “You were right, we have descended to the level of monsters.”

“Don’t.”

Ailwyn struggled with the latch as Anders stepped out of the shadows with Aashif.

“I suspected you might lose your way, Brother Ailwyn, but I hoped not.” They joined Ailwyn by the iron lady, Anders’ expression sad.

“Help me.” Moaned Danni.

“This is wrong.” He gestured to the blood on the floor.

“The Fallen are about to descend on the order, Ailwyn, with their hoard... more if you let her out.”

“And whose idea was that, Anders? We should have stopped this madness when we knew they were waking their kind. We should have waited.”

“You’ve never understood strategy, have you? Twenty years ago, when Lilith woke Abaddon, you wanted to move, and now you want to wait! And free one of them too. I have to ask if your heart is really in this fight, Ailwyn. Have you switched sides, like Richard did?”

Ailwyn squared his shoulders, fists curled at his side - a fighting stance. "*You* stopped us confronting Lilith, Anders."

"Because they keep slipping away!" Shouted Anders. Aashif remained impassive but stepped back, Ailwyn and Anders both furious. "We catch one in a hundred, and the rest die, reborn in new bodies, and then we hunt them all over again!"

Ander's eyes blazed and spittle flew from his lips, and Ailwyn's anger morphed into a terrible realisation. "Oh my God, you're mad."

"This is our chance to confront them all!"

"You didn't even discuss delaying with the council, did you? When did you tell them just how many Fallen were being woken?"

"Tonight we fight the lords of hell and imprison them forever."

Ailwyn eyed Anders with absolute horror. "We can't beat Beleth! Never mind their combined might, there are too many Fallen. They'll win and He will be freed."

Ailwyn turned to Aashif "You've broken our most sacred vow in your arrogance." He then turned to the metal casket. "Danni was right. We've become monsters and unleashed hell."

Aashif shifted, uncomfortable, but Anders shook his

head in disgust.

"Lock this traitor up, Brother Aashif, he will stand trial tomorrow."

"There won't be a tomorrow!"

Aashif took a tentative steps forward, but stopped under Ailwyn's glare. "Don't you dare, you little shit!"

Ailwyn shook of his head and heaved a great sigh. "Richard was right all those years ago, and I've been so blind. Tonight I'll fight and die with the order... God help the world tomorrow."

Ailwyn approached the metal casket, watched closely by the others. He leant close, both hands on the metal. "I am sorry, Danni. I guess I'll see you in hell soon enough."

Attack

Everyone in the Order was battle trained, even the clerical and admin staff. They had offered for the elderly to retreat, but everyone had decided to stay, and the call was out for everyone abroad to come home. Most had, and the monastery was packed beyond capacity with warriors. As the sun set, a female warrior, Olive, sat tense before a bank of screens - CCTV from the exterior, the gates and grounds, and also the interior, including Danni in her iron casket. Another roll of thunder, louder this time. Closer. Then a BUZZ from the intercom by the front gate, and she focused on the image of a huge, iron gate secured with heavy bars.

A low mist clung to the ground outside the gates, obscuring the ground. Parked outside, Marbas, in a black, government car by an intercom.

“FBI.” He held a badge up to the camera.

“The Order is locked down, you’ll have to come back in the morning.”

“Fetch Brother Anders, Sister, he will want to see me.”

“Not tonight, Sir.”

The sentry refocused the camera on blurry outlines behind the FBI car – the shape of other vehicles, behind him. She reached down for an alarm under the desk as, behind her, Brother Jerome entered into the room. She glanced over her shoulder, then back at the screens as he approached.

"Believe me, he will want to see me. Just go and get him." Marbas was saying into the intercom.

Jerome produced a knife and quickly, expertly, cut his 'sister's' throat – but not before she pressed the alarm, which flashed throughout the monastery. He twisted her body aside to protect the equipment from the great gush of blood, then dropped her on the ground, without sparing a glance at her gasping, twitching body.

Outside, the huge gates swung open and the black car drove in. The gates remained wide open as the car drove up the gravel, and the rumble of thunder louder grew louder... along with something else. A deep growl. A hell-hound stepped out of the fog and roared at the gates. It sniffed, then stepped through - and yelped as its feet touch the gravel, before dissolving into mist, neutralised by protective wards that flared brightly, but then fizzled out, their power spent.

Lilith followed the car in a black van, which she drove at speed through the gates, followed by 3 coaches and more cars. Buried under the gravel on the drive were the first tier of defence, activated when the alarm went off. Metals spikes sprang up to shred tires and sent the vehicles skewing into the grass. A coach levered open its doors and 4 Fallen jumped down, to run to the monastery, but as their feet touch the ground they howled and erupted into balls of flame. Their brethren pressed their faces against the glass, watching the van as it screeched to a stop on the grass. Waiting.

Lilith climbed into the back of the van where Tarel, Belial and Armers crouched in a semi-circle.

Beleth was chained to the floor and panel walls, roaring at them. His piggy eyes sparkled with malicious intent, mostly focused on Tarel, but no intelligence lurked there and as much as they could in the small space, the Fallen kept out of his reach.

"Get your fat arse back here, Abaddon!" Ordered Lilith, and the van rocked as Abaddon squeezed into the back.

"Get the fuck on with the chant you idiots!" She shouted into a radio, broadcast to all the coaches.

Together they began to chant, their hands forming circles, moulding the air. Thick, black smoke formed in wisps around their fingers. Tarel leant over to open the back doors of the van as the mist grew into clouds of smoke that drifted out onto the ground outside. The shadows solidified into hell-hounds, who leapt off towards the distant monastery... but as they ran over the ground, they yelped, many dissolving back into mist. Beleth threw back his head and roared.

In the surveillance room, Ailwyn made the sign of the

cross over the female monk's body, her throat slit ear to ear. A guard escorted him, shocked to realise there were traitors within the Order.

"Call for backup then review the feeds, see if we can see who did that." The young man nodded, "And watch the door!" Ordered Ailwyn.

He turned to the screens, splattered with blood, and eyed the open gate on one camera. Another camera showed the black van with fog and hell-hounds streaming out of it, and yet another showed the faces of hundreds Fallen, pressed against the glass of 3 coaches. For a long moment he watched them, one by one, begin chanting, their mouths moving in unison in a deadly spell. With the spell, the coaches filled with thick, cloying smoke that oozed out of the doorway and broiled across the grass towards the monastery.

"God help us."

He touched his ear, an earpiece. "Detonate underground ordinance in the grounds. All of it!"

He switched feeds again, to focus on the van. "Rocket launcher on the black van."

Timed with his command, the van on screen replicated - dozens of identical, black vans all over the grounds. It was impossible to tell which van was real and which was an illusion.

"Which one, Brother?"

"Fire at will, get them all." He ordered as he scanned the feeds from the grounds, the torrent of smoke now lit by fiery eyes. Hells hounds materialised in flashes, only to dissolve on the holy ground, but they were relentless and seemingly endless, getting ever closer to the monastery.

A series of BOOMS shook the surveillance room and several cameras went dead. Ailwyn switched again, to see one coach totally destroyed, its remains scattered over the grounds. Another coach was on fire and Fallen streamed out, screaming as they touched holy ground, but many of them able to stagger on, the protection worn out by the advancing hell hounds. The ground was losing its power, and the 3rd coach was completely undamaged. Ailwyn shivered as the camera recorded their hungry expressions as they peered longingly at the monastery. God, thought Ailwyn, what had we done?

His attention was grabbed by the hell hounds who drew nearer the monastery. A ring of warriors surrounded the building. They braced and the first hounds reached them, along with the thick mist. In flashes, Ailwyn saw a female Buddhist slash and cut the hounds with two blessed swords. A man in a turban swirled a wicked curved blade in great arcs around him, cutting through the hounds. Two Muslim monks, a male and female, fought back to back, surrounded by baying, snapping hounds. One lunged, knocked over the male, and he was instantly engulfed in snarling hounds that ripped him apart.

Next the Sikh and Buddhist were both are overcome by the hounds, and Ailwyn wondered where Anders was, but didn't have time to dwell.

"Fall back to the monastery." He ordered.

One by one, all the exterior camera feeds switched off.

"Secure the entrances and protect the fountain, ensure we keep praying." He switched feeds to the quadrangle as more guards rushed up to join him.

"Check the feeds, find who killed our sister, and find Brother Anders." He instructed.

The wall of broiling black mist touched the monastery wall.

"They're coming! Brace."

While the others were occupied, he switched to external feeds and found Harry outside the eastern gate.

Harry had driven around to the eastern gate after leaving the monastery. They were seventy or so miles from the nearest habitation, but he'd prepared for a wait and had coffee and snacks with him. He'd parked up and dozed in the car, until the first explosion sounded from behind the high wall.

He'd jumped out when more explosions sounded, shaking the ground under his feet. He recalled Ailwyn's instruction not to return, and the monks were clearly expecting trouble. Harry debated calling for backup, but didn't want to land Danni in more trouble. Besides, despite his scepticism with Ailwyn, he could *feel* the presence of evil. It oozed over the wall and coated him with a sickly feeling of contamination.

Another boom accompanied by billowing smoke over the wall of the monastery, and he pulled out his phone, but then put it away again and instead shot the lock in the door. He slipped into the Order's grounds, and nearly fled out again. Outside, the night had been crystal clear but inside the wall, visibility was a few feet.

In the dark fog, two red lights focused on him. They loped nearer and he backed up against the wall as a massive hell hound ran, snarling, towards him. Harry shot again and again, but the hound kept coming – until it landed on a ward that flashed brilliant, blinding white. With a wail of agony the hound vanished and Harry scanned the fog.

As he watched it grew thinner, contracting away from him towards the monastery in the centre. He checked his phone but saw he had no signal. Wary, no, he amended, terrified, he ducked back out to his car for his bullet proof vest, then returned and crept forwards.

Ailwyn saw Harry approach and could only hope he was alright – he couldn't spare anyone to check on him, not that they'd be able to reach him. He looked at the feed to Danni - the casket in a pool of light, as the feed lights flickered.

The locks on the Iron Lady rattled, and the camera went dead.

Children lose protection

Over in Scotland, Amy was asleep in a small, messy bedroom with few toys, a small night light beside her. A loud CRACK woke her with a start. Instantly fearful, she looked wildly around the room, her hand automatically reaching to her wrist, to Danni charm bracelet.

To her dismay, the small wooden beads were cracked, scattered about her bed.

"Danni?"

She turned to the bonsai tree and saw, to her horror, the pot was cracked in half. New shadows danced in the corners of her bedroom, the monster she had been hidden from for so long had her scent again.

In the monastery cell, the Iron Lady rocked from side to side, and clasps holding it closed rattled and slid open by themselves.

In Sweden, a little boy woke up, screaming. On his windowsill a flowerpot had shattered with enough force to cover his bed in dirt. Another protective gift from Danni, and now, in the corner of his room, shadows danced.

In the monastery in Thailand, Naiyana, Achara and the children whose tattoos Danni removed all doubled over in pain, gripping this stomachs. The abbot, in meditation, felt a cold breath over him and ordered the monastery closed, as he hurried the survivors into the temple.

“We must hide you here until this passes.” He advised them.

“What if it doesn’t?” Asked Naiyana.

“Then we are all doomed.” He replied. In his head he made plans for the worst case scenario. Something had struck him as off with Brother Anders, before they’d got the call that had sent them rushing from the monastery.

In Australia… in Central and South America… in Asia… all over the world the children helped by Danni over the years lost their protective charms. And with their loss of protection, the monsters sniffed them out again. Still tentative and unsure, they circled around the children so suddenly revealed to them again. In the Netherlands, Iona was by a lake with her family. Her gaze went blank, then she started screaming.

Florin grabbed her and ran back to the caravan, to find his mother staring in shock at their home.

"This is it, Florin." She stated, hurriedly getting her phone out.

"What happened to the wards?" Asked Florin, desperate as his daughter kept screaming.

"Danyal is awake."

Back in the cell, the iron lady wobbled and the metal bulged.

A moment of silence settled and the Iron Lady went still again.

Then the front of the casket exploded off, to fly through the air and SMACK against the far wall. Danni fell out, holes in her clothing rimmed with blood, covered in punctures from the spikes inside the torture device, her eyes pure black.

She raised a hand to examine the holes in her flesh of

her hands, her wrist, forearm... all of which closed before her eyes.

Back in the van Beleth could scent death and was winning his battle with the restraints, which strained, close to breaking. Exhausted, the Fallen stopped their chanting and the flow of smoke stopped – but outside the van, the world was now covered in an oily, filthy smog.

Lilith leant over and pushed Belial out of the van. He screamed as fell and scrabbled to get back in – until he realised the ground no longer burnt.

"You fucking bitch!" He shouted.

"Get the others off the coach, if they haven't moved already. I want them storming the monastery."

"What about Beleth?" Asked Belial.

Lilith turned to Beleth. "Bring one of them here."

Belial and Tarel ran off together into the fog and soon returned with a grinning Akibeel.

"Akibeel, well met." Greeted Lilith. "I have an important task for you."

He joined her at the van and his face fell when she saw Beleth. Before he had time to speak, Tarel shoved him into the van and Beleth fell on him.

Tarel then climbed in and looked deep into Beleth's eyes. "Beleth. You need to wake up now. Remember who are and awaken."

Beleth focused piggy eyes on her.

"You are Beleth."

He threw back his head and roared, but when he looked back at her, intelligence had returned to his eyes.

"I am Beleth, of the first created angels."

"Now a king of hell." Tarel replied and he roared in rage.

"A king, Beleth, a king in a frail, pitiful body." Said Lilith.

Beleth looked down at his body, his consciousness slow to wake up. "You don't have long before you burn through this body, it is too weak for you." Lilith said as Tarel cautiously drew nearer. Beleth was one of their most powerful soldiers, but his rage made him difficult and dangerous, even to her.

"We are here to free our master, Beleth, and get our long delayed revenge on His Chosen."

Beleth nodded and relaxed and Tarel unlocked his chains. He pushed passed her, out of the van, and turned to run to the monastery. They could feel the other Fallen running by in the smoke, their presence like black holes, their intense hatred focused.

Tarel laughed out loud and jumped out of the van to follow them, a more cautious Lilith behind. She wanted to expend the Order's protections as much as possible before she risked herself, and was relieved that a horde of Fallen remained and hundreds of hell hounds. They spread out around the monastery to encircle it, then all charged at once. Windows and doors were smashed or ripped off, and the Fallen flooded inside, followed by the mist.

Completely lost in the fog, Harry tried to follow the sounds of gunfire. A shape loomed before him, and he was relieved to pick out a human outline.

"Hey!" He called.

The shape approached him and Harry picked out 2 black eyes, before a man ran at him with a knife. Harry shot him twice in the torso, then waited, frozen, expecting him to leap back up. The fog thinned, pulled towards the building, and Harry stayed at the edge, tense, ready to fire.

Ailwyn watched the footage on their cameras, mostly useless in the thick fog but full of blurry running shapes

– dozens perhaps hundreds of Fallen who still remained. He turned to the other guards.

“Brother Jerome killed her.” Stammered one monk, horrified to watch the Fallen overtake his brothers and sisters.

“Kill him if you see him, but otherwise focus on the Fallen.”

Four others were in the room with him, all terrified. *“And I brought this down on you.”* Thought Ailwyn.

“This is our great battle, we cannot let them achieve their goal.” He told them, before making the sign of the cross. “Remember you fight with God at your right hand.”

He smiled at each of them, a feral grin, and they responded with a roar.

“Let’s join the fight!” He shouted, and they ran from the room.

Outside a shattered window, a female Muslim warrior lay on her back, pinned to the ground by four hounds, each with teeth sunk into wrists and ankles. Flames burnt her skin where the hounds bit, and she writhed and screamed.

The mists parted and Beleth stepped through, hungry eyes focused on her. The Monk went completely still, teeth gritted against the pain, as Beleth produced a knife and dropped to his knees beside her. She spat in his face.

Beleth grinned and plunged the knife into her stomach. Looking into her eyes, relishing the agony on her face, he ripped a hole. Then he buried his head inside the wound, greedy hands pulling out her intestines, as Lilith ran out of the mist.

"Beleth, no!"

Beleth swallowed – then sat upright and his back arched. A bright glow started in his mouth, still trailing bloody entrails. The glow spread down his body and intensified, until his bones shone through his skin. Lilith backed up, then turned and ran away as Beleth exploded. Around him, the 'hounds' dissolved into smoke.

The monk was splattered in her own gore - but she smiled, at peace. "You stupid fuck, we're holy!" then she breathed her last.

Lilith screamed in rage at the waste of Beleth as a manic Wormwood ran up, screaming in ecstatic rage and bloodlust. He was once one of the 'fair angels', and in Lilith's fury she riddled him with bullets, furious with Beleth wasting himself in useless gluttony, furious at all the stupid Fallen.

Every step towards the monastery had cost the Fallen, not that she cared, as long as they reached their prize. From hundreds there were down to dozens as they threw themselves into battle with no thought or strategy. Not that she had expected any better, they had allowed the expendable Fallen to lead the charge, assisted by the hell hounds. None of them were scared of dying, the concept held no real meaning for them, but none wanted to go back to Hell, or even Otherworld. None of them wanted to forget again when they did manage to get back into this world in an inadequate human body – they all hungered to release their real if twisted, powerful forms when Lucifer was finally free to walk this world. Hungered to the point of madness, another curse of the Fallen.

As Lilith watched, the Fallen spirit of Wormwood pulled free of its pitifully frail human vessel. She had picked her lieutenants carefully, and they were all still alive. They were inside the monastery grounds and so very close to Lucifer. They would not fail. Those who remained all tasted and smelt Lucifer, he was so tantalisingly close. The loss of Beleth was a blow, but they still had more Fallen than they'd thought possible. Lilith shot Armers a snide look – she would be sure to tell her master it was her idea to create a mass awakening, while he had wanted to stick to scheduled rituals.

As if reading her thoughts, he met her gaze.

"Would you like to lead us into the monastery, Armers?"

"I'll follow you, Lilith."

They looked around to see Abaddon disappearing into the smoke ahead of them, and hurried to catch up.

In the entrance hall, two monks fought Marbas, but he defended himself with ease as they attacked from either side. A cut and thrust, overstepped, and Marbas pierced one monk's throat. The other lunged forward, cutting a deep gash on Marbas chest, but Marbas pivoted and impaled the other Monk on his sword.

Elsewhere Ailwyn fought Belial, both with swords. Ailwyn was bigger, but Belial was lighter on his feet and stronger. He danced around the old monk, clash, clash, the pair well matched, but behind Ailwyn, Jerome approached, knife in hand. Ailwyn sensed him at the last minute and hacked at Belial to gain time to turn, but Jerome slashed a dagger into Ailwyn's leg, and he collapsed.

"Master, I am here to serve."

Jerome bowed to Belial, who laughed in delight and raised his sword to finish Ailwyn off, but Ailwyn produced a gun and shot Belial in the chest.

"No!" Screamed Jerome.

Belial staggered back as a flower of blood blossomed on

his chest, while Jerome ran at Ailwyn with a scream. Calm, Ailwyn raised his gun and shot Jerome, but he gave Belial time to stagger off. Ailwyn shot after him, but missed as Belial rounded a corner.

Ailwyn sagged to the ground and shrugged off his robe, and cut strips to make a bandage for his leg.

The mist was now concentrated around the main monastery building, but even there it was thinning fast. Harry picked his way over bodies, dazed by the carnage. He checked his phone intermittently, but still had no signal.

He paused beside a brick building, as old as the monastery, and heard whimpers from inside. He carefully eased open the door on an infirmary. There were beds either side of the room, all full of wounded men and women, and other people had been dragged in and left on the floor, but he couldn't see any doctors or nurses.

He did spot two people who were arguing over someone in a bed, and something about them stopped him calling out. He slipped in and crept closer, and the hair on the back of his stood up on end. As he drew nearer he saw they were armed and arguing over the a very old man, who was already grievously wounded, fighting for the right to kill him.

"He killed me! I know him, he killed me!"

"He took my body too." Shouted another, shoving him.

Harry eyed the wounded all around him, some of whom were trying to get up. He made eye contact with the old man they fought over, then shot the men in the back. Two quick shots, BAM-BAM, and the atmosphere changed immediately. He squinted and thought he saw 2 dark shapes tug from the bodies and ooze into the ground.

"Are there any more of those... things?" He shouted, feeling sick. "In here?"

A woman nearest him shook her head. He considered – he knew basic first aid and some of these people were bleeding out before him.

"Go." Said a woman, reading his thoughts, "We will tend to each other."

"I'll come back as soon as a I can." He told them. He hated leaving them, but he had made himself a promise to help Danni.

He made sure they were armed – those who were able to fight – and slipped back outside where the mist had faded even more. He hurried over a wide stretch of lawn, feeling painfully exposed, and made it to the front door. He had stepped over so many bodies he quickly gave up counting, but the entrance hall stopped him in his tracks. Liberally splattered in gore, he could barely find his footing as he stepped through bodies.

He hesitated. He could still hear distant gunfire and had no idea where Danni might be kept, so he decided to look for information in Ailwyn's office. Jumping at every shadow, he made his way up there, relieved when he didn't encounter anyone.

He let himself in, his nerves screaming at him as he cleared the room, cursing himself as an idiot to be in this situation. Unsteady footsteps approached and he swung his gun to the door, his hands unsteady, as Ailwyn staggered in.

"Detective?" Asked Ailwyn, puzzled and wary, then relieved. "I am glad you are here, but you shouldn't have come."

Harry noted instantly that Ailwyn was hurt and hurried to help him, directed to a first aid box and then a crutch Ailwyn used when an old injury flared up. As he patched him up, and told him he needed stitches, Ailwyn filled him in.

"You need to take Danni as far away from here as possible." Finished Ailwyn.

"But… you're saying you lost?" Asked Harry, trying to process. He couldn't believe Fallen Angels were rampaging the monastery… but he had seen them with his own eyes.

Ailwyn cut him off by getting to his feet and limping out of his office, "We're not lost while I live, and you must fight another day. I'll take you to Danni."

Harry followed him through a maze of corridors, deep underground, to a cell. When Ailwyn opened the door, their torches picked out the medieval torture device in the middle of the room, its spikes covered in blood.

Harry paled as he eyed the monstrosity. "Tell me you didn't put anyone in that?"

Ailwyn shone his torch around the room and found Danni lying on the ground, her clothing punctured and blood stained.

"Danni!" Exclaimed Harry, as he ran over and, gently, felt for a pulse.

Ailwyn joined him, but Harry batted him away, "What kind of animals are you? How could you do this? You're supposed to be men of God?"

Harry stroked Danni's cheek, "Danni, can you hear me? I'm gonna take you away."

Danni's eyes snapped open.

"We'll make sure we shut this bastard monastery down forever."

Danni's eyes were pitch black, and she seemed not to recognise Harry.

"Danni? Go with the detective. Please." Said Ailwyn.

Danni's eyes flashed amber and she turned her attention to him. "You're too late, *Brother* Ailwyn of the Church of England."

"Can you walk, kid? I'm sorry I couldn't get here quicker." Said Harry.

Danni pushed Harry away, and he fell heavily to the floor, while she sprang to her feet.

"Danni? Or Emma? It's me, Harry?" He asked.

She cocked her head and studied him, briefly, then turned to Ailwyn. "This is what you wanted, Brother. Let's go and meet my kin."

"No, Danni, I was wrong. I am sorry."

"He's a sick old bastard, Danni. Leave with me, we can get out." Harry patted his pockets, remembering a picture one of the Cutchogue children had given him, "Look, Katie drew this for you. She wants to meet you."

He held out the piece of paper with a stick figure child beside a yellow angel with huge wings, "You saved her life."

Danni eyed the paper with disdain. "Why are you here?"

"To rescue you!" Harry grinned, but his smile faded

when she didn't respond.

"If you're still here when we finish, I will kill you myself." She stated, before grabbing Ailwyn's arm and dragging him from the room.

"Go, Detective. Get as far away as you can." Managed Ailwyn, before he was pulled away.

In the quadrant, the mist had never taken a hold with proximity to the holy water. Soft spot lights illuminated the giant fountain and the semi-circle of six prone monks, heads pressed to the ground, bravely suicidal as they ignored the sporadic bursts of gunfire, their prayers a soft, background chant. Around them, twenty members of the Order, of different sexes and religions, stood facing out with automatic rifles.

Danni dragged Ailwyn onto a balcony overlooking the yard and hid in the shadows, warning him to make no sound.

Eloheli, a former angel of the Seal, ran forward. Once radiantly beautiful, now rabid looking with glowing red eyes - to be mowed down by gunfire. A hail of bullets erupted from the shadows, cutting through the monks as they wildly tried to return fire, and Ailwyn turned away, but Danni grabbed his chin and forced him to watch.

More Fallen appeared and their bullets took out two of the praying monks, even as the others ignored the chaos, and certain death, and continued their prayers as their 'guards' were felled around them.

Below, in the courtyard, Anders stepped out of the shadows. Opposite, an exultant Lilith strode out to meet him, followed by Abaddon then Marbas, their clothing liberally splattered with blood. Behind them Tarel and Armers, both cut and bloody, supporting the fatally wounded Belial between them, his torso drenched in blood.

"Take me to Him now, I'm dying." Ordered Belial.

Two praying monks still remained, intent on their task, as Lilith pointed a gun at Anders. Ailwyn inhaled, perhaps to shout a warning, but Danni yanked his arm up behind his back, then placed her free hand over his mouth.

"Watch." She said. Keeping to the shadows, she made him face the quadrangle below and whispered in his ear. "And we'll see what you think about forgiveness and redemption when you are the victim of betrayal."

In the courtyard, a calm Anders slowly raised his weapon - and shot the nearest praying monk in the head, before moving on to the next. Distant, sporadic gunfire still sounded, but even with the rumble of the waterfall, the silence seemed huge as the chanting stopped. Anders dropped his gun and faced the Fallen.

"I will take you to the one you seek."

Betrayed

Up on the walkway, Ailwyn mumbled a surprised curse, but Danni tightened her hand over his mouth to stop him calling out.

"Kill him, Lilith!" Shouted Belial, blood gushing from his mouth as he struggled to retain consciousness. "Come on, hurry up, I have to meet him *now*."

Belial coughed up more blood and sagged between Tarel and Armers, as Lilith considered.

"We can find our own way. I can sense him."

"You can, but you need me to open the prison."

"Shoot him, Lilith! Get on with it-." Shouted Beleth.

"Oh shut up!" She said. She pivoted and shot Beleth between the eyes, and Tarel and Armers dropped his still twitching corpse without a glance.

"Who are you?" She asked.

"Brother Anders."

"You're the one who got the Crowley's grimoire to me." Stated Lilith, working out events in her head, and Anders nodded again.

"What?" Asked Ailwyn. "No! That grimoire was destroyed?"

"Shhh, brother, quietly now." Danni held him close to

whisper in his ear. “Brother Anders found it and made sure it got into Lilith’s hands.”

“No! Why would he?” He mumbled.

Danni twisted his arm painfully. “Shh. Watch and find out.”

“How many of your number are left?” Asked Anders.

Lilith cast a quick look around, but shrugged. “Not many. Maybe a dozen, but it matters not. All our brethren will all be free in this world soon enough.”

“Come, I will take you to Lucifier.” Said Anders, before leading them away from the quadrangle. “I advise you avoid the water.”

“Oh, Anders, what have you done?” Moaned Ailwyn.

As the group below vanished into the monastery, Danni pulled Ailwyn back from the edge. Tiny beside his bulk, she slammed him against the wall and stepped up close.

“Is this what you wanted? As you were torturing me to do your dirty work? As you made me summon them here?” Ailwyn’s hand grabbed Danni’s wrist as her hand encircled his throat. “Your Order dead, all the Fallen freed?”

Ailwyn looked deep into her bottomless eyes and dropped his hand - defeated.

"Lucifer free?" She added.

"I'm sorry, Danni." Managed Ailwyn. "We should never have treated you the way we did. We failed. I failed. In everything."

"And Anders? You must have known he was corrupted?" Danni dropped her hands from his throat and Ailwyn took a ragged gasp, but made no attempt to defend himself.

"I... I wasn't paying close enough attention." Croaked Ailwyn and Danni cocked her head, studying his reaction. "Listen, Danni, let Harry take you away from here."

"Why? There is no hiding from Lucifer once he's released on this realm." Danni looked away, into the middle distance, lost in thought. "He is truly beautiful you know. Once the most beloved of all angels."

Danni looked back to Ailwyn and tilted her head further in a strangely inhuman gesture. More like a bird, or a reptile. "You do understand what will happen when he is free?"

"He will take his vengeance on humanity." Replied Ailwyn.

"You think?" Her voice was strangely flat and inflection free. "So why did do it?"

"I didn't... I tried to stop them summoning the Fallen

when I realised how many were awake but… they didn't think we'd be defeated."

"How could you not be?" Still her voiceless was strangely lifeless and Ailwyn shivered. Had he done this to her?

"We will survive. There are outposts of the Order…"

"You think you can survive the Morning Star in all his power and raging glory?" She asked.

"Lucifer can be beaten. He can be contained." Said Ailwyn desperately, not ready to concede their total defeat. "We've done it before…"

"And what of the people the unleashed Fallen will kill first? What of their followers, in the military? In governments all over the world? With their fingers on big red buttons."

Ailwyn sagged. What had they done? They had failed their sacred duty – failed all of humanity.

"Even if you could contain them again, which I doubt, Lucifer isn't your real problem." Her next words took his breath away.

"The minute Lucifer walks the earth, the angels will come."

She pointed skyward to heaven.

"Angels?" Ailwyn struggled to understand, hope dawning. "The angels will come here? They will help us!"

"You've met angels, did they appear to give a shit about humanity?"

"I've met fallen angels."

She eyed him with her strangely blank expression, tinged with incredulity.

"They are the other side of the angelic coin. You've read the holy books. You've read Revelations. No angel holds humans in high regard, Brother."

Her amber eyes bored into Ailwyn's.

"Any why would they? You're greedy, selfish, arrogant, destructive and entitled – and look what you've done to this beautiful world. The angels hate you." Danni's blazed amber, but she looked skyward, away from Ailwyn, thinking aloud. "The second that the angels in heaven feel Lucifer free, here on earth, they will come in force to here to fight him, not protect you."

She allowed a few minutes to sink in, before finishing.

"You've brought about Armageddon."

She watched the words sink in, the horror on Ailwyn's face, then she stepped back.

"Come on, you get a front row seat."

She pulled Ailwyn's arm over her shoulder and half-carried him into the bowels of the monastery. As they left the balcony, Gamon crept into the quadrant below, followed by a nervous Harry. The dog looked up towards her, then released a soulful howl of distress.

Deep underground, Anders led the Fallen into the chamber of the dead. Lilith, Abaddon, Tarel, Marbas and Armers were joined by 20 surviving fallen angels, who passed through the Order's dead. Anders kept his down as he passed between the tombs, but the Fallen behind them look around gleefully.

"Your ancestors are not at all happy about your betrayal, Anders!" Stated Tarel.

Marbas and Tarel giggled, but Anders ignored them and continued at a stately pace. On either side of the path the ghosts of the dead Order lined up to stare hatred at the Fallen in their midst.

"All those centuries fighting us, then you lead us here of your own volition!" Said Lilith, eyeing Tarel with glee.

"Feel their impotent anger, Lilith!" Laughed Tarel.

Marbas and Tarel laughed so hard they had to hold each other up. Abaddon laughed too, an effeminate giggle, even Armers cracked a smile.

"I like parading right passed them." He peered into the dark, "I think I recognise some of them from my former lives! I believe I put some of them here."

Anders stopped and turned back to face the Fallen. He saw Tarel wave to the tombs and his face tightened.

"They did not understand how corrupt humanity is. That sickness has broken the earth itself, there is no remedy for it."

The crypt echoed back his words to him.

"Humanity cannot continue. For its own sake it must be purged, as God once did in the great flood."

Tarel gasped for breath while Lilith grinned at her.

"They don't seem to agree with you."

She tapped his forehead, gifting him with Sight, then gestured to the sarcophagus. His eyes widened as the chamber filled with the ghosts of The Order. They stared in utter contempt and anger at Anders, who opened and closed his mouth. The weight of the dead guardians' condemnation settled on his shoulders and with a cry, he turned and ran ahead.

He was still fumbling with keys to a huge, iron door when Lilith caught up with him.

"Too late for second thoughts, Anders."

Anders looked over her shoulders at the rows upon rows of his ancestors.

"I stand by my decision!" He shouted at them.

His hands steadied and he unlocked the huge door, and the sound of a torrent met them.

"The prison of the Fallen." He shouted over the noise.

Danni supported Ailwyn down the stone stairs to the chamber of the dead. She paused as she heard laughter carry from ahead, wanting to time her moment to catch up with them. Her eyes had returned to normal by the time they reached the bottom, but her lip was curled in contempt, and she still moved with a grace more reptile than human. As she dragged Ailwyn, limping, into the chamber, she tapped his forehead, gifting his with Sight, and he saw the ghosts for the first time.

His footsteps faltered and Danni had to drag him between the columns, with thousands of accusing eyes stared at him.

"What..?"

"Meet your ancestors. Witness to your failure."

Ailwyn looked side to side, aghast. "Oh God, their souls are still here..?"

“The angel of death can’t come near the Fallen, Ailwyn, not until the end of days. Azrael is unable to come near this place, so he cannot escort them to the peace they yearn for.”

“They’re... *all* still here? Trapped?”

The ghosts, thousands of them, eyed Ailwyn in condemnation, and he staggered as he absorbed the suffering of his predecessors.

“You’ve left them in agony for centuries.”

Ailwyn stopped and managed a 360 turn, seeing row upon row of them, trapped down here beside the Fallen’s prison. The ghosts of the order, as one, turned their backs on the path.

“Don’t worry, Azrael will be here soon. You’ll meet him, along with the full heavenly Host.”

Ailwyn passed out. Danni caught him as he fell, dropping her shoulder to hoist him up. With barely a grunt, she hefted him onto her shoulder and carried him, blood from his leg leaving a drip-dripping trail.

Lucifer Freed

The prison of the Fallen was a huge cavern lit by bare light bulbs, the recesses full of shadows. The sound was deafening as millions of gallons of water crashed onto a small island surrounded by a deep trench that the water vanished into, to be recycled and sent back up to the top to be blessed in an endless cycle. A wall of water and behind it, dim shadows of figures, still as statues. Along one wall of the dungeon, torture devices from the throughout the age - a rack, a wheel, a cauldron and iron lady. A table with iron tools, knives and mallets.

Lilith, Armers, Abaddon and Tarel and Marbas and all the other 20 Fallen Angels crossed to stand before the water, Anders to one side. Momentarily frozen, until Danni arrived with an unconscious Ailwyn over her shoulders.

"I see I'm just in time." She said brightly.

Lilith growled and raised a gun to shoot her, and Danni hid behind Ailwyn's body.

"That's not very nice, Lilith. You wouldn't be here without me."

Abaddon waved Lilith down as Danni, watched by everyone, carried Ailwyn towards a large, wooden crucifix propped against a wall.

"You're far too late, you bitch." Shouted Lilith.

Danni dumped Ailwyn, feet first, and he moaned.

"You will not gain our master's forgiveness, not at this late stage." Stated Lilith.

"Not after you put him here." Added Armers.

Anders shot Danni a surprised look, but he didn't even exist to her. She grinned and winked at Lilith. "Oh I dunno, he always had a soft spot for me, didn't he, Lily? And he's always preferred me to you."

Lilith growled again, an animal sound of rage.

"Before you dispatch this body of mine, let me remind you of the problem of Otherworld."

The Fallen eyed her in confusion.

"*I* am the key. I can open Otherworld." Said Danni, "You need me."

"What do you mean?" Asked Abaddon.

"Once we release Lucifer, the heavenly host will arrive." She waited for them to nod, "There are too few of you to fight them, *and* you're in weak human forms. How will you fight the angels in these pitiful bodies?" She asked, gesturing to her own body.

The Fallen thought about it.

"How can you help?" Asked Abaddon.

"I can cross worlds at will." Danni's eyes flashed black and she grinned.

Armers caught on first. "We've unlocked the Underworld but not Otherworld." He stated. "If we're to stand a chance we have to take our real forms in this world."

"And let all the others in." Finished Danni. "In their true forms."

Ailwyn shot a sickened look at Anders, who paled.

Armers inhaled sharply, "That's why Asdodeous wanted you! That's why he didn't share his secrets with us. He wanted you for himself, alone."

"I reckon he figured that if he could come and go, he wouldn't need Morning Star, and then our heavenly brethren would never come." Said Danni.

"Once Lucifer is free we'll have the strength we need." Screeched Lilith. "We don't need her!"

"Once Lucifer is free you will have broken the covenant so when the angels arrive they will be in their heavenly raiment." Stated Danni patiently. Overly patiently, with a heavy dose of patronising. "*We* will still be trapped in these bodies, unless *I* open all the doors between all the worlds."

"Don't do this, Danni." Begged Ailwyn.

“Do it then. Open Otherworld to this plane, allow our bodies through.” Demanded Abaddon, overriding Lilith.

“I intend to. But I need to time it for the moment you free Lucifer.” Replied Danni.

“No! She’s planning something!” Shouted Lilith. “She betrayed us before, she’ll do it again.”

“Then we’ll let Lucifer deal with her.” Said Abaddon.

Danni grinned. “Now, I’ve got my offering, what did you all bring?”

She eyed their guarded faces with delight.

“Oh you know how much Lucifer craves love and attention,” She dropped her voice to a dramatic whisper, “Since he fell out with father.”

She scanned them. “Did you bring a present?”

“We’ve brought his freedom.” Replied Tarel, unsure.

“I brought the best present. I brought him you, the ultimate traitor.” Replied Lilith, grinning.

“There you go, another reason not to shoot me, though the rest of you are fucked.”

Before they could answer she turned back to Ailwyn.

“See, I got thinking. Brother Anders here pretends he’s doing the right thing... He might even believe he is.”

Danni held Ailwyn upright against the cross. "But we've all seen into his soul and it's as black as ours would be, if we had souls..."

They all watched her, and she eyed them over her shoulder. "Brother Ailwyn here is a good man – a weak but innocent human to behold what we achieve."

Tarel giggled, but the others look sceptical as Danni addressed Anders. "The iron nails and mallet, if you please."

Anders hesitated, but Tarel shoved him towards the bench. Grim faced, Anders picked up a mallet and two thick, iron nails. Danni beckoned and he crossed to stand beside her.

"You must nail Brother Ailwyn's to the cross." Tarel laughed with delight as Anders hesitated.

"Come on, the master wants to be free." She goaded.

Anders placed a nail against Ailwyn's flesh, then hefted the mallet. SMACK, with a single stroke, he drove it into Ailwyn's hand. Ailwyn uttered yell of pain and his struggles tore the flesh on his hand, before Danni slammed him back onto the cross and, effortlessly, pushed his other hand against the wood.

Ailwyn focused immediately on Anders, ignoring pain. "Anders, no! No, please stop this madness. I beg you!"

Tarel's giggles increased, "You're right, Danyal, I like it!

Start begging, Brother!

Anders, now fervent, looked into Ailwyn's eyes as he placed the second nail on his palm, while Tarel laughed out loud.

"Humanity has strayed too far, Brother. We have grown depraved. We are not fit to inhabit this beautiful world ."

"That's not up to you to decide!" Shouted Ailwyn, to the Fallen's delight.

"It is too late. The day of reckoning is as hand."

"No! No, Anders, you must stop."

WHACK, he slammed in the other nail and Ailwyn nearly fainted again, but his weight on the nails roused him. Danni looked to Anders with an evil grin.

"Now, Brother Anders, turn off the water."

Danni took Anders by the shoulders and turned him back to the others.

"Danni! Danni, I know you're in there. Please, in the name of God, stop." Ailwyn struggled and blood poured from his hands and the wound on his leg.

"I'm not sure He's interested in your pleas, Ailwyn, not anymore. You seemed to think I wasn't worthy of him anyway?"

“Turn off the water, Priest.” Shouted Armers.

Abaddon shoved Anders towards the water-wall.

“Open this prison!”

Anders took a step back, then ran and jumped into the waterfall. He vanished into the water, long enough for the Fallen to become uncomfortable, but then the deluge suddenly stopped until the water was just a trickle from the cavern ceiling.

Hundreds ‘iron ladies’ were suspend from chains from the ceiling, and the dripping water hissed and evaporated as it touched them. Anders stood in the centre of the island, his hand on a lever, soaked.

“Come back here, Human.”

Anders headed back towards them, picking up speed to jump the crevice. As he landed, Abaddon stabbed him in the stomach repeatedly - stab, stab, stab, hissing with pain as his dripping garments sprayed holy water on his hand. He then lifted Anders off his feet and hurled him against the wall, to crumple to the floor at Ailwyn’s feet.

“I can feel him!” Said Marbas, and the Fallen turned their attention on the island, in awe.

“I can feel all of them.” Added Lilith, eyes glowing.

Tarel hopped up and down in excitement. “At last!”

A deep, rumbling voice filled the huge room. "Get me out!"

Danni leapt effortlessly over the chasm, watched by a hopeless Ailwyn. She navigated the iron caskets towards the centre of the island, the other Fallen close behind. She paused beside one casket, which rattled.

"Asmodeous." She muttered, and Asmodeous roared in response.

She edged around it to head to the centre. All the caskets were sealed closed and wrapped in chains but this one was most heavily secured, entirely circled in heavy iron chains. Danni came to a full stop before it.

The world around her vanished, leaving her alone with the casket.

"My love." She whispered, stepping close. "Do you know me?"

"You betrayed me." Replied a deep voice – at once beautiful and terrible. Lucifer.

"I did." She replied. "Just as you betrayed all of us when you asked us to follow you."

"I did." He replied. His beautiful voice filled the cavern, full of a deep aching sense of loss. "You most of all, my love."

Lilith edged forward, unhappy that Danni was speaking

to their master.

"Do you regret it? What we did?" Danni asked.

"Every hour, every minute, every second." The terrible, haunting sadness emanated from the casket, and tears welled in Danni's eyes.

A pair of lights appear in the casket, bright eyes that pinned her with a stare. "And also never."

She stepped forward and placed a hand close to his face as she pressed her cheek to the metal, heedless of her skin as it blistered. "I'm sorry."

From his position on the wall, Ailwyn cried, matching the tears that streamed down Danni's cheeks, as he prayed forgiveness for his failure – and for a quick end for mankind.

"And now they will pay. For my fall, for my pain, for my loss... and for holding me here. My wrath will know no bounds."

Lilith yanked Danni back. "I never betrayed you, my Lord."

The others approach in a semi-circle and bowed.

"Get me out of here!" Lucifer's voice was deafeningly in the room, and the Fallen ran to the casket and hacked at the chains, all except Danni, who wiped away the tears from her eyes.

“I need to draw the runes to open Otherworld, quickly. We need the doorway ready the second he’s released.” Stated Danni. “Tarel, find chalk or something, Armers, you must help me.”

Tarel pouted, but ran back to the main room while Danni paced the circumference of the island.

“I’ll draw the first runes, you can check them, then repeat them around the island until we have a full circle.” She told Armers, and Tarel jogged back with 2 lumps of chalk.

As Danni measured, the other Fallen tried to break the chains around Lucifer’s casket.

“We need an axe for the chains.” Stated Lilith, and the Fallen ran back to search for tools.

“Soon, Master, you will be free.” Giggled Tarel as Danni dropped to her knees and began to draw runes, a mixture from all the ages and cultures, tainted by dark Satanic runes.

A star, and Danni whispered “Morning Star, light bringer. Most beloved.”

A tear fell on the stone as she moved onto the next drawing, 2 legs “Travel.” Said Danni. “Travel. Worlds. Realms. Dimensions. Between.”

An ankh “Life. Live. Opening. Key.”

A flat basket with a handle, "vessel, chalice, life force, container." She said.

2 joined semi-circles, "Mouth, speak, order, command." She said.

A seated pharaoh, "King."

She drew an amended ankh that sizzled into the stone, "Blood. Sacrifice. Death. Rebirth."

The drew fasters – a spinx, a star, a column with crosses over it, an eye with an intricate pattern under it, and as she spoke the runes burned into the stone.

"Gatekeeper. Goaler. Liberator. Usurper. Opening. Fracture. Death. Rebirth."

Armers examined the work, wary of betrayal.

"What order are they repeated?" He asked.

"This order." Replied Danni. "This exact order, with the incantation to bring them to life. You continue here, I'll work backwards. We must time the completion of the circle with the exact moment we liberate Lucifer."

Lilith shot Armers a look, but he nodded.

"This will work." He studied them again for a moment, then grinned and shouted, "We have our portal to Otherworld!"

He dropped to his knees to continue writing. Danni

rushed to the start of her runes and began rapidly recreating the pattern, working backwards. As they wrote, the Fallen attacked the central casket, hacking at the chains with axes, hammers and chisels.

One by one the chains broke and crashed to the ground. The Fallen rushed forward, pushing and shoving each other as they grabbed the chains, heedless as their skin blistered and burnt.

“Hurry up!” Lucifer shouted, his booming voice reverberating through the stones.

Finally the chains were all broken’ leaving 3 clasps holding the casket closed.

“Get back, you fuckers, all of you, out of my way.” Shouted Abaddon.

Danni and Armers drew closer to each other, the circle nearly complete.

“Finish the circle, I’ll activate the portal in the middle.” Ordered Danni as she got to her feet and jogged around the caskets, back to the centre.

Armers hurriedly drew the final runes as Abaddon released the first clasp.

A BOOM echoed through the chamber. From Ailwyn’s position against the wall, the view of the island prison blurred and the ground shook.

Lilith pushed Abaddon aside to release the second clasp.

The BOOM repeated, louder, and a wave of air pressure flattened Ailwyn against the wall. He thought he detected a misty outline between him and the island. A vast shape that should not have fit inside the chamber. Then the distinctive sound of beating wings.

A cold, icy sweat broke out on Ailwyn's brow as an unmistakable new presence arrived in the prison. Where the Fallen were overtly vile and corrupted, this presence was icy, burning cold.

The Fallen focused on the metal casket and Danni squatted beside the central lever for the waterfall. Armers ran to join them and fought with Marbas, Abaddon and Lilith for the honour of releasing the final clasp as the whole casket vibrated. From all around, the trapped fallen angels woke up to their presence – and so did the angels. They hovered at a doorway to this world, on the brink of stepping in with Lucifer's freedom.

"Let me out!"

"Release me!"

"Get me the fuck out of here!" They yelled, vying for attention in a Babylonian chorus of languages.

Abaddon, by far the biggest Fallen, won the battle as he

threw first Lilith then Tarel aside, then punched Marbas in the head. He reached for the final clasp.

“I wanted to save you, my love.” Said Danni.

Lilith was back on her feet, furious. She turned to Danni, momentarily puzzled by her words, until she saw her hand reach for the lever to restart the waterfall as the Abaddon and Tarel opened the casket. “Nooooooo!”

From his position on the wall, Ailwyn watched as the casket door opened. He got a glimpse inside, before his view was obstructed by a massive figure that solidified before his eyes, mist coalescing into a terrifying substance with massive wings. The temperature of the prison seemed to drop and rise at the same time – a bone aching cold and a flesh melting heat.

BOOM, BOOM, BOOM. More vast figures dropped from the roof, shaking the foundations as they began to take substance in blinding, dazzling light.

Then Danni grabbed the handle and pulled. A loud rumble and the Fallen eyed Danni in horror, Marbas already running towards her. He neared her as the holy water hit. A torrent engulfed them and they blazed white, their screams carrying over the water, then, one by one, the blazing light lights faded into wisps.

“Danyel!” Screamed Lucifer, in rage and anger and, worst of all, soul-destroying sadness.

Ailwyn watched the vast sentinels dissipate again, understanding but not comprehending what had happened. He realised Lucifer had been freed – for split-second, and that the heavens had responded. He saw the Fallen, he had felt their vileness. He had spent his entire, adult life fighting to prevent this... and yet, it was one thing to believe and another to have proof.

He sagged, close to unconsciousness, his brain unable to process. Anders sat against the wall at this feet, one bloody hand clasped to his stomach, equally dumbstruck.

Judgement

Danni burst from the fountain of water and stood for a moment eyeing Anders and Ailwyn, as they gaped at her in amazement. Ailwyn's already overloaded brain noted that all her wounds had totally healed – the cuts and punctures, and the burns.

Ignoring him she crossed to Anders, stopping to scoop something up of the ground, before she squatted beside him. She opened her hand, which held his crucifix. She examined it, running her finger on the outline of Jesus.

"This has great power when you believe."

"You can touch it?" Gasped Anders.

"I could always touch it. I didn't touch it before out of respect... See, I do not believe - I *know*. Who created us, and what waits on the other side." She reached for Anders' free hand and placed the cross on his palm.

"You are dying, Brother Anders." Danni tapped her finger on the figure on the cross. "And I advise you spend your last breath praying to this son of the new covenant to intercede."

She closed his hand around the cross.

"Because you're about to meet his Father, the God of the Old Testament. " She looked Anders in the eye. "The unforgiving God of vengeance and retribution." She got to her feet. "And you should be very afraid."

Anders opened and closed his mouth, unable to talk - but Danni had finished with him. She stepped up to Ailwyn and using just her fingers, pulled out the first nail, her skin blistering from the touch of the iron. Ailwyn moaned and collapsed, supported by Danni. She reached to the other nail and pulled it free, then hefted him over her shoulder.

With a grunt of effort she carried him out of the prison, back to the chamber of the dead. The ghosts turned to them in surprise as she entered, and Danni eased into the water with Ailwyn. She lay him on his back, supporting his weight.

He had no energy to move at first, and instead just stared at her in confusion – and awe.

"What happened? Why didn't you die?"

"Brother Ailwyn, there are bodies everywhere and the authorities will be here soon." She said.

He continued to gape at her, and she cupped her hands to scoop up water. "Drink. This water will help heal you, and you have much to do. You cannot let the police or FBI overrun here. They cannot find this prison."

Dazed, Ailwyn drank and his strength did return.

"I thought you'd opened the worlds? You *helped* them? Then you didn't?" Ailwyn looked between Danni and the water. "The holy water doesn't hurt you?"

She laughed, a bitter sound. "It seems not, though it's not exactly comfortable."

Ailwyn was completely overwhelmed.

"I created a doorway. But all magic has multiple purposes, something humanity doesn't understand. It can open *or* it can close. I have made your prison stronger, but also weaker if they break out." She shook him, "Ailwyn, my wards can be undone and reversed, when they really will open all the worlds. Your Holy Water will deplete quickly if it's not replenished, and then the Fallen will escape."

He blinked rapidly, to her frustration.

"You must replenish the holy water and you must stop the police. Urgently."

Ailwyn blinked, still dazed, and Danni shook him again, harder.

"Ailwyn! What are you going to do? You cannot let the authorities in, they can never know what you have here!"

Ailwyn finally seemed to come to his senses.

"I need the phone line, I'll make some calls." He heaved himself up and waded to the side. "I'll call in everyone from around the world... everyone we have left."

She crossed to the side, to hop up and pull her legs out of the water. "Hurry!

He grabbed the stone of the side, but his expression turned puzzled as he noticed his hands - the wounds had closed, leaving 2 ragged scars.

"You will always bear the stigmata, as a reminder to keep this place safe, Father Ailwyn."

He noticed that she'd changed his honorific as she got to her feet and leant over to offer him a hand. "Others like Anders will come."

"I will be vigilant."

Danni expression turned angry. ""You'll do more than that! You *allowed* Anders to do this. *All* of you used torture! You delighted in pain."

"And we were willing to murder a baby." Added Ailwyn. "The rot started with you, where the Order truly lost its way. I am so sorry we treated you so badly." His head was overflowing with thoughts – the many implications after the last few hours. "You are right to condemn us. Condemn me."

Her held was still held out for him to take, and he grabbed it. Danni lifted him up, out of the water, "And you committed another very great wrong to your own kind."

She pointed to the nearest sarcophagus, with its silent,

beseeching figure. “Ignorance is no excuse. You have kept these souls in torment for hundreds of years.”

“I will remove their bodies, all The Order’s dead.” Agreed Ailwyn.

“Do that. Move them far from the Fallen so that Azrael can take them away and finally give them peace.”

Danni marched off, and he watched her back.

“What are you?” He shouted after her.

Danni didn’t answer and after a moment he hurried up the stairs behind her, to ensure any remaining warriors didn’t attack her.

“The Fallen who are awake but not yet here, the summons still resounds in their heads. They will make their way here in the coming days.” Her voice carried down the stairs to him.

Ailwyn jogged after her, surprised to find that despite the battering, the wounds and exhaustion, he had a spring in his step. His jog accelerated until he was running up the stairs after her.

Harry had sat for a while in the chamber, eying the torture device, at a loss about what to do. Eventually he decided to leave, to head back to NYC and warn Sam that… that 'something' was coming. Confused and distressed, he headed back up but got lost in the warren, until he heard a panicked dog barking.

He'd followed the sound and found that 2 of the foul people had cornered Gamon and were teasing her with a knife. Lunging, slicing, then backing away, Harry shot them both in the back without a thought.

The dog slunk over to him, low to the ground, and he'd stroked her to calm her, relieved to find that her injuries were superficial. Then Gamon had run off and Harry followed, back to the giant waterfall. Harry was out of ammunition, but when he saw the dead monks around the fountain, still kneeling, shot as they'd prayed, he was overcome by a profound sadness. When Gamon refused to leave the quadrant, Harry had sunk to the ground beside her, compelled to pray for all the dead – for the first time in years.

Redemption

Danni and Ailwyn emerged into chaos, blood, death and pain. Windows were smashed and walls were destroyed or fire-blackened, and small fires still burned. Ailwyn had spread word that Danni was not to be harmed, then phoned his contacts, stating the Order was fine and to stay away, then he followed Danni to the entrance.

She stood outside in the rising sun, and the full scale of devastation became apparent.

The grounds were churned up with gaping holes from ordinance and small fires still burnt. The three coaches were destroyed, their frames peeled back like giant, blackened bananas. Several outbuildings were smashed and broken while the main monastery had gaping holes in the walls and smashed windows. And the dead littered the ground – some Fallen but more from the Order. Hundreds of dead.

Coming through the still open gates was a convoy of assorted vehicles – caravans, campervans and huge RV's, pristine hire cars.

"FBI?" Asked a wounded monk who hobbled out, supported by another, but Ailwyn shook his head. It wasn't any government force or authority, but he wasn't sure what it was.

He ordered the exhausted warriors to arm themselves as a big RV parked and a hugely muscled and tattooed man climbed out. He totally ignored the monks to focus of Danni.

"Kazia put out the word in the US, we have been preparing since she met you in the Netherlands." He stated, although he eyed Danni warily.

"She wasn't sure what side you'd picked, but... the Romani have responded to the call for help." The man eyed the wreckage, and finally focused on Ailwyn. "What about the police?"

"They'll stay away for now but I don't know how much time we have before someone comes snooping. They must have heard the explosions in New York City." He replied.

"This place will never be secret again." Stated Danni, then looked up to the sky, "And if a satellite happens to pass, footage of the devastation will be all over the web, then the authorities will have to investigate."

The Romani man eyed the carnage as others joined him and still more cars arrived, including the Abbot from Wat Marp Jan, who had brought dozens of saffron clad monks. Behind them, more cars pulled up and Alex got out.

"Muma Alice sent us." He eyed the carnage and whistled.

"You need to clear these bodies. A pyre is too visible

and it'll stink. If you got diggers, we could enlarge these craters and bury them." Suggested the abbot, surprising them all with his practicality.

"Do it, " said Ailwyn, "but just the Fallen, and treat them with respect. Their parasites have fled, their remains are mortal and once housed people. And gather our brothers and sisters, they will be taken far away for burial."

They organised into teams, a group to find and tend the wounded, a group to dig vast graves, another to put our fires and yet another for the most important job of all, the sanctification of the holy water into the prison, led by the Abbot.

Then Gamon bounded up to Danni, ecstatic as only dogs can be, Harry behind, with a lopsided, tentative grin. Danni knelt beside the dog and allowed to her lick her face, nearly smiling.

"Sweet Jesus." Harry looked around, "It's almost like you had a battle with fallen angels and nearly invoked Armageddon." He laughed shakily, then eyed Danni with concern, "Are you alright? I should have tried harder to reach you..."

Danni knew his concern should touch her but at that moment she was struggling with her emotions. Something inside her was awake, full of memories she didn't recognise, and she felt removed from everyone around her. Still, he *had* come for her, and just maybe he had helped her after all. Her gaze slipped to Alex, who held himself back from the others, and she tried to remember the person she'd been a few short days ago in Louisiana.

The Romani setup camp and by nightfall, mass graves had been dug and filled with the now empty hosts of the Fallen, all buried in a mass grave under tonnes of earth, with the promise of a memorial. The Order's dead warriors were laid in crypt under the chapel, ready for transportation. The Romani negotiated a contract for rebuilding, wreckers had started clearing the burnt out cars, and Ailwyn had fended calls from the authorities. He claimed the order had experienced a huge gas leak, but that it was fully under control.

At midnight, a meeting was called. A few Muslim, Jewish, Sikh, Christian, Buddhist and Hindu warriors had arrived, too late to fight, and they joined their injured compatriots, but they were now outnumbered by the other creeds the Order had previously rejected.

Ailwyn addressed them, welcoming all and thanking them, ushering in a new era of cooperation, and acknowledging that all had their part to play in fighting the Fallen. He was voted leader, and promised that things would change. He also vowed to move the prisoners to a new, secret location, and then made it clear that Danni was not to be hunted again. She was of the Order now, in whatever capacity she chose.

Harry watched the meeting for a while then slipped away to search for Danni. He eventually bumped into Alex and together they climbed to the top of the monastery, where they found her with Gamon, looking out over the assembled masses, hundreds of them, with small campfires punctuating the night.

"So I gather you're the hero, right?" Asked Harry.

Danni snorted but Ailwyn joined them. "Yes, she is."

Danni still wasn't sure what she felt about him. He'd colluded in torture and murder, but she had to acknowledge that letting the Fallen go free was not an alternative. And she had also killed for a cause.

"You've got some nerve even coming near her!" Spat Harry, and with Alex they stepped up either side of Danni.

Ailwyn merely nodded his agreement. "What will you do now?"

Danni had no idea. She'd lived on the run for so many years, the thought of peace was totally alien to her.

Still, that was a background thought, just a distraction really. Churning in her head were her new memories. She could vividly picture ancient Egypt, Rome, Constantinople, and many other times as if she'd been there. She had also *known* the Fallen – as in recognised them. Lucifer in his cold, painful prison flashed into her head, and the heart-wrenching sorrow she felt as she betrayed him. And how had she managed that? The spells she'd created used arcane knowledge that did not belong in this world.

She eyed Ailwyn – he had asked her who she was and she still didn't have an answer.

In her pocket, her hand brushed on a folded up piece of paper, the picture Katie had drawn for her. The picture reminded her of all the children she'd protected over the years, who were vulnerable again now. She thought vaguely it was a good thing that she could still worry about anyone. She would start by retracing her steps to help them again, but after that?

"I could use your help securing the new prison, when we work out where to place it." Ailwyn said after a while. "And how to transport them."

Harry scowled at Ailwyn, but Danni shrugged.

"You're better off leaving them here. The truth is out that Lucifer is in this realm." Her skin tingled when she said his name, and she thought she heard a distant, wail of anger and misery, and she shivered. "You'll always be tracked eventually, wherever you go. As long as you keep up the praying, your prison is well protected."

"Just pretend to move it, Brother. You're good at deceit." Added Alex.

They turned their attention to the scene below them again. Fairy-lights switched on as the group dispersed, the strains of music and singing and snippets of laughter carried up to them.

"What a difference a day makes." Said Harry, "I never want to experience that again! Give me a wholesome serial killer any day."

Danni eyed them sideways – Gamon, Alex, Harry, Muma Alice, Kezia... even Ailwyn. She had found... friends.

"Danni, you once asked me if I believed in redemption. In your redemption." Said Ailwyn eventually.

Danni stiffened.

"I do believe." Stated Ailwyn, picking his words. "It is not my place to say what happens after this life, but I do believe you are not damned for eternity."

"Whoever I am?" asked Danni.

"Who you are is a good person." Stated Ailwyn. "And I am serious about you always having a home here." Said Ailwyn, "It doesn't matter who, or what, you are, you are one of us."

Harry raised his eyebrows at Danni. "I've got some kids in New York who'd love to meet you in person. They said you spoke to them, while they were captured."

She left with Harry that night, with an open invitation to

Muma Alice, to all Romani camps and, of course, the Order's many monasteries all over the world. After New York, she would go to Amy in Glasgow and back from there. After that, she didn't know and decided that she didn't care.

THE END

I hope you enjoyed Fallen, thank you for reading it! I will revisit Danni at some stage, but in the meantime, I have attached extracts from two other books. **DRUID**, a supernatural, historical thriller, and **INHERITANCE** an epic fantasy for young adults, both available/soon to be available on Amazon.

Extract from DRUID:

DRUID

AD 150, England: When a trail of bodies points to the gods' displeasure, an outsider challenges the might of the Druids in a deadly battle of power and magic.

The mighty Druids. Judges, law makers, healers, seers and story tellers. The conduit of the gods.

It is not advisable to turn your backs on the Druids, and even less advisable to catch the attention of gods – and Arian has done both. The capricious gods send attackers to her home, forcing her to the mighty city of Titelbhe to trade for new supplies, just two weeks before Samhain and the Dark Half of the Year.

And Titelbhe is a city in crisis. A wild boar, a manifestation of chaos, has killed the heir, Prince Igrid. The harvest is poor, a calf is born with two heads and milk turns sour as sidhe roam freely. As panic spreads, a child is savagely attacked and Arian intervenes. A child who turns out to be Princess Oife, daughter of Prince Igrid, granddaughter of the chief, Queen Neala. Disasters escalate and Arian realises the royal line is being setup, as dark magic stalks Titelbhe.

Arian knows she must leave and she has re-stocked for a lonely winter. The Druids are coming and her father, once a Druid High Priest, has taught her arcane knowledge they will kill her for possessing. Knowledge and magic she can use against the darkness, and she realises that the gods have placed her in Titelbhe... Also, something unexpected has happened. Neala and Oife, even the arrogant Prince Caen, have welcomed her into their family, and without her help they will be charged before a corrupt Druid court and sacrificed.

As a Wicker Man is built, Arian must decide if she will flee back to lonely isolation, or stay to defend those she loves, and confront the might of the Druids.

Chapter 1

200 men and women followed Prince Igrid over an undulating, empty plain towards a vast forest. Their mottled clothing acted as camouflage, so they seemed to appear and disappear, flickering in and out of existence. Lunar watched them from the sky, her cold light turning night into monochrome day and casting strange shadows that seemed independent of their owners.

The night had a hint of magic and a touch of Otherworld.

Igrid stopped at the edge of the forest and raised his right arm, fist clenched. Tall, muscular, with long black hair in corn-row plaits, there was little in this world he feared. He surveyed the forest, full of deep shadows and movement, despite the stillness of the night, and caught the suggestion of faces in the branches. This was the Green Man's territory, and he did not always take kindly to human visitors.

He asked the Green Man's permission to enter, then said a quiet prayer to Druantia, goddess of protection. The others reached the forest threshold in a long line and stopped, each saying their own prayers. This final hunt of the year meant the difference between a lean and a comfortable winter – but it was also a warrior's test, to be completed alone, against the forest's bears, wolves and wild boar.

A lone wolf answered Igrid's prayer and a finger of dread prickled his spine. Stifling the feeling, he dropped his arm, then pelted into the forest. Silent but swift, the others followed.

Inside the forest, contrasting shadows and bright light confused the senses, but Igrid ran, unerring as he navigated branches and treacherous roots. The ancient trees grew bigger, their mighty trunks dwarfing him, until the clumsy sound of breaking branches brought him to an abrupt stop. Loud grunts to his left and he approached a bright clearing where a huge wild boar scratched the ground, its great curved tusks rooting for food. Fully focused on the boar, Igrid fitted an arrow to his bow but as he lined up his shot, a cold knife plunged into his belly.

He shouted in anger and pain as his attacker twisted the blade, sliced sideways, then pulled it free. The boar squealed in rage as Igrid dropped his bow to hold his stomach together, but a shove pushed him to his knees as the boar attacked.

Igrid punched the boar away and reached for his own knife. His life draining away, he gathered the last of his strength and threw his knife to thud into the muscled thigh of his attacker. A grunt of pain brought fleeting satisfaction that vanished as he saw his attacker's face, the face of his friend, then the boar was on him again and, with sickening ripping sounds, eviscerated him. Tossed around like a rag-doll, Igrid bit back his screams until the pain faded. He felt the pulling on his intestines, but from a long way away. As his eyes glazed over, his last focus was the moon.

"Avenge me." He begged Druantia.

A whispering answered Igrid, the conversation of the sidhe. Above the canopy, the trees exploded as hundreds of crows took flight, their discordant croaks shattering the silence.

A large but shallow cave. Herbs and charms were hung from roots in the ceiling and, on the ground, stones inscribed with chalk runes were placed in a circle. Within the circle, piled furs for a bed and a fire, which cast strange shadows on the walls.

Arian slept peacefully. Gaunt but fit, around 16, her long blond hair plaited and threaded with beads. Aside from her gentle breaths, the silence was absolute – until the sudden, harsh *caw-caw* of crows.

Arian's eyes flew open and she instantly noted the fire's distorted shadows. Wide awake, she slipped off her covers and rolled, as a spear slammed into her bed. A shout and a second spear thrummed into the ground by her leg, and Arian rolled again, reaching for a square of leather with a few possessions on it, which she bundled into a makeshift bag.

A shouting, angry mob poured into the cave with flaming torches as another spear shot past her head. Arian launched to her feet and dashed to the back of the cave, but an arrow grazed her shoulder as she escaped into a tunnel.

“After her.” shouted their leader.

“I ain’t following no witch into her lair!”

From a dark tunnel, a panicked and confused Arian listened. The cave held her entire life – charms, food, furs, weapons and shelter, and coming into winter it was certain death to leave them. Why had these people attacked her, how did they even know about her?

“She woke up, but we didn’t make no sound!”

“Black magic.”

A sickening memory surfaced; 2 weeks ago, the desperate, agonised cries of a baby had drawn Arian from the forest, and she’d cast secret healing runes to save its life. There was nothing black about her magic, but it was forbidden, and this was her reward for showing compassion.

“I had witchbane on my arrow, she’ll be dead by morning.”

On cue, a searing pain hit her wounded shoulder.

"Idiot! The Druids want her."

Already frightened, Arian's blood ran cold at the mention of Druids. She fled blindly into the pitch blackness, ricocheting off walls in her panic. She ran, forced into the domain of things best left undisturbed.

For a long time, her footsteps and laboured breathing were the only sounds in the relentless darkness until a distant tap-tap of something, perhaps more feet, from ahead. Arian stopped to listen, but the blood roaring in her head muffled other sounds. She continued, the pain in her shoulder worsening with every step.

Distracted, Arian took too long to notice the change in smell. Damp had been replaced by a fetid stench, and her skin prickled. She had taken a wrong turn, but she had no strength to retrace her steps.

Phosphorescence gradually lifted the darkness and the tunnel became visible around her, the path littered with animal bones. The sound of rushing water carried as she reached a junction – left was cold and dark, right was blindingly bright and warm; Duidelf's lair. An insatiable river goddess who lured 'pilgrims' to her icy depths.

"Come to me, Arian." A soft voice urged. "I will heal you."

The light pulsed and her dizziness increased with her escalating panic. She'd escaped Duidelf before but today she was vulnerable, and the goddess sensed it.

"Let me help you, Arian."

Arian took an involuntary step towards the goddess, then grabbed the charm bracelet on her arm. A trickle of resolve and protection, enough to turn her away. She gathered her failing strength and ran back into the darkness.

The sun was rising when Arian staggered from underground into a bright, airy cave, high in the mountains. Her larder for medicines, herbs were tied in bundles and kindling was stacked, ready to light. She collapsed next to her fire pit but, hands shaking badly, was unable strike a spark with her flint ... but a fire sprang to life. Arian grimaced, was she now in debt to the fire god Cacus? Dizzy and faint, she realised she was near death when her debts would be counted. In her delirium she supposed that was better than repaying them while alive.

She grabbed herbs and dumped them on a flat stone. With the last of her strength she ground them, splashing water from a stream to make a paste. Rough and lumpy, she shoved the mixture on her burning shoulder, then she slid to the floor, unconscious.

The sun had set again when Arian finally woke, and Lunar once again cast her cold light into the cave. The arrow wound still throbbed, but the fierce pain had abated. With a groan she sat up, to discover a pool of vile smelling pus under her shoulder.

Her head clearer, she noted the fire still burning hot - and impossible, the wood inside the flames un-burnt. Adrenalin surged, and she recalled the crow's cry that had woken her and saved her life. Her debt to the gods was growing, but why?

Worried, Arian grabbed berries from her meagre store and went to the mouth of the cave to look out over a vast forest far below. There was no path, only a precarious climb which was impossible in her condition but going back was also impossible. Duidelf would be furious, and alert, but even if she evaded her, the villagers would be waiting in her cave. She'd need more help to survive, she realized grimly… which arrived as a fat pigeon to flew into the cliff-face and dropped dead at her feet. Whoever, or whatever, wanted her alive was really keen, and it was never good to have the attention of the gods.

Behind Arian the fire flared up and radiated a ferocious heat that cast twisting shadows on the walls. The hairs on the back of her neck rose, and she turned slowly. A shadow on one wall grew larger and solidified – a tangible, human shape with tall antlers and fiery eyes.

She lowered herself to the ground and kneeled, battered by the waves of heat. Then the fire abruptly died and when she looked up again the shadow was gone.

Terrified and bewildered, Arian tried to place the deity from the Druid pantheon but failed, her knowledge incomplete. The question resurfaced – what did it want from her? Gifts always came at a price...

"The gods play with us for entertainment." Her father's voice replayed in her head, stoking her fears and bringing a pang of sadness. Since his death two years ago, she'd been on her own. Always on the move, always hiding from people. And from the Druids.

Arian tried not to despair as she took stock of her meagre belongings. She had a charm bracelet of wooden beads for protection, which she'd carved under her father's watchful eye. She had plenty of herbs for medicines and cooking, but that entailed trading with people who would want to hand her over to the Druids, or save the time and just kill her. She also had flints, some hoarded coins and 2 other items – a golden torque, her father's, which she could never sell, and a bronze goblet that belonged to her mother. The goblet that always shone and never tarnished.

She examined the strange cup and, as usual, wondered at its origin. Her father had once been a High Druid, until his wife had given birth to triplets. Arian was first, born with a caul over her face and about her shoulders. His wife still in labour, a servant had kidnapped Arian and hidden her. While Arian's father, Brin, had searched for her, Arian's mother and her 2 baby sisters had been sacrificed. The loyal servant had saved her life, and Brin had fled the Order with Arian and spent the next 14 years teaching her everything he knew about magic and Balance – all of it forbidden knowledge. Arian didn't remember the servant, who'd died that first winter, but her father had drummed into her that the Druids would never give up hunting her, their sacrifice incomplete.

As always, the goblet sent an unpleasant tingle through her hands and she set it down. She had no choice, she would have to trade and hope to remain anonymous. And if possible, she'd sell the goblet and be pleased to be rid of it. It was beautiful, surely it would have enough value for her to buy furs, or a new cooking pot.

Arian ate and gathered healing herbs for her shoulder and the numerous cuts and scrapes her dark escape had inflicted. Then she selected herbs to sell, as she decided there was only one place she could go to trade; Titelbhe, a vast trading hub with no resident Druid advisor. Her main problem was time. She only had 14 nights until Samhain, when the barrier between worlds thinned and Druids would descend on Titelbhe to protect the city and liaise with the sidhe for a prosperous year. Arian's anger flared at the thought of Druids 'protecting' anything. Samhain was the night when faeries, the aes and dubh sidh, crossed over to grant favours or make mischief. The Druids would be there for their own purposes that had little to do with help.

She wasn't sure if it was a stray breeze, but the fire flared up. Her main problems, she amended, were Druids, her shoulder, people - and the gods.

Extract from book one of the Inheritance YA series-
Inheritance

The vast, mining city of Wall has one focus: priceless, coveted diamonds, capable of holding and magnifying magic. For countless centuries, the inhabitants have dug ever deeper in their quest for wealth, and eventually their digging unearthed more than gemstones.

They woke something best left undisturbed, and the ripples are felt around the world. The Unnamed King, a Sisterhood of Witches, monarchs, advisers, courtiers and courtesans, all hear the siren call of evil.

And five unwitting orphans are the focus of the call. Tilda and Alex, homeless petty criminals, also the distant descendants of dragons. Jess, who is a Weir, a magical mix of bloodlines capable of creating new and strange life. Si and Sal, descended from mages who are trapped in The Castle – once a bastion of learning, now a living entity imbued with hatred, pain and stolen power.

Five teenagers who hold the world in their hands... and who the world is now hunting.

Because far, far away, a wounded entity is stirring. Like a bloated spider, it takes its place on a web that extends across the world, and resumes seeping its poison. Discord it calls itself, and its only rivals, the Dragons and Mages, are long gone from the world.

Inheritance: Chapter 1

A small prison cell in a dungeon is not a good place to start a story, but that was where I found myself.

Such a stupid, stupid way to get caught! I had been hiding in a secret compartment above the throne room, there's an alcove with armour, and behind that, a step up to a ledge and a hidden compartment. I could see and hear everything going on in the throne room, but not be seen myself.

I had pilfered breakfast and taken it to my hideout; it was all so easy I had got cocky I guess. I'd taken more food than I could easily carry, so I couldn't jump up onto the ledge. No one could see me though, never, not if I didn't want to be seen, it was a trick I had. My little bit of magic, and I relied on it, so maybe I had made too much noise as I put the food up ahead of me then prepared to climb up.

I certainly wasn't prepared for what happened next. Everyone was looking for me, everyone in the city, because of the huge reward on my head, but no-one could find me. I evaded them easily – and then suddenly I didn't. I stare at my ankles, shackled in flimsy silver cuffs with a slender chain between them. Someone had attached them to me, and the minute they had touched my skin, as I began to climb up I presume, I had collapsed. Dropped like a stone to the floor, unconscious. Then I had woken here.

Whatever these were, my body was reacting badly to them. My skin was tingling, like insects were crawling up my legs, or my skin was trying to escape the chains. I held up my hand and saw it twitch, the skin changing colour momentarily, the bones seeming to elongate before going back to normal.

I was not scared at that moment. I did not feel violated, in fact my body seemed quite happy with what was happening and while it didn't like these chains, it welcomed whatever changes they seemed to be triggering. Besides, I had long since learned that many things are outside my control and my reactions were what mattered; not moaning about something I couldn't change, that was just depressing and futile. How could an orphan of Wall feel any different? I wondered again why I was 'wanted'? I had no idea why there was a huge reward for my capture, I was totally bemused by the hunt for me. What had I done to warrant that? That was, of course, why I was hiding behind the throne room, trying to find out before escaping. Not that that was easy, I should add, for I live in a walled city with only one way in or out – the sea, but I could stow away on a ship, I felt confident.

"Move."

I looked up to see a huge guard in the doorway, holding the door open. Behind him were two rows of guards, three on either side of the door.

"Are all those guards all for me?" I asked.

"No talking, no touching, just walk between us," he replied, not looking at me.

He looked apprehensive I thought, and I was the only one here. Was he scared of little me? I caught sight of a shape beyond the guards, an impression of a person from movement and shadow that vanished when I looked hard. I continued looking for a moment and my vision seemed to sharpen. I zoomed in, seeing the walls of the dungeon in fine detail, the feldspars in the hewn granite walls suddenly clear, as if I had a magnifying glass.

"Move!" The guard repeated, and I jumped, waking from my daydream. That was odd!

Slowly I stood up and looked at my chained ankles. I lifted a foot to test it, and was surprised that the chain stretched now, although it had not done previously. Tentatively I stepped forward and found walking would not be difficult.

I made my way to the door of the cell, noticing that the burly guard flinched as I neared him.

"What, you gonna hit me if I talk?" I asked, as I stepped past. Could he be scared of me, I wondered? There was one way to find out. I stopped walking, a half-formed

notion of rebellion in my head - and the chains on my ankles bit, sinking deep into my flesh.

I yelled, collapsing to the floor.

The pain was excruciating, but stopped as quickly as it hard started, and I lay for a moment getting my breath. The skin on my legs felt warm, and waves of heat rushed down my body towards the chains, but curiously there were no cuts. My body seemed to hate the chains now though, enraged by them, wanting them off.

"Move!" The guard said for a third time and I got up, once again the chain stretching so I had full movement.

I glanced at the guard and thought I saw a flicker of something like sympathy for me, quickly gone. The thought that he might be scared by me was funny actually, I am a pitiful little thing, if I say so myself. I am tiny and woefully undernourished, probably fifteen years old; scrawny was the term usually used for me. As I walked, I thought, if he's not scared of me, yet I have so many guards and, of course, these shackles, what was he scared of? I looked around again and saw the shadow up ahead, vanishing in front of us up the stairs, and felt a cold shiver go through me.

Magic.

There was magic in the air, which was terrifying him and, in fact, all these guards. There was major magic everywhere, of course, since the teenage Weir Queen had taken control out of nowhere, which was about the time the order for my capture had gone out. We were all used to magic of course, used it every day, but there had been no one truly *powerful, not for centuries.*

But that shadow thing flitting up ahead, was that what was scaring these tough men? Or was it their new ruler who had, after all, just deposed their previous masters? On the street, rumour had it she could kill with just a word, which was scary enough. It must be extra unsettling to be so big and muscled, and yet so powerless, I thought.

I was mounting the steps at this point myself. I did not scare easily. As I said, this isn't because I'm particularly brave, but because I've been in danger ever since I could remember, and you cannot live in a constant state of fear. I am puny but fleet, cautious and inventive, so I got out of most scrapes by not getting into them, and I couldn't immediately see how to get out of this one. That Weir Queen was a worry, a very frightening lady.

"Ouch!"

I was so preoccupied, I stubbed my toe. Hard. I was in bare feet and the stone steps were irregular. As I stumbled, the shackles around my ankles bit and I screamed and fell, bouncing all the way back down the stairs. There were guards in front and behind, the big burly guy immediately behind me, none of whom attempted to catch me or stop my fall. I tumbled back to the bottom, my ankles burning with agony, shoulder, knees and elbows hitting the stone steps painfully on the way.

"Stop it, stop it." I screamed, curled up in a ball.

My ankles felt as if molten metal was being poured over them, then abruptly the pain stopped. There was no residue of pain, no lingering burn or bruise on my flesh, but my legs pulsed, blood raging angrily through my veins. I leant over and touched the cuffs, screaming again as they bit into my fingers and ankles once more.

I tucked my fingers into my armpits, then squinted at the chain and cuffs on my legs. My heart was racing, and I could see the blood coursing down and up my legs, under the skin, to the feet and back up. My feet seemed to be changing shape, getting longer and scaly, then back to normal. I glanced up at my guard, who was hovering nearby. He didn't seem to notice anything strange.

Looking back again, my legs appeared normal, short and dirty; it was only when I focused on them intently that I could see my blood vessels pumping and my skin changing. I shut my eyes and shook my head, then got slowly to my feet. I looked up the stairs, where the shadow person had gone, and shouted.

"It is impossible for me to walk if you keep crippling me with these chains! I get the message, I'm coming."

The guards looked up the stairs where I had shouted, but there was no answer. I glowered at them, in a foul mood now, but I started up the stairs again.

The dungeons are a long way down so the walk up took a long time. As we got higher, and left the dungeons, we started meeting other people and crossing other corridors. Always the guards would silently fan out in front of me and stop people coming near me, 'Mr Burly' sticking by my side. Up and up we went, the surroundings getting noticeably plusher.

Eventually we stopped outside the throne room, not far from my previous hiding place. The doors swung open, and I was admitted into the presence of the Weir Queen. She looked up and laughed with delight when she saw me, gesturing for me to be brought forward.

"Dragan! You led me on a merry chase trying to catch you, but that's all over now. Let me have a look at you."

The guards prodded me with a spear and I walked forward until I stood ten paces in front of her, where I stopped. No one asked me to stop. The guards had fallen back and no one stood between us, but the Weir Queen had no reason to be afraid of anyone; she did not need guards. Magic crackled about her, radiating out, sizzling at her finger tips.

"How did you manage to evade me for so long?" She tilted her head and studied me.

I kept silent, my limited form of rebellion, and she frowned. The chains around my ankles responded, sizzling against my flesh but not painfully.

"You really are a runt of a thing, aren't you? Could you really be one of them?"

She looked uncertain about something and I stared back at her, unsure what to do but determined not to back down. Behind her a shadow flicked over some thick curtains before flitting across to the throne. The Queen inclined her head as if listening, keeping her eyes on me.

As I waited I studied her. She said I was a runt, and she was right, but she wasn't all that great herself. At a guess, she was a year or two older than me, but looked just as scrawny. The large crown had extra padding and still looked precariously large on her head. Her cheekbones were pronounced, not from any aristocratic breeding, but like me, she had lived on very little food for a long time.

"How did you hide from me, Matti?"

I started, surprised. My full name is Matilda Dragan, but my friends call me Tilda, and there are very few of them. Nobody used Matti, but the name stirs a memory... once, long ago, someone had called me Matti, hadn't they? I shrugged it off. This witch queen could call me anything she liked! If I was going to object to anything, that was the very last in a long line of things I would object to. The thought made me smile slightly, which caused her eyes to narrow.

"We'll see soon enough. If it you're one of them, I will know all your secrets, and if it isn't... well, you won't last, and then it is immaterial." She smiled nastily. "Chair for Matti, over there."

She pointed to a spot several feet to her right, and a chair was carried over. I looked at her uncertainly before walking over to it, totally bemused now. She was completely mad, this queen. Why would she hunt me, arrest me, put me in chains and then have me sit in a throne room with her? I looked at the others in the room, but everyone avoided my gaze. They were clearly all terrified, full of bright, false laughter and chatter, quick to respond to anything the Queen had to say. How many of these people had been at this court with the old ruler? What had happened to him? He had been fair enough, I guessed, if a bit old. King Wells, on the throne for years with fourteen squabbling children waiting to take it from him, and then the witch queen had stepped in and swiped it from all of them! Some rumours said the heirs were now in the mines under Wall, others said she had massacred them in their sleep... others said she'd killed them with dark magic. The thought was unsettling, and Tilda moved on quickly. They certainly weren't here anyway.

"Now Matti, I have some entertainment I think you'll enjoy."

She interrupted my ruminations and I sat down as the Queen clapped her hands. A door to the side opened and a huge man was dragged in, hands bound behind him and a hood over his face. He was pushed so he fell hard onto his knees.

The Queen stood up and approached him, walking around him in a circle before pulling off his hood with one hand, then grabbing his hair with the other hand and yanking his head back so he stared up at her.

"Matti, I believe you know Alexander?"

Her body had been between us, obscuring my view, but she stepped aside now and turned him to face me. It was my friend, a big lumbering simpleton I'd teamed up with when we were young. Sometimes he protected me from others, sometimes I protected him when his stupidity got him into trouble. I didn't know how old he was, a bit older than me physically but years behind mentally. His big blue eyes stared at me, his black hair tousled, his heavily muscled body hunched and bruised.

"Alex?" I asked, looking sadly at him, then at the Queen.

Was this why she wanted me? Had poor Alex mentioned me? What did a dumb brute like him have to do with anything? I suddenly felt angry, and stared hard at the Queen, defiant.

"Our murderer, brought to justice! The first act of the new Queen, looking after her people." Said the Queen.

There was a smattering of applause and cheers from the courtiers. There had, indeed, been a terror on the streets for nearly a year now, a terror who had stalked the city, torturing and murdering indiscriminately the rich and poor, but that was not Alex.

"He's no murderer." I replied before I could help myself, which sent a murmur around the court.

"Alex, what do you like to do to people?"

Alex sat up with an effort and looked at the Queen.

"I pull them apart, while they are still alive." Alex turned to look at me, "I like hearing them scream."

"No! What are you saying? Alex, It's me, Tilda! Do you remember? You never hurt a fly; you hate hurting things." I turned to the Queen, furious. "What have you done to him? Alex would never hurt anyone and, and... he can't even talk properly! You've cast a spell on him."

The Queen flicked a lazy finger, gesturing up and then towards me. Alex got to his feet slowly and wobbled over to me. His body was the same, his face, but his eyes were different: they seemed to glow with a cold fire and I shivered as he stared at me. The Queen snapped her fingers, and the bindings came away from his arms as he got near me. He placed his hands on the arms of my chair and leaned in close.

"I remember you," he stated, looking into my eyes while

I stared at him, mesmerised.

The Queen watched us intently for a moment and I noticed the shadow flicker back to her. I raised my hand to his face, but she snapped her fingers again.

"Music! You will dance for us, Alexander!"

A folk song was started by the court musicians, and to my surprise, Alex started dancing, a line dance, which he is most unsuited to with his hulking form. He started singing, and the courtiers all laughed at him.

"Stop it," I said, embarrassed for him. Alex hated people looking at him, and this was so cruel.

The song was a well known folk-song, a duet for a man and woman. As he sang the female part, I looked at his face with horror. It changed.

As he sang the female section, his features softened and elongated, his eyes slanting and his jaw softening, a tiny bit but making him entirely female. His beautiful deep blue eyes, his face - everything about his face belongs to a beautiful woman. Then for the male part, his face changed back, back to Alex, but with strength, not a simple-minded Alex. He was very handsome, but his vacant brain left his face unanimated, his mouth always partially open. Now he was all there, the weakness gone, but the irony is the dance, the silly line dance that made him look so stupid.

"Love me, build me up a home and marry me," he sang again the female part again, and his face shimmered and changed, his voice even sounding feminine. That was when I got an unpleasant feeling, an absolute certainty - I had to stop this.

I looked up at the Queen, who was watching him and laughing. Behind her, shadows swarmed up and down the walls, excited, emitting a thrum of noise.

"Stop this!" I ordered, no longer timid, I knew something very bad was going to happen if it continued.

She laughed even more loudly and I stood up, walking to her throne.

"You have to stop this. You don't know what you're doing." My voice was level.

I knew the consequences of contradicting this witch, but I had a strong feeling that the alternative much worse, a feeling or maybe a memory buried in my brain.

"Matti! Excellent, you must dance with him as well. Alex?"

Alex came up behind me and grabbed me roughly, swirling me in front of him, then pulling me into an embrace. His arms were like iron around me, pulling me in close, and I looked up to see his features shift again.

"Don't do this. You have no idea what you are playing with. You will destroy us all!" Then I pointed to the wall

behind her and courtiers gasp, shocked by my courage. "Don't listen to those things, they are lying to you and manipulating you. Whatever they said is a lie, please stop this."

Alex pushed me away clumsily as part of the dance, singing the female part, his face changed again. His sleeve rolled up and I saw a bracelet wrapped several times around his wrist and up his arm. Silver, rippling, just like mine.

He pulled me back to him roughly and I thumped against his chest. I grabbed hold of his face and forced him to look down at me, inadvertently touching the bracelet on his arm, which sent tingles along my arm.

"Alex, it's me, Tilda! Please stop this." He changed again, female, and pushed me away roughly, letting go so I crashed to the floor.

My legs tingled. It knew about those chains somehow, and my body was preparing for battle, waking up after a long sleep, and I am not sure I can stop it. Alex is the same, waking up, and this is not good, somehow I know that. I can't break the chains, but I could fight their affect.

"Your Majesty, please. You must stop this; you must take these off." I tried to be respectful, get her attention, but it is no use.

The Witch Queen laughed.

Suddenly the walls of the throne room seem to throb and shake, a high window shattered and the Queen laughed harder while the courtiers huddled together, nervous. Alex stopped singing and dancing and turned to stare at the Queen.

There was another tremble, like a small earthquake. I realised the Queen had no idea what was happening, not really. She might be a powerful witch but she had no idea what she was unleashing. I looked around wildly, not sure what I needed, but sure I'll recognise something useful. I stopped as I noticed the sceptre the Queen is holding.

"Stop this now, you stupid cow!" I shouted at her, getting her attention.

"How dare you!" She raised the sceptre over her head, pointing one end at me, but then changed her mind. "Come here," she snapped, and I felt a compulsion to go to her.

Gladly, I stepped forward, but paused as I neared Alex, grabbing hold of him, wrapping my arm through his.

"I said come here," snapped the Queen.

I kept hold of Alex, using him as an anchor against the compulsion that pulled my legs. I didn't budge, causing her to storm over to me. She planted the staff on the ground and raised her other hand to strike me, which is when I desperately lunged for the top of the sceptre.

The instant I touched it, I pulled it tight to my body, the queen, pulling her so she fell into Alex, and creating a circle, a bond with the three of us touching each other.

There was a flash and we vanished, leaving the throne room. I heard a howl of disappointment behind me, see several shadows rush out from the walls towards us, but they are too late.

****

Tilda sat up with a start and inhaled deeply. She was opposite a very ancient woman with wrinkles on top of wrinkles, the queen and Alex slumped unconscious on the floor. They were in a huge, featureless space, dim half-light making everything grey, nothing else to see except the four of them.

"Where am I? What's going on?" Matilda asked, looking around wildly.

"What else do you remember?"

"Wha..? Where's the throne room?"

"You came here when you touched the sceptre, remember? You were telling me what happened."

"No... yes... maybe. How did we get here? Where are we? It... it seems familiar, but I've never been here before?"

"Are you sure?"

"Who the hell are you?" Matilda asked, angry and scared.

The old woman leant close and interrupted. "Tell me your first memory of Wall."

The crone puffed on a vile smelling pipe and it blew the smoke in Matilda's face and she travelled back in time to her childhood.

****

I was of running, running away from the Catchers.

A gang of children pelted along the top of the Wall, fleeing the Catchers who were rounding up stray children to take them away to the place of no return. Down to the mines. I was filled with fear, barely keeping ahead of the big men who ran after us, flicking weighted ropes around our ankles that tripped us up.

I darted into a narrow alleyway then slid sideways under a low platform that held vast rubbish bins. Other little feet ran past me, then I heard the footsteps of the Catchers and I held my breath. If they had seen me slide under the platform it would be all over, no one ever came back once they had been caught. The footsteps slowed outside my hiding place and my heart skipped a beat, but then they accelerated again and ran past me.

I looked along the alleyway to see a Catcher chase a small child and grab her. She screamed, but he squeezed her neck and she collapsed. This was their magic: they touched your shoulder and you collapsed.

I watched him pick up the child and walk back past my hiding place, greeting more Catchers, before walking back the way they had come, no doubt picking up the other children they had caught. I waited in my hiding place until it was dark, cold and miserable, but I remained silent. That was before I discovered my magic, how to be invisible when I wanted.

Anyway, at last I crept out, legs numb and stiff from inactivity and cold. At the edge of the alley I peered along the main path that runs along the edge of the wall. It is empty now, and I walked quickly to the left, sticking close to the wall. I come upon a manhole cover, which I levered open, then jumped jump down.

Other children looked up at me, but I ignored them and squeezed past them to my space beside the wall with a small window onto the Outside.

****

Matilda snapped back to the present.

"Your space?" Asked the Crone.

"Everyone had a space..." Replied a surly Matilda.

"You'd been there before and had your own space."

"I... I... what does it matter?"

"That was not your first memory. How did you know

about the Catchers?"

The old woman looked intensely dissatisfied, but Matilda just shook her head, confused.

"I don't know."

"Humph." The old woman puffed more smoke at her. "Tell me when you met Alex?" her voice receded, as if coming from far away.

****

The city of Wall towered over a desert on three sides, the fourth side bounded by a raging sea that was impassable 9 months of the year. Wall is, basically, a city inside a high wall. A really high wall, with multiple levels, the richest people living topmost, some of whom even had gardens on top of their houses. Traders and jewellers, lots of jewellers as diamonds were Wall's single export, nobles and artisans, your usual city I supposed, plus the runaway orphans, who had warrens through all the levels that they navigated in their daily struggle to steal food and avoid the mines under Wall.

Wall's livelihood comes from underground. The city mines the finest quality diamonds in the world, and people make the dangerous journey here to trade with us. The city is huge, covering many miles, and some large estates grow fruit and vegetables, but not enough to support everyone. The workers that go down the mines have to be fed, so we lead a precarious existence based on trade. These same workers live underground too, the bulk of the city being underground in the maze of tunnels created by generations of miners.

I was contemplating this as I sat on one of the ledges overlooking the desert. They dotted the exterior wall like a giant's ladder and I'd discovered them a while ago. As it was summer, Wall's food was plentiful as the seas were open for trade and I had stolen enough bread to last all day and was content to just bask in the sunshine. It was safer than most places in Wall as no one ever looked outside, and if they did, they would need to crane their necks to see me. The biggest danger was of falling into the desert far, far below, so it was about as safe as it was possible to get.

I liked it here, I liked the solitude. Then I saw them approaching below, glancing up at me every now and then, looking directly at me as if they knew where I was. I guessed they understood there was a chance I might fall, and with a gasp I wondered how high they could jump. The city wall towers hundreds of feet over what we call simply 'Outside'. I had found a rope fastened to an exposed pipe on the outside of the wall and used it to climb down to this ledge, nearly half way down. Could they jump up and reach me here?

I looked down as several of the beasts wandered over and sat directly underneath me. This was the closest I had been to them - and they were terrifying. They were covered in points, like quills on a porcupine, only they were easily twenty feet long and the quills were more like swords, rustling and stirring as they moved. Their mouths were similar to a dog's muzzle, lined with two sets of sharp teeth. Some time before I had witnessed a fight between three of them, two against one. They had torn it apart then eaten it, though the two victors had left limping and bleeding.

They were called Wyens and were invincible, at least to humans if not each other. To recap, to the east of Wall is a treacherous and stormy sea. To the north, west and south is desert and Wyens. You can see forests and rivers and mountains in the distance, but I would never travel there because Wyens attacked all humans and ripped us to shreds before eating us. Our criminals all went over the wall. Particularly nasty criminals were lowered to the ground to be eaten alive, while others were merely pushed, having the fortune of dying quickly upon landing. Any transgression, including homelessness, and you were sent underground to the mines, but major crimes or 'desertion' from the mines, and you were sent to the wyens, which is what happened to many of the older orphans on the streets.

There are no gates in our outer wall on the land side. There are massive gates in the harbour wall on the seaward side, but nothing on the land. I had wondered many times who had built these walls; how they had managed to do it without the Wyens eating them? There was a growl below me and I backed up, closer to the wall, my hand groping for the rope. Then I fell off the ledge as someone jumped down and landed beside me. I squealed and scrabbled frantically until a hand grabbed me and pulled me back to safety.

I closed my eyes, trembling, for several minutes. When I opened them, I looked up, and then continued looking up until I met the eyes of a giant. He had a lovely face, big deep blue eyes, but his slack jaw and vacant expression told me he was not all there, not at all. When he was sure I had recovered my balance, he reached underneath the ledge and pulled out another rope, then began to climb down towards the waiting Wyens. I grabbed his hand then.

"No, stop! They'll eat you," I told him, but he gently removed my hand and continued down the rope. I squeezed my eyes shut and put my hands over my ears, curled up on my ledge, and waited.

After some time I didn't hear screams or snarls so I peered down, wrapping my hand around the rope above so I would not fall. To my amazement he was standing in the middle of a circle of the beasts, and they were licking a pot he held out for them.

When they had finished, he put the pot into a sack which he fastened to his back, then turned and began to climb back up the rope. I was tempted to scurry up the rope and run away from him because he scared me, but instead I waited, stepping back when he got level with me.

He didn't glance at me, but instead took the next rope

and climbed up to the top. It was getting dark now, but I could see the Wyens below as dark shadows, prowling the base of the wall. I waited until he got off the wall before taking the rope and climbing up carefully after him. At the top I paused and peered over, but he had gone.

I didn't see him for a long time after that. There was another roundup and I was sitting safely on top of a building when I saw him lumber by below me, towards his spot on the wall, a big bag over his shoulder. He was very big, but he wasn't mentally all there, and despite his size he was still a child. I watched him walk to the corner, when a Catcher came from the opposite direction, pulling a hand cart piled high already with children.

They met and the Catcher looked dubiously at him.

"What's your name?" He looked him up and down belligerently.

"Alex," he replied slowly.

"You're a big lad, you would work well in the mines. Who owns you?"

"Alex," he repeated, and the Catcher smiled.

"Well, a stupid brute won't tell tales, eh?" He reached forward and clamped his hand on Alex's shoulder, and then Alex collapsed.

I bit my lip in indecision: one rule of the wall was to mind your own business. My hand nudged a large lump of rock, which I picked up experimentally. The Catcher put down his cart and, with a heave, started dragging Alex. With surprising strength he hoisted him up by his arms and rolled him into the cart.

I looked at the children already in the cart, small, thin and doomed and, almost without thinking, I threw the rock onto the Catcher's head. With a groan he touched his head before collapsing to the ground. Now what? There were bound to be more Catchers around, they never ventured out alone.

I climbed down the wall quickly and experimentally tried to drag the cart, for I was fairly puny. To my surprise it moved easily, on quiet, well-oiled wheels, perfectly balanced to make pulling the cart easy. But now where to take it?

I kept going the way the Catcher was facing, turned a corner and then ran straight for a few blocks, heading towards the sea wall where there were big warehouses. I didn't hear the whistle of the Catcher's alarm, not until I approached the back of some old warehouses I knew were poorly maintained.

I dropped the front of the cart and ran to a door of one of the buildings at random, the most decrepit looking, and began tugging frantically at it. There was a rusted padlock and I tried to prise off the bolts holding it into the rotten wood. I was surprised when a large hand reached over mine with a metal pole. I looked up to see Alex lever the padlock off the door, pulling out the screws fastening it place, then pull open the door.

I ran for the cart and pulled it in, then Alex pulled the door closed behind me. None of the other children were stirring yet, but we managed to push the cart inside and pull the door shut before anyone saw us. I then squeezed out of a hole in the corner and pushed the padlock back into the screw holes. You would have to try the lock to realise it was loose, and I thought we were safe enough, safe as anyone ever really was on the Wall, I reckoned.

Back in the warehouse, the other kids came around while Alex and I peered through holes in the wall and watched the Catchers in their search for us. The kids sat up and climbed out of the cart, sensibly realising they had to keep quiet. Some came to join us as we watched, others went off exploring the warehouse.

As it got dark, one of the kids, a dark-haired girl, called us over.

"We found food," she said, and I turned to see a group of children gathered in a circle.

"Someone needs to keep watch," I replied, and the girl nodded. Another nod to a smaller kid who came up and took my place, peering outside while I dropped down and joined them by the food.

Alex followed me, and I was surprised by how light he was on his feet, hardly making a sound.

"You saved us," the girl stated, looking at me.

I looked at Alex, who also stared at me and I shrugged, embarrassed.

"Maybe we ought to help each other more, us kids." I hadn't really thought that before; it hadn't even occurred to me, but as soon as I said it, it seemed right. "They gang up on us all the time, right?" I smiled at her, and after a minute she smiled back.

"I'm Katie, and that little shrimp over there is Maggie, my little sister. Have some food, it's good."

I settle down and pick up some cheese and cured meat, a real feast. Alex joined me, hulking down beside me.

"How did you get Alex on your side? We've seen him walking about but he never pays anyone any attention. Did he help you rescue us?"

I looked at Alex, who was eating happily.

"I don't know. He was caught and, well, I managed to knock out a Catcher and then, well... I ran off with the cart. I'm not sure it was such a good idea, actually. They're going to be really angry with us now."

Katie nodded but shrugged. "It'll pass. I have somewhere we can keep out of their way. A disused tunnel section in the north."

I shook my head. I rarely go underground.

"There's a whole area that caved in ages ago, and everyone avoids it. We've been hiding there for a while now. We only go surface to get food, but with this stash we could last a long time."

I shuddered at the thought. Unlike everyone else in Wall, I hate going underground, but she had a point. I look at the other children gathered.

"Do any of you have homes?" I ask, sure they will all be orphans like us.

Everyone shook their head except for a tall skinny boy, who stared at us through narrowed eyes.

"Do you want to join together?"

"They will just catch us easier if we're together. I'm not sticking around," he stated, and some kids looked at him and nodded too. There are twelve of us, I quickly count, which is a big group.

"True," I nod, "but with a group we could have lookouts, and we could work together if they do find us."

The boy spat in disgust and stood up.

"Well, it's your lookout, but I'm not staying." He grabbed a wheel of cheese and ran, to the hole in the

corner then out into the night. Two other children, a boy and girl, grabbed their own food and followed after him, leaving nine.

"If he's caught he knows where we're headed," said Katie, looking after him.

I wasn't concerned about them, though I was sure they would be caught. "Well, if any of us are captured that will also be true. Besides he doesn't know precisely. I'm in. What do you all want to do?"

The remaining children nodded and I realised that aside from Katie, Alex and I, they were all very young, none more than five, I would guess. There must have been a disaster underground very recently, for they cannot have been above ground for long. Most children had parents who were miners, but there were many accidents in the mines, so a lot of stray orphans.

"Katie, have you been with this lot for long?"

"No, Maggie and me stick to ourselves. We came up top for food and the Catchers found us. I thought we were done for." Katie shivered and I looked to the others, suddenly curious.

"How did you get up top?"

"We followed a cat," said one little person.

"Were your parent's miners?" I asked the same child, and they all nodded and look sad.

"Did you all come up together?"

"Yes, we were collected from home yesterday, but we heard them talking," replied the same child. "They said we were small enough for the chimneys but our parents told us we must never go in the chimneys."

All the children shivered, and I got a picture in my head of near vertical shafts between the mines where air was pumped below. These got blocked, so small children went through them daily, cleaning them so they didn't get suffocate the miners below, but many fell to their deaths.

"There was a cave-in. All our parents are gone, but I saw a cat go up a dark tunnel and decided to follow it, and the others followed me," said a small boy.

The children all looked at us with big, wide eyes, trying to be brave, struggling against tears.

"That's why the Catchers were all out today, after this little lot here." Katie spoke behind me.

"Hey, you've got a new family and we'll look out for each other, right?"

The children cast big, wide eyes at Katie, who hesitated. She assessed their size – their ages – daunted by the number of inexperienced children we were collecting together. Then she nodded and began packing up the food into small bags.

"We'll each carry as much as we can in food. It's a long walk but we should reach there by morning."

We packed up everything edible we could find, looking in barrels and finding a store of apples that cheered all of us up. We had meat, cheese and apples, all well preserved.

When this is divided up, Alex picked up the biggest bag and waited by the door for us, expectantly.

"OK, Katie, you lead the way."

We trooped out in a line, Katie at the front, me at the back of the little kids, Alex trudging behind me.

It was a long walk to the North, but we made it and made our camp there very successfully. I've lived there ever since that day. We all collected orphans whenever we could and stuck together. That was our 'code', if you like, making us very different to the other waifs in the city. We never turned anyone away and we shared what we had.

Until the Weir Queen made a concerted effort to find us.

****

Matilda came back to the present again, both puzzled and, by now, frustrated.

"What is this about? Where are we?" Matilda looked around the cave, grumpy. "What the hell is going on, Old Woman?"

"I cannot answer that, but you can – you must find that out yourself, and you do not have much time left here." She puffed away, the smell truly vile.

"Well, can't you help me at least? I mean, you brought me here and these memories aren't exactly useful."

"Stupid girl! You brought yourself."

The crone paused while Tilda digested this, but before she could form any new questions she leant forward again.

"Who were your parents?"

"I don't know! I never knew them... Well, I don't remember them."

"Your first memory was on the Wall, running away from the Catchers. How old were you?" The hag leant closer and looked intently at Matilda, blowing more smoke in her face.

"I don't know! I don't have a birthday. Seven or Eight I guess."

"Yet you can't remember anything before that?"

Matilda shook her head, puzzled and, for the moment, distracted.

"I never thought... I don't remember anything?"

The crone sat back, puffing away.

"I thought of something before we came here. I recognised something stirring in me, in Alex, like I nearly remembered something... what was it?"

Matilda looked at the crone, flapping away the smoke.

"Do *you* know what's happening? You must know how we got here, you were here already?"

The crone clicked her tongue in annoyance. "Concentrate! Not why or how, but *who*! Who are you? Who is Alex? That is what you need to answer, and you don't have any time left here now, you must go back."

"No! Something terrible is about to happen back in Wall." Replied a panicked Tilda.

"When you get back you will have but a few moments. There will be confusion, and you will not be noticed at once. It is a shame you cannot take the Queen with you, but there will not be time. Take Alex and leave Wall immediately. The chains are gone but the effects can't be stopped now, they are in motion."

The crone's voice was fading and it was getting lighter.

"Wait, how did we come here?"

"Ha ha! You really don't know anything, do you?" The old woman relented a bit. "I do not know much, this is a surprise to me. What I do know I'm not allowed to say but bring the diamond in the sceptre and, whatever you do, keep Alex with you."

"Who are you?"

The crone cackled, receding gradually.

Printed in Great Britain
by Amazon

47531433R00258

Uruk
The first recorded city,
2,000 years before Christ.

But Uruk was not the first ever city.
An older city existed in Mesopotamia –
until someone invited the devils in.
Razed to the ground and all traces scrubbed from the records,
it was not the first time the ungodly had reached out
for humanity, and it would not be the last.

Some call these devils the Fallen, and organised religions,
united in a secretive army called the Order,
stand sentinel against them.
The Fallen and the Order search for the one who can
permanently open the door between worlds and let them in;
the one fallen angel who repented. Danyal.

Both sides suspect that 22 year old Danni is the human host
to a dormant Danyal. Kidnapped at birth by a rogue monk
from the Order, raised on the run and perpetually hunted,
she's adept hiding, even as technology makes evasion harder.
But now her adoptive father is dead and the net is closing in.

Stalked by the priests and fallen angels,
Danni must confront her extraordinary skills -
her innate knowledge of all languages,
her ability to cross between worlds, her Sight and her
baffling memories, with the uncomfortable feeling that
she is a host for something other.

As opposing hunters close in on their prey,
Danni must pick a side in the battle between
Heaven and Hell.

ISBN 9798666684726
90000
9 798666 684726